THE BEST WEEK THAT NEVER HAPPENED

DALLAS WOODBURN

Month9Books

Copyright © 2020 by Dallas Woodburn

THE BEST WEEK THAT NEVER HAPPENED by Dallas Woodburn
All rights reserved. Published in the United States of America by Month9Books, LLC.

Trade Paperback ISBN: 978-1-951710-11-8
ePub ISBN: 978-1-951710-12-5
Mobipocket ISBN: 978-1-951710-13-2

Published by Month9Books, Raleigh, NC 27609
Cover design by The Leaf Book Design

Month9Books

PRAISE FOR *THE BEST WEEK THAT NEVER HAPPENED*

"A poignant and gripping heart-tug of a page-turner filled with heart and hope. I couldn't put it down. Magic." – Jennifer Niven, New York Times bestselling author of *All the Bright Places* and *Holding Up the Universe*

"Dallas Woodburn weaves a bittersweet love story between star-crossed lovers—thwarted not only by distance but also by insurmountable tragedy. This captivating, poignant story is perfect for teens on the brink of discovering who they are and what really matters in the time they have left." – Natalie Lund, author of *We Speak in Storms*

For Allyn and Maya:
Every week I get to spend with you is the Best Week of My Life.

A long life may not be good enough, but a good life is long enough.
—Benjamin Franklin

The Fish That Swim up the Waterfall

At Akaka Falls, on the Big Island of Hawaii, there is a fish called the o'opu alamo'o. These fish are born in the waters above the falls. Their babies drift in the current all the way down the falls, down the river, and out to the Pacific Ocean. There, they grow into adult fish.

When it is time, they begin to swim back from whence they came, up the freshwater streams toward Akaka Falls. At the base of the waterfall—which is more than four hundred feet high—they do an amazing thing. Using a sucker on their bellies, the fish climb up the sheer cliff wall, painstakingly making their way up and up and up, until they reach the top of the waterfall. There, they hatch the eggs of the next generation of o'opu alamo'o, new fish that will make the same journey.

The o'opu alamo'o, you see, understand that life is a cycle. We could all learn from these fish. Sometimes we must hoist ourselves up waterfalls in our own lives, back to our origins, back to where we began.

DEADLY TRAIN ACCIDENT IN VIRGINIA

Sixty-eight people were killed and hundreds wounded in a commuter train accident on the Northeast Corridor from Philadelphia to Washington, DC, on Monday. The train unaccountably derailed, and the first two cars careened into the mountainside, killing sixty-seven passengers along with the train conductor. Eight passengers remain missing.

Authorities have not announced the cause of the accident and are withholding further details pending further investigation by the National Transportation Safety Board.

Vigils are being held for the victims in Philadelphia and Washington.

hey tegan,

i know it's been a while. i was just thinking of you randomly today and that time we followed the sea turtle. remember how we thought we could chase her all around the world? bet we could have, if your parents hadn't called you in for dinner.

are you still mad at me? i hope not, because i miss you. i'm not mad at you anymore. i'm sorry for ghosting you. truce?

—kai

PART ONE

MONDAY

When I open my eyes and sit up, everything is dark. My brain is cottony, and my eyes won't focus. I can't remember where I am or how I got here. I'm not afraid. I mostly feel … empty.

The warm air is humid and heavy. Beads of sweat trickle down my back, even though I'm wearing a thin tank top and jean shorts. I take a deep breath. Then another. I am sitting on the bare ground, hard and bumpy. There are rocks, sharp and pointy as blades. Impulsively, I slip one into the pocket of my shorts. Protection.

When I stand, I hit my head on something hard. A sloping roof? A shelf of rock? Has someone kidnapped me and taken me captive underground? I should be terrified, but I'm mostly confused and curious. Something about this place seems familiar … but whatever the memory is, it remains out of reach, like wisps of clouds passing through my brain, impossible to grasp.

Gradually, my eyes adjust to the dimness. Black walls of rock surround me. I begin crawling forward on my hands and knees, a strange anticipation fluttering in my chest. If I'm lost, why do I have this hopeful feeling? The rocks graze my bare knees and sting my

1

palms. My eyes blink against the darkness. And then, I see it—a shaft of light, up ahead. I crawl faster.

The roof of rock slopes up and up until I find myself in a large dark chamber. A shaft of light streams down through an opening in the ceiling, like the Pantheon in Rome, which I think I've visited before, or maybe I've just seen pictures. Right now, my memory isn't working all that well. It feels as if I'm half-asleep, waiting for the details of my life to come into focus.

Suddenly, a figure steps into the shaft of light. I freeze. His back is to me, but there's a spotlight on him, like an actor onstage. There is something recognizable in the way he carries himself: the breadth of his shoulders and the slant of his hips. As I scoot a little closer, the rock falls out of my shallow pocket and plunks onto the ground. A soft *thud* is loud in this hushed chamber of stone. The boy turns, glancing around.

When I see his face, my breath catches in my throat.

Kai.

The sight of him brings a memory into focus: the last time I saw him in person, three years ago. He looks exactly the same as he did then.

He stares in my direction, but his expression is utterly blank. *Does he recognize me? Can he even see me in this darkness? Or is he looking past me, lost in thought?* I stand, ducking my head to keep clear of the ceiling. I am about to call his name when he steps out of the light, vanishing as quickly as he had appeared.

I slip the rock back into my pocket, and then I follow him.

The last time Kai and I talked, it did not end well. I was angry with him about something. And he was upset with me too. He was so upset that he said he needed space and hung up the phone. Thinking about it now makes a rain cloud sit heavy in my chest. *Why would I ever fight with Kai? He is so easygoing and gentle—he never argues with anyone. God, I must have done something terrible to actually make him angry. What did I do? How can I make it right?*

I need to catch up to him so we can talk. Then I can explain, or maybe he can explain to me. And then I can apologize. And then things will be okay between us again.

When I reach the shaft of light, I tilt my head back and gaze up. The light filters into the rock cavern through a round hole about the size of a dinner plate. Through the hole, I can glimpse clear blue sky. Wisps of cloud skitter past.

With a flash of recognition, I know exactly where I am.

The lava tubes.

Our place, mine and Kai's.

Three years ago ...

"Meet me tonight at the lava tubes," Kai said. His brows were knitted together, his tone urgent. His fingers lightly touched my hip. "So we can, you know. Catch up."

"I'm not sure," I hedged, glancing at my parents in the distance. They were distracted, gathering our snorkel gear and dumping our dirty towels into the laundry bin at the resort kiosk. Expecting me to be following right behind them. If I didn't hurry, soon they would notice my absence and start bickering.

"I don't even remember how to get there," I said to Kai.

"Don't worry, it's simple—I bet you'll remember as you go along. Follow the path along the edge of the golf course. You hit the parking lot, and the path turns to gravel and veers down to the lava tubes. You can't miss it, really. I still go there all the time."

All the time. *His words made me flinch inside, which surprised me—I didn't have a crush on Kai. But then why did I hate to imagine him bringing other girls there? Maybe because the lava tubes were special: the hideout we had discovered as kids, the place we had spent those magical summer hours dreaming, pretending we would run away together. Silly plans. Childish games. Still—it hurt to think of him there, without me. With someone else instead.*

I turned away. "Look, it was great to run into you, but I should go … "

"T, please." He touched my shoulder, and I couldn't help myself. I paused, turned back around to face him. "It's our place," he said. "Remember?"

Our place. *The look in his eyes was so earnest.*

"Okay," I whispered. "I'll see you there. Midnight." Then I reluctantly pulled away, heading up the sandy hill to my waiting parents.

I'm not buried in some scary underground cave. I'm somewhere familiar and safe: the secret hideout of my favorite childhood vacation.

As I gaze up at the bright-blue daytime sky through the round hole in the rock roof, memories come flooding back about a different sky I once glimpsed through that hole—night, star-studded.

Kai is here somewhere. I need to find him.

In the distance, a faint glimmer of sunlight marks the cave exit. I plunge toward it through the darkness, memories of that night swirling through my mind. Memories of the last time I was here, three years ago.

Three years ago …

I couldn't remember when I had ever been so nervous. You're being stupid, I told myself. Get a grip, Tegan. I prided myself on having nerves of steel. Public speaking, drama auditions, sports tryouts and championship games—I strode through it all with a calm smile on my face. So why did the idea of a midnight excursion with Kai make me so jittery?

It's just Kai, I reminded myself. Your random childhood friend from a lifetime ago.

Kai was born and raised here on the Big Island, and I had come here with my parents on vacation when I was eight. I first met Kai on the beach when he accidentally knocked over my sandcastle. For the rest of that vacation, he and I were inseparable. I had been devastated to return home. Back then, neither of us owned smartphones. We hadn't kept in touch. I had always wondered what happened to that little kid I once knew.

For some un-pin-downable reason, seeing Kai again on this trip seemed like a gift from the universe, a remnant of my past washed up onto the shore of the present. Life had been so complicated and difficult—

my parents tried to act as if this trip to Hawaii was a normal vacation, but even I could tell it was a last-ditch effort to save their marriage and keep our family intact. Kai was a reminder of a time I was nostalgic for, a time when everything was right in my innocent little world. A time I yearned to go back to.

I slid out of bed and crept through the dark hotel room, carefully stepping past my snoring parents and the land mines of half-empty suitcases, and snaking cords belonging to laptops and phone chargers, until I finally reached the oasis of the bathroom. I changed into a sundress, leggings, and my favorite cozy sweater, the only warm thing I'd brought to Hawaii. I didn't dare turn on the light to put on any makeup. I pulled my hair into a low ponytail, grabbed my mini flashlight from my backpack, and slipped out of the hotel room and down the outdoor hallway until I reached the beach.

That time of night, the beach was deserted. I kicked off my sandals, relishing the cool sand on my bare feet. During the day, the sun baked the sand, making it too hot to step on for more than a few seconds. As kids, Kai and I would race each other from the ocean across the huge swath of scorching white sand, to the Popsicle cart behind the snorkel gear rentals. The trick was to run fast, your toes barely brushing the ground. Still, we would gasp, "Hot! Hot! Hot!" as we ran. By the time we reached the relief of grassy lawn, we usually forgot to care about who had won the race. It felt like both of us had won, turning our tongues into rainbows, dangling our feet in the pool. I would always order cherry. Kai would mix it up—sometimes pineapple, sometimes lime, sometimes blue raspberry—depending on his mood.

My friendship with Kai was like the sand beneath my feet. As kids, our friendship was midday-sun sand, its heat immediate and strong. In the years since then, the sand had cooled. What was our relationship now? Were we still friends? Was he the same person I remembered?

A breeze teased strands of hair out of my ponytail and brushed them into my face. The moon was a glowing china plate in the sky, so white and smooth it looked artificial. I had expected my stomach to be a riot of butterflies, but now that I was actually out of the hotel room, making my way toward the lava tubes—toward Kai—I felt a strange absence of nerves. It seemed like I was separate from myself, watching my actions from a distance. Like I was a character in a novel, turning the pages to see what would happen next.

From the beach, I headed up the path skirting the edge of the golf course. At night, the golf course was abandoned, the golf flags flapping forlornly in the breeze. A pair of seagulls strutted across the green as if they owned it. Across the parking lot, the path turned to gravel. I turned on my flashlight, aiming its narrow beam at the uneven ground, and willed myself not to trip. My nerves had returned with a vengeance. Every step took me closer to Kai. What was he expecting, exactly? What was going to happen? What did I want to happen?

At school, everything was different. I was different. There I was Tegan, captain of the soccer team. Tegan, leader of the student council. Tegan, straight-A student, never shy about raising a hand in class, the girl everyone wanted as their lab partner. I had friends, sure, but sometimes I felt separate from the other kids. No guy had ever asked me out—unless you counted Mark Teng inviting me to lunch that one time so I'd help him with his science fair project. And I'd had little crushes here and there, but all of them faded within a few months, like seeds that hadn't been given enough water to grow. My focus was firmly on the future—achieving, striving, succeeding. I was determined to be the first one in my family to attend a four-year university. That goal underlaid everything I did, pushing me toward perfection. I could take risks on the soccer field; I could make a fool of myself in front of the entire student body by acting out some goofy skit at an assembly. No sweat. But I couldn't take risks outside of the careful parameters I had set for myself. Getting drunk at some party? Nope. Making out with random guys? No, thanks. I'm sure some of my classmates thought I was boring, but I didn't care. I told myself it would all be worth it, that day I got my acceptance letter in the mail.

Which is part of what made this whole sneaking-out-late-at-night-to-meet-some-guy-I-barely-knew thing so surreal. I didn't do stuff like this. Maybe I was fooling myself, expecting Kai to be the same guy I knew as a kid. Maybe he was a total asshole. Maybe he was a creep. Maybe he just wanted to hook up. What if he expected to? I mean, I was meeting him at midnight in a deserted cave in Hawaii. Nobody knew where I was. Maybe this was the stupidest thing I had ever done.

I stopped in my tracks, breathing in the cool, damp air, trying to decide what to do. I almost turned around and headed back up the path, back to the hotel room, back to my (hopefully still sleeping) parents. But then I remembered Kai's buoyant smile, the kindness in his eyes, and the way it had been so normal talking with him even though we hadn't seen each other in years. Deep in my gut, I trusted him.

So, for better or for worse, I kept walking.

The path began to slope downward, and I knew I was getting close to the lava tubes. Soon, the path turned left around a bend, and my heart thudded urgently in my chest. When I rounded the corner, there it was. Like a place out of my dreams, it looked exactly the same as I remembered.

The entrance to the lava tubes—tunnels created from hardened lava hundreds of years ago—was dark with shadows. My grating footsteps on the gravel sounded especially loud in the hushed night. A flashlight beam bobbed into view at the cave opening. I clicked my flashlight off and on and off again, a greeting.

"Tegan?" Kai said. "Is that you?" He didn't shout, but his voice carried in the quiet draped around us.

"It's me," I said, clicking my flashlight back on and crunching down the gravel path toward him. A flash of memory: our eight-year-old selves, planning to hide out here and live like the Boxcar Children so I would never have to return home. Because that summer, leaving had meant the end of the world. Of course, no vacation lasts forever. The world Kai and I had created had predictably ended. My mom had soothed me on the plane ride home, stroking my hair as I cried in her lap.

"You made it," Kai said when I got close enough to see his face. He was wearing a collared button-down shirt and board shorts. There was a knot in my stomach, but then he smiled, and the knot relaxed. His smile was the same smile of the friend I had known before.

"I was surprised how much I remembered from when we came here as kids," I said. "Plus, your directions were good. Very thorough."

He laughed, and I laughed—it was good to laugh, even though what I'd said wasn't particularly funny. The laughter helped ease the weird tension buzzing between us.

"Come on in," Kai said, gesturing for me to go ahead. I cautiously stepped forward, ducking my head under the low opening. I had forgotten how dark it gets inside the lava tubes. The hardened rock was black and smooth, with a richness that was different from the ordinary gray rocks back home. This rock was ... magical. It had seemed that way when I was a kid, and it still seemed that way now. This rock had poured forth from the deepest recesses of the earth. Touching it was like touching the distant past and the distant future at the same time.

Soon the cave roof sloped up enough to stand. I gazed above us at the hole I remembered in the cave ceiling—through it, I could glimpse a star-filled sky and the bright moon.

"*Gorgeous night, huh?*" *Kai said from behind me.*

"*Yeah,*" *I murmured, turning to face him. A camping lantern and two beach towels were spread out on the ground.* "*What's this fancy setup?*" *I asked, teasing, trying to sound more casual than I felt.*

"*Oh, just a little something I had my butler drag out here,*" *Kai said, matching my tone. He bent down and switched on the lantern. A bright glow warmed the cave. Instantly, the surroundings seemed homier. I settled down onto the green-and-blue striped beach towel.*

"*So,*" *I said.* "*Tell me everything.*"

"*Everything?*"

"*Yeah. Like, what have you been up to the past seven years?*"

Kai grinned. "*Not much to tell. Surfing, school, working on my parents' boat.*"

"*Oh yeah—a fishing boat, right?*"

Kai eased himself down onto the other beach towel. "*No, it's a tourist boat. Dolphin excursions, manta ray snorkels.*"

"*I did a manta ray snorkel, the last time I was here.*"

"*I know. That's how we met.*"

"*What?*" *I laughed, thinking he was making a joke, but Kai looked serious.* "*What are you talking about?*" *I asked.* "*We met because you knocked over my sandcastle.*" *The moment was still so clear in my memory. Kai had washed up onto the shore in a giant rogue wave that completely destroyed my painstakingly constructed castle. He had seemed like a creature of the wild ocean—a mer-child, seaweed tangled around his legs and salt water soaking his hair. I had been angry at first; it was not the most opportune moment to begin a friendship. Soon, though, Kai won me over with his quick smile, his easygoing nature, and a pink seashell he'd found buried along the shoreline. By the end of that day, we were two peas in a pod, two hermit crabs sharing the same shell.*

"No, we met before the sandcastle, when you and your parents came onto our boat," Kai said. "You had signed up for a manta ray snorkel. You were the youngest one there by far."

"That's right," I said, remembering that night: the dark water lapping against the boat, the salty smell of the wind, and the cold shock of the ocean, even with our wet suits on, when we dropped anchor and dipped ourselves into the water. "But, wait—how do you know that?" I asked.

"Because I was there," Kai insisted. "I had to convince my parents to let you do it. They said you were too young, but I promised I would watch you the whole time."

I scrunched up my nose. "You mean, like a babysitter?"

"No, like—like a friend." He flopped down onto his back. After a moment he raised himself up on his elbows. "You really don't remember, Tegan?"

I shook my head. "I'm sorry. I don't remember you being there."

He laughed a little to himself.

"What?" I asked.

"Nothing. Just—I obviously didn't make as big of an impression on you as you made on me!"

I blushed. I hadn't meant to hurt Kai's feelings. "So what did we talk about, this actual first time we met?" I asked. "Maybe it will jog my memory."

"We didn't really have a conversation. I remember handing you the wet suit, but I was too shy to say anything."

"You, shy?" I nudged his foot with mine. "I don't believe it."

"You're one to talk! My mom thought you weren't going to make it out there with those manta rays. 'That little girl is gonna pee her pants,' she told me."

I laughed. "Your mom said that?"

"Yep. Listen, we've seen grown men freak out when the manta rays come. Total panic attacks. We all thought you would get scared and want to come back to the boat. But I can still see you, jumping right into that water without a backward glance. And when it was time to go, you came swimming back to the boat like you'd had the time of your life, without an ounce of fear or remorse."

"I didn't want to leave. Those manta rays were magical." I picked at a hangnail and sighed. "We didn't make it out there this trip. I wish we had. My parents could use some magic right about now."

Kai's brow wrinkled in concern. "Everything okay?"

"Yeah, it's fine. I mean, no, it's not really fine; they're getting divorced, I'm pretty sure. It seems inevitable at this point. This whole trip has been like a ticking time bomb."

"I'm sorry to hear that," Kai said softly. He was the first person I had told—the first time I had even really admitted the words to myself— which seemed strange, as I barely knew him. Maybe because I was on vacation, far away from my normal life, I felt comfortable talking to him about things I would never have voiced to anyone back home.

"Thanks. Anyway, I don't really want to talk about my parents right now."

"That's cool," Kai said, scooting up so his back was against the wall opposite me. His knees were bent, mirroring mine. "If you ever want to talk about it, I'm here."

"Thank you," I said. I could feel that tension settling in between us again, buzzing like electric sparks. He was looking into my face, his eyes deep pools of amber in the lantern's glow. I looked away, at the shadows on the rock behind him.

"Give me your phone," Kai said.

"What?"

"Here." He handed his phone to me. "Put your number in, and I'll do the same in yours."

I pulled my phone out of my sweater pocket and slid it along the beach towel toward him. He typed in his number as I put mine into his phone, saving it under Your Old Friend Tegan. *I don't know what compelled me to reinforce the friendship component of our relationship. Maybe it was the romantic glow of the lantern, the tucked-away feeling of the caves, the flickering tension that sprang up between us out of nowhere, like flames that could leap out of control at any moment. I had that teetering-on-the-edge-of-a-cliff feeling—it would be so easy to close my eyes and let myself fall down into the unknown. But it was terrifying, that feeling. I preferred to be standing firmly on stable ground. So I did my best to pull back from the cliff's edge.*

I cleared my throat and slid Kai's phone back to him. "So tell me about school," I said, changing the subject to the mundane. "What are your friends like?"

"They're cool. Funny. You'd like them. They all can't wait to graduate and get out of here, always talking about moving to the mainland. I say they don't know what they have right in front of them."

"You don't want to move to the mainland?"

"Naw, not really." Kai grinned, the same grin I remembered from childhood slowly widening across his face. "Why move anywhere else when you already live in paradise?"

"Hard to argue with that," I agreed. "If I lived here, I wouldn't want to leave either. I'm gonna have a hard enough time tomorrow."

"I can't believe you're already leaving tomorrow. I wish I'd run into you earlier. There's so much I want to show you!" Kai moved his leg over, just a little, so his foot brushed mine.

I swallowed. "Do you have a girlfriend?" I asked abruptly, inching back toward the cliff edge I'd tried to avoid.

Kai seemed taken aback by the question. Was he blushing? "No," he said. "Flyin' solo." He paused, studying me. "What about you?"

For a half second, I considered lying and making up a boyfriend. How would Kai ever know? But I'm a horrible liar, for one thing. And I didn't want to lie to him. I wanted him to trust me as I did him, even if I never saw him again after this night.

"No one for me either," I said. "At least, not yet." I bit my lip, realizing the words sounded much different—much flirtier—than they had in my head.

Kai groaned. "I wish you weren't leaving tomorrow!" he said.

"I know."

We looked at each other. Kai's eyes were strikingly familiar and new at the same time.

"So ... tell me about your family," I said. "The last time I saw you, I think Theo was four? I remember we buried him in the sand, and he got upset."

Kai laughed. "He's eleven now. He's always following me around, trying to copy whatever I do. It can get annoying sometimes. My other brother is Paulo. He's five. He can get away with anything because he's the youngest. He's super cute, and believe me, he knows it."

"I'm so jealous. I've always wanted siblings."

"You can have one of mine!" Kai said. "Seriously, though—you're right. I'm lucky. My mom says my brothers and I will appreciate each other more when we're older."

"I bet that's true. And how's Makana the Magnificent?" Makana was their grizzled boxer dog. I had met him once, when we were kids; he loved playing in the waves. He had raced over to us and licked my cheeks. I usually felt apprehensive around big dogs, but I hadn't been the least bit

14

scared of Makana.

"Oh … " Sadness washed over Kai's face, and my heart sank. "He got sick—cancer—and he was too old for treatment. We had to put him down last year."

"Kai, I'm so sorry. That must have been really hard."

"The hardest part actually wasn't the moment when he died. It was right after, when we were left with this shell that looked like Makana but wasn't him anymore. I wish I could remember him as alive and vibrant, but it's tough not to think back on that final image of him."

We lapsed into silence. It would have been natural for Kai to ask about my family, but I wondered if he was avoiding the topic because of my parents' impending divorce.

After a few moments, he said, "Sorry, don't mean to be a downer. Tell me something you're passionate about."

"Passionate?" The word intimidated me. "Um, I don't know. School? I'm aiming to go to college, so school pretty much consumes my life."

"What's your favorite subject?"

"It used to be math, but now it's science. My physics teacher was really awesome. She helped me see the world in an entirely new way. There's all these hidden mysteries and magic lying beneath the surface of things."

My friend Andrea would have rolled her eyes if I geeked out like this, but Kai looked impressed. "I think science is really confusing," he said. "I wish I could see it the way you do. 'Magic' is about the last word I would associate with science class."

"Here, I'll give you an example," I said, not even trying to hide the enthusiasm in my voice. Pretty soon, I would start waving my hands around as I talked—something my dad did too. He claimed it was "part of our Italian heritage." My hands only started waving around when I was excited about something. I never even noticed myself doing it.

"Did you know that trees talk to each other?" I continued.

Kai shook his head. "No way."

"Yep. Scientists discovered recently that trees communicate with each other through tiny roots in the soil."

"What do they talk about?" Kai asked.

"They send distress signals about drought and share nutrients with other trees. Like, a birch tree will send carbon to a fir tree, and then in the winter, when the birch tree doesn't have any leaves, the fir tree will send over some carbon. It's really amazing. We've always thought of trees as these independent organisms, competing against each other for water and sunlight, but actually they have this entire social network."

"Well, that is freaking awesome," Kai said, genuine wonder in his tone. "I'll never look at a tree the same way again. Tell me another one."

I laughed. "You make it sound like I'm telling stories."

"You are, in a way. True stories. I always thought science was memorizing formulas or studying diagrams in a textbook, but you make it interesting." He spread his arms wide, as if to take in the entire world around us. "Tegan Rossi, I can't believe I'm saying this, but you just might make me fall in love with science."

Fall in love. *My face grew hot, and I looked away from him, gazing out toward the cave entrance. Darkness. Nothing but darkness. Inside our cozy halo of light, in this secret hideout from our childhood, it was as if we were the only two people in the universe.*

"Tell me another one," Kai said softly. "Please?"

"Okay." I crossed my legs beneath me. "Have you heard of Schrödinger's cat paradox?"

"Um, no."

"Basically, it's a thought experiment. Imagine you put a cat in a steel box."

"Why? What'd the cat do?"

"Just go with it. In the box there's also a bottle of poison, a hammer, a radioactive substance, and a Geiger counter."

"A Geiger what?"

"It measures ionizing radiation. So when the radioactive substance decays, the Geiger counter detects it. This triggers the hammer to smash the bottle, releasing the poison, which kills the poor unsuspecting cat."

Kai shrugged. "That's okay. I've always been more of a dog person."

I nudged him playfully. "Anyway, the whole point is that until you open the box, the cat is both alive and dead at the same time."

Kai scrunched up his eyebrows. "Wait—what? That's not possible."

"I know, it's kinda trippy. The way my teacher explained it is that since radioactive decay is a random process, there is no way of predicting when it will happen. So there's no way of knowing when the cat will die. You have to open the box to observe whether the cat is alive or dead."

"Okay ... " Kai said. "I'm still following ... "

"Until you open the box, there's no way of knowing which state the cat is in, so you have to treat it like all possibilities are correct. So the cat is both alive and dead. That's the paradox. It's like, my aunt had this breast cancer scare—and thankfully, she's fine. The tumor was benign. But she said when she was waiting for the results, she was in this weird limbo state. She both had cancer and didn't have cancer."

"I'm confused," Kai said. "You can have cancer and not know about it, right? Just because you don't know about it doesn't mean it doesn't exist."

"That's true. And until my aunt got the test results, both possibilities existed at the same time. She both had cancer and didn't have cancer. The cat was both alive and dead."

"Huh," Kai said. "I'm not gonna lie—I still don't really get it. But I liked listening to you explain it. You're crazy smart. And it's cute when

you get all excited and wave your arms around as you talk."

Now I was definitely blushing. I crossed my arms, to rein them in. "I've been talking too much. So what about you? Tell me a big dream you have."

Kai tilted his head back, looking up at the small circle of starry sky. "I know it's, like, impossible to do this as a career. But I want to be an artist."

My eyebrows shot up. I never would have pegged him for an artist. "Wow! That's really cool. What kind of art do you make?"

"I've done some painting and collage. Last year, I discovered wood carving, and it's become my jam. My dream is to open my own art gallery one day."

"That would be amazing, Kai! I have no doubt you will. I remember your determination when we used to dare each other to do those silly stunts in the pool."

Kai laughed. "If only real life were as easy as doing a headstand or holding your breath underwater."

My phone beeped, and I glanced down. It was a text message from Andrea, about this new TV series she'd started watching and wanted me to watch too. I felt a pang that I'd be heading back to my real life tomorrow. No—today. I squinted at my phone, not believing my eyes: 12:52. I could have sworn only minutes had passed since I'd arrived at the lava tubes.

"Crap," I said, shoving my phone into my pocket. "I should probably head out soon."

Kai leaned back and groaned. "Ow," he said, sitting up and rubbing his head. "Lava rock is unforgiving."

"Tell me about it," I said, pulling my right arm out of my sweater. "I still have the scar to prove it." I stretched my arm out to him in the lamplight, and Kai scooted forward to study it. Our bodies were so close that I could lean forward and rest my forehead against his, if I wanted to.

The scar was a narrow line, slightly raised, running parallel to the vein doctors had used the few times I'd gotten my blood drawn.

"Oooh, that turned into a good one," Kai said, gently running his thumb along my scar. I shivered. "Sorry," he said, releasing my arm.

"It's okay," I said. It hadn't been a bad shiver. Part of me wanted him to lightly touch my arm again.

"I think about that night all the time," Kai said softly. "Most exciting night of my life, running away with you."

"Maybe we would have made it, if only I wasn't such a klutz," I joked. It wasn't true—even if I hadn't sliced my arm open, even if Kai hadn't run for help, it wasn't like we could have really hidden out in this cave forever. They would have found us in the morning.

"We could still do it," Kai said. "Run away." His eyes met mine in the lamplight, a question in his expression. I knew what he was asking. And I knew what I wanted to answer. But I was scared to let myself go. To relinquish control.

So as Kai leaned toward me, I turned away. His lips grazed my hair. I pretended I didn't notice. "Thanks for inviting me here tonight," I said, scooting back and standing. "It was really great to catch up."

"Yeah, I'm glad we did this."

"I guess I'll … see you around."

Kai bent down, gathering up the beach towels. "I'll walk back with you," he said.

"Oh, you don't have to do that; I can take care of myself." It irked me when guys acted like they needed to be "protectors" for girls.

"I know," Kai said. "But I should be heading back too, and I thought we could walk together." He handed me the lantern and widened his eyes. "Maybe I'm scared to walk back alone, okay?"

He laughed, and I laughed, and things felt better between us, almost like the kiss attempt had never happened. The walk back to the hotel passed quickly—I was aware of every minute ticking by, grains of sand slipping through my helpless fingers. We kept to safe subjects, like funny YouTube videos and stories of grumpy teachers and our favorite bands. Kai told me about this local musician who sometimes played at a restaurant down the road called The Blue Oasis. "I'll take you there," Kai said. "Next time you're in town." And even though it was never going to actually happen—my parents were splitting up, and I probably wouldn't come back to Hawaii for years, and Kai and I likely wouldn't talk again after this night—his words made me hopeful.

So I smiled and replied, "It's a date."

We were back at the hotel, standing at the edge of the outdoor hallway that led to my room. A lamp glowed a few feet away, casting our shadows against the wall. In the distance, the waves were a rhythmic hum.

"Well, I guess this is goodbye-for-now, Tegan Rossi," Kai said.

"I'll miss you," I blurted out. I didn't know why I'd said it. Past 1:00 a.m., and I was tired, and suddenly the last thing in the world I wanted to do was to go back into that room where my parents slept, to my normal life that quite soon was going to shift into something grayer and lonelier. Besides, it was true. I had always wondered what had happened to Kai. After seeing him again now, I was definitely going to miss him.

"I'll miss you too," Kai said. He pulled out his phone from his pocket and waved it at me. "That's why we should stay in touch. And then you'll come visit again. Next summer?"

"Maybe. Yeah, okay." I smiled, taking in his mess of dark hair, his strong nose, his dark eyebrows and big, expressive eyes. There was no way I'd be back next summer.

He opened his arms for a hug, and I leaned into him. Underneath his cologne I smelled something else, sunscreen or salt water. Maybe he spent so much time in the ocean that he always smelled a little of salt. His arms around me were solid and warm.

"I'm horrible at goodbyes," I mumbled into his chest.

"I know," he said. "I remember from last time. That's why this is just goodbye-for-now."

I gave him one last squeeze, pulling back to look at his face. "Goodbye-for-now, Kai Kapule. Thanks for tonight."

I'd been too scared to kiss him earlier, but now I wished he would try again. His brown eyes held mine. I couldn't read his expression. He leaned in, and my heart surged. His lips brushed my cheek—sweetly, gently—only for a moment, and then he stepped back, releasing me.

I hesitated. He looked as if he wanted to say something else. But when he didn't say anything, I walked up the path toward my hotel room. I turned around, just once, to see if he was watching me. He was. He smiled and held up his hand in a goodbye wave. I waved back. I felt sure it was the last time I would ever see him.

Then I turned the corner, and that was that.

I was never actually going to run away with Kai that night. But kissing him—really kissing him—would have been a metaphorical running. Running toward something new, something I wanted but was afraid to want, something that I couldn't control and that might have disrupted my carefully balanced plans. Kissing him would have meant I needed to be vulnerable. To let someone else in.

Every day after that night, I wished I had kissed him. I wished I had said yes. I wished I had let myself fall from the edge of the cliff.

I stumble across the threshold of the cave into a warm Hawaiian afternoon. After the dim light of the lava tubes, the sun is especially bright, and the colors around me seem more intense than normal. Lush green grasses, bushes with bright-yellow flowers, palm trees drooping with brown coconuts, and, in the distance, the sparkling blue of the ocean. The dirt path is exactly the way I remember it, winding up from the lava tubes toward the golf course and the resort where I stayed with my parents.

My parents. Are they here? Did we come to Hawaii on a family vacation? For some reason, I can't remember the flight over. Maybe I went to the lava tubes to meet Kai again, but I fell asleep. Maybe I bumped my head and lost my recent memory.

No, that can't be right. Kai wouldn't just leave me in the lava tubes. Unless he was running somewhere to get help for me, like he had when we were kids and I hurt my arm.

But I would definitely remember if my parents were here together because it would mean they could stand to be in the same room again—something that hasn't been true since the divorce, not even at my high school graduation. They sat on different sides of the auditorium, and I had two separate graduation parties: one with my mom's family and one with my dad's. Andrea thought it would be special to have two parties, but it just made me tired and sad. It would have been so much better with everyone together.

If my parents are here, trying one last time to knit our family back together, it will be nothing short of a miracle.

I glance around for Kai, but I don't see any sign of him. Not even a trace of footprints in the dust. I don't know what else to do, so I head up the path, the same path I walked with Kai three years ago. Maybe more memories will come back.

Three years ago …

My phone vibrated with a text before I'd even slipped my key into the lock and let myself back into the hotel room. When I glimpsed Kai's name on my screen, I felt an undeniable surge of happiness.

> Kai: next time let's have more than 1 aloha ok?

I read the text multiple times, but it remained a riddle. I replied with a confused emoji and a series of question marks.
A few seconds later, my phone vibrated again.

> Kai: aloha means hello & goodbye. today i had to say hello & goodbye to u at the same time = only 1 aloha

As I read his words, a wave of bittersweet emotion coursed through me. Nostalgia? Regret? Hope? I wanted to race back down the hall and chase after him, but I told myself that would be stupid. We would have to say goodbye all over again. I was leaving tomorrow, and that was that.
I was trying to decide what to text back when my phone vibrated again.

> Kai: next time u owe me 2 separate alohas. it's too hard

```
to say goodbye when we just said
hello
    Tegan: i know. what if i call u
when i get home & say aloha?
    Kai: not as good as in person,
but i'll take what i can get
```

Looking back, that's when our friendship truly began again. The next day, I called him when I got home, as promised. We've talked pretty much every day since.

Against the sapphire sky, the palm trees shimmer like a mirage. I'm wearing thin flip-flops that slap against the ground with each step. The path has transitioned from sandy dirt to black asphalt that practically steams in the humid heat. As kids, Kai and I wondered if you could really fry an egg on a hot sidewalk. We decided to perform an experiment, and Kai stole an egg from his parents' fridge. Tragically, before he reached our designated meeting place, the egg broke in his shorts pocket. He told me that he could never again reach into a pocket without remembering, too clearly, the gooey feel of raw egg against his fingers.

I reach the crossroads where the path splits in two. One branch winds down along the perimeter of the golf course—toward the beach and the resort—while another veers off to the right, toward town. I'm about to turn left, the way Kai walked me back to my hotel room three years ago, when I spot something in the distance.

A small figure with dark hair cresting the ridge. Heading toward town.

Kai?

The figure is too far away to tell whether it's him or not.

Still, it's something. I turn right and hurry up the path. After a few steps, I break into a run, my flip-flops slap-slap-slapping the ground, sounding like a drum, like a pulse, like my frantic, hopeful heartbeat.

Two months ago ...

"There's only one thing I want for graduation," Kai began. There was an unusually cautious tone in his voice.

"Let me guess ... " I said. "A new kitty?" It was a carried-over joke from I didn't even remember when—I was a cat lover, but Kai preferred dogs. We had an ongoing battle over which was a superior pet, even though Kai had no experience with cats, and I had no experience with dogs. Sometimes I talked to Olina, his family's dog, when Kai and I FaceTimed. I refused to admit that she had totally won me over with her playful barks and wagging tail.

Kai laughed, but it sounded strained. He cleared his throat, then said, "All I want for graduation is for you—Tegan, please—will you come visit? Even just for a few days. It'll be so great! We can relax on the beach, hike Akaka Falls, go snorkeling ... "

It was two days before finals began, and I was a hot mess of stress and sleep deprivation. Nothing sounded better than stretching out on a beach towel in the warm Hawaiian sand, waves rolling in, my best friend squinting at me in the sunshine. Graduation seemed far enough away to be another lifetime. So I let myself surrender to the deliciousness of the daydream. I didn't think about what it might mean, or what might happen, or how everything might change. I sighed into the phone and said, "That sounds like absolute perfection."

"Really? You'll come?"

"Yeah. Let me just get through finals and check with my mom, and then I'll book my plane ticket."

"Okay, perfect. That sounds perfect. I'll talk to you later." It was like he wanted to get off the phone before I changed my mind. "Call me if you need a study break."

"Thanks, will do. Bye."

As I hung up, a spark of doubt flickered in the back of my mind—was I really going to do this? Visit in person and risk opening the Pandora's box of whatever feelings Kai and I had for each other? Staying on the shore was so much safer than diving into the uncertain, choppy ocean waves. I was already mentally backpedaling: People's plans change. Kai will understand if I can't come. *I resolved to deal with it later and opened my textbook to continue my long trek up the mountain of final exams.*

Before long, I've caught up enough to see that yes, the figure I'm following is definitely Kai—same jet-black hair, tan skin, broad shoulders. "Kai!" I shout when I get close enough. "Kai! It's me, Tegan!"

He stops and turns. My heart leaps. But instead of smiling, he looks confused.

And when I reach him, and get a closer look at his face, I feel uneasy. Something is off. He looks a lot like Kai, but ... something is different from the friend I remember. He looks like a Kai impersonator. All the individual features are there, but when you put them together, it doesn't add up.

I rest my hands on my knees and bend over, my breath ragged from running. My feet hurt. Sweat trickles down my back. My heart is beating fast, and not just from exertion—I feel suddenly nervous, and embarrassed, and shy. I thought that when I saw Kai again in person after all these months apart, we would be instantly comfortable together, and it would seem like I'd never left Hawaii. But now that I'm standing here with him, I feel ... awkward. Uncertain. Maybe following Kai was a bad idea. Maybe I should have turned left at the crossroads, toward the hotel, and looked for my parents. After all, I still can't remember what Kai and I argued about. Maybe he's angry with me.

"Tegan?" Kai says. His voice sounds different too—slightly higher than I remember. "You're Tegan?"

I nod. "Look, I know we got in a fight, but I can't remember anything about it. I don't even remember how I got here. Please, can you forgive me for whatever I did and help me? I need my best friend right now."

"Okay, sure. Let's go find him."

"Kai, please. Don't act like you don't know me."

Then he smiles, and I know even before he says anything else: this person is not Kai. His smile is different.

I step backward. "Who are you?" I ask, my fists clenched.

"I'm Theo," he says, laughing. "C'mon, I'll take you to Kai. He's probably at the shop. I was headed that direction anyway."

Theo. Kai's younger brother.

My tension and fear melt away into relief. I bound forward and give him a hug. "Theo! Wow, I can't believe it—the last time I saw you, you were a little kid! Sorry about burying you in the sand, by the way."

He pats me on the back agreeably. "It's okay. No hard feelings."

"Kai's kept me up-to-date about you," I say, breaking away from the hug.

"You too. Believe me, I've heard a *lot* about you."

Does he mean that in a good way or a bad way? I can't tell. It strikes me that he might know why Kai and I got into a fight. I could ask him. But I bite my tongue and decide against it. I'll wait to talk to Kai directly.

I follow Theo down the path toward town, excitement burgeoning in my chest. I can't wait to see Kai.

Kona is bigger than I remember—there's a chain supermarket now, plus a Costco and a Target. Still, downtown looks mostly the same: surf- and snorkel-guide kiosks, clothing stores, knick-knacky tourist shops, casual seafood restaurants. Even though it's a weekday morning (today is Monday, according to Theo), lots of people are out, walking and window-shopping. You can spot the tourists by their sunburns, tacky T-shirts, and big floppy hats.

Kai sent me a tacky T-shirt as a Christmas gift one year: bright pink with white hibiscus flowers, plus a sunset in the background. It was also three sizes too big, so I wore it as a nightgown. My favorite gift he ever sent me was a puka shell necklace. Unlike the factory-made ones some kids at school wear, my necklace was a single puka shell attached to a thin gold chain. I wore it all the time and got so many compliments, until I lost it a few months ago. I searched everywhere, tearing apart my bedroom and my mom's car, but no luck. It must have slipped off at some point while I was wearing it. The chain was very delicate, easily broken. I never had the heart to tell Kai that I lost it.

Now, following Theo as he weaves around people and bikes and street vendors, I mourn the loss of the necklace yet again. I wish I had it on—to show Kai how much I love it, as if by association I can prove how much he means to me.

I'm more nervous to see him than I expected to be.

Theo glances back at me. "We're close!" he says. "It's up on the next block!"

Kai works at a tourist shop that sells carved wooden dishes, signs, and decorations. He told me a little about the shop when he first got the job last year, but he seems pretty indifferent—doesn't love it, doesn't hate it. His boss is "chill" and will let him bump up his hours to full-time when he graduates; plus, the work is easy. His real love, he says, is carving, but working at the shop will pay the bills. Last we talked, he was planning to move out of his parents' house right after graduation and get his own studio apartment downtown. I always tell him he should go to college, study art or business—it could help him open his art gallery one day. But Kai always replies that college is too expensive and he doesn't need it. I think he's just scared, and I've told him so. *Maybe that's what our big fight was about.*

I'm so lost in thought that I don't notice a girl backing out of a doorway, holding an enormous cardboard box. We bump right into each other. The box wobbles in her grasp and tilts, spilling papers onto the sidewalk.

"Oh my gosh, I'm so sorry!" I bend down to gather up the mess. The girl sets the box down on the ground.

"No big deal," she says. "It was my fault. I couldn't even see where I was going."

We smile at each other, and I feel a jolt of recognition—she looks familiar. Dark hair streaked with burgundy highlights, charcoal eyeliner rimming almond eyes, a small stud of a nose ring, barely noticeable, in her left nostril ... but I can't place her.

The girl, meanwhile, seems suddenly flustered. She hurries to gather up the papers, which I see now are leaflets and postcards advertising an art show. I thought she was coming out of a shop, but it's actually a gallery.

I hold up one of the postcards. "This looks neat. Mind if I take one?"

"Sure," she says, not meeting my eyes.

I slip the postcard into my back pocket and neaten the rest of the stack before handing them to her.

"Thanks," she says, hefting the enormous box into her arms again.

"Do you need a hand with that?"

"No, I'm fine." She sweeps past me, walking in the opposite direction of Kai's shop. I stare after her, puzzled by her sudden coldness. *Did I do something wrong?*

Then I feel a tap on my shoulder and whirl around.

Theo stands there, looking impatient. "What happened? You were right behind me, and then you disappeared."

"I'm sorry. I literally bumped into someone and had to help her—"

Theo smiles: all is forgiven. "It's okay. I was just worried. Kai would kill me if I let something happen to you."

"I'm ready now. Sorry."

As if no longer willing to trust me on my own, Theo grabs my hand, giving me a look that says, *This means nothing, okay?* It reminds me of a babysitter holding a child's hand in the supermarket so they won't get separated. Together we wind our way down the sidewalk, weaving around carts selling coconut water and sidling through clusters of slow-moving tourists.

After what seems like only a few seconds, but must have been minutes, Theo abruptly stops in the middle of the sidewalk. He drops my hand. "We're here," he announces.

I look up at the storefront. Tiki Island Decorations & Designs. Yep, this is it. Kai always jokingly refers to it as The Tiki Room.

I take a deep breath and follow Theo inside.

A little bell jingles as we push open the door and walk into the shop. It is a small space, crowded with wooden items stacked on shelves, displayed on tabletops, and even hanging from the ceiling. It is like we have climbed inside a tree. The shop is empty. Reggae music plays softly in the background.

Theo saunters straight into the heart of the store, but I linger in the entryway. It seems suddenly like my whole life depends on what happens next. I quell the urge to push back open the door and flee into the street. *This is Kai*, I remind myself. *Kai, your best friend.* But the nerves don't go away.

Crowded against the front window is a fake Christmas tree decorated top to bottom with wooden ornaments—"HAND-CRAFTED," a sign proclaims. Trying to distract myself, I walk over and study the display. Some ornaments are smooth wooden globes, surprisingly light in my hand. Most of the globes are painted with images of surfers, dolphins, ocean waves. My favorite ornaments are the wooden snowflakes, paper-thin, so delicately carved it is impossible to imagine an actual person crafting them. Maybe, despite the sign's promise, these are machine- produced. I take one in each hand and compare them. It's clear they are different: one has six narrow points while the other is broader, like a starfish. *Could it be possible each ornament is unique, like real snowflakes? That would definitely mean they are hand-carved.*

The bell jingles. I glance over.

There he is.

Kai.

In the two seconds before he notices me, I observe him as a stranger would. He's carrying a plastic takeout bag—lunch, probably. His black hair is shaggier than the last time we FaceTimed, which alarms me. How long has it been since we've talked? He seems taller and sturdier than I remember. Board shorts, simple white T-shirt, sunglasses perched on his head. He looks bored: his expression is everyday, mundane, when you're not expecting anything unusual to happen. Then he sees me and does a double take.

"Tegan?" he says.

I'm still holding the snowflake ornament. I raise my hand in a little wave.

His mouth falls open in shock. "What are you doing here?"

Before I can respond, he drops the takeout bag right there on the floor, runs over, and envelops me in the biggest hug of my life. Just like that, all my nerves melt away. His arms around me are warm and strong. He smells like fresh laundry and coconut sunscreen. I make a wish: to stay wrapped up in this moment forever.

But eventually, Kai pulls away. He looks at me, an amazed smile lighting up his face. "I can't believe you're here. I can't believe you surprised me like this. How did you find the shop?"

"Theo showed me."

"Ah, so Theo was part of your master plan, huh? I thought he's been acting kind of weird lately."

I open my mouth to explain, but no words come. I don't know where to begin. How do I tell Kai that Theo hasn't been helping me—that actually, I have no clue what I'm doing here?

Unless … maybe he's right. Maybe I *have* been planning this big surprise with Theo, and somehow I bumped my head and got amnesia and forgot everything that's happened recently.

But no. That's not right either. Because Theo was surprised to see me too—he didn't know that I'd come here to Hawaii.

"I see you found one of my pieces," Kai says, nodding at the snowflake ornament in my hand.

"Wait … you *made* this?" I hold up the snowflake against the light, admiring its intricate detail all over again.

Kai shrugs. "Yeah, I've been playing around with snowflakes lately. They're fun to carve, and a challenge, because every one is unique."

"Gosh, these are exquisite, Kai. I'm going to buy this one."

"No, don't—I'm making one for you, actually. I was going to mail it for your birthday, but maybe I'll finish it in time to give it to you in person."

The unasked question—*How long am I staying in Hawaii?*—lingers in the air between us, but we both ignore it.

"I had no idea you have such skilled hands, Kai Kapule." I'm going for funny and playful, but it comes out sounding different. I blush, focusing my attention on attaching the ornament back onto the Christmas tree display.

"There you are!" Theo says, appearing at the end of the aisle. "I've been looking all over for you, bro! I couldn't find Mr. Kenu either."

"He's probably in the back taking a nap," Kai says. "I stepped out for a minute to get lunch. Things have been really quiet all day … until now!" He wraps an arm around my waist in a half hug. I let myself lean into him a little.

Theo smirks at us. "How come you didn't tell me Tegan was visiting? This is big news."

"You can cut the crap," Kai says, laughing. "You got me, Theo. I had no idea you were in on Tegan's surprise."

Theo doesn't need to respond; his confused expression says it all. Kai looks down at me. "Wait … so Theo wasn't in on the surprise?"

"No," I admit. "I just ran into him."

"I was over at the golf course making a delivery," Theo says. "She came running after me, calling out your name."

Kai's arm drops away from me. My throat tightens. Maybe now it's all going to come out—our argument, our silence, whatever I did that made him so upset.

"T, that doesn't sound like you," Kai says, his brow furrowed. He always teases me for being so organized, for wanting to arrange every careful detail in advance. "So you haven't been planning this for a long time? Did you come here spur-of-the-moment?"

"You're always saying my life could use more spontaneity, right?" I laugh, but Kai and Theo do not.

I look down. Despite all the wood-carved artwork filling the shop, the floor is, ironically, not wood—it's linoleum tiles.

Kai grabs my hands in his. "Tegan, what are you doing here? Is everything okay?"

"I don't know," I say, pure panic hitting me like a train. "I can't remember."

Ten years ago …

"We're almost there," Kai whispered. His hand was warm in mine as we crept together along the shadowy dirt path toward our secret hideout. At my elementary school, I never held hands with boys—doing so would immediately result in teasing exclamations of "Cooties!" from the other kids. But, here in Hawaii, everything was different. Kai and I grabbed each other's hands without thinking—when we went snorkeling and saw an especially cool fish, when the Popsicle cart emerged onto the pool deck in the afternoons, when I glimpsed a beautiful seashell nestled in the soft sand. And now, as we tiptoed through the descending darkness, it seemed normal to hold hands, to make sure we stayed together.

The last scraps of sunset were already fading from the sky; evening was falling quickly. Soon, my parents would expect me to come in from the waves. I wondered if they had noticed my absence yet.

I stumbled in my flip-flops, stubbing my toe on a rock. "Ow!"

"Are you okay?" Kai asked. "Do you want the light?"

I ignored my throbbing toe and tugged him forward. "No, I'm fine." Kai had a flashlight, but for now it was in his pocket. We would turn it on once we were safely in the lava tubes. We didn't want anyone to glimpse us sneaking away.

The day before, a lump had formed in my throat while I ate my cherry Popsicle, realizing how little time was left before my vacation ended. I would have to say goodbye to Kai. I would have to return home. I gave Kai the rest of my Popsicle because I wasn't hungry anymore. When I tried to talk, I had to shake my head and bite my lip to keep from crying.

Running away was Kai's idea, but I latched onto it immediately, thinking of my favorite book: The Boxcar Children. *I'd always loved the idea of surviving on my own, building a home out of nothing but my own resourcefulness. Kai and I would have a wonderful time living in the lava tubes. I imagined us playing in the ocean all day, pilfering food from buffets at the resort, and sleeping each night in our hideout. No school, no chores, no parents, no rules. It would be paradise.*

Kai had gathered supplies from his house: a picnic blanket, two pillows, a jumbo bag of trail mix, gummy worms. These he had placed inside our hideout earlier in the day. I wasn't able to bring my suitcase; it would have aroused suspicion. All I had were the clothes on my back and the sandals on my feet. And my lucky charm. I reached into my shorts pocket and rubbed my fingers against it—a small, smooth rock with sharp edges and a point at one end. Like an arrowhead. I'd found it in the lava tubes the first time Kai took me there. Without quite knowing why, I'd slipped it into my pocket. I'd wanted to bring something back with me—some evidence that this place existed, that my experiences here had really happened. Touching the stone, I became a brave adventurer.

Before too long, Kai and I reached the entrance to the lava tubes. Our secret hideout. We crept across the threshold, and Kai let go of my hand to grab his flashlight. Suddenly, there was a loud THUNK from outside. Scared, I darted forward, deeper into the cave. My sandal slipped on the slick floor, and before I knew it, I was falling sideways. A sharp rush of pain. When Kai clicked on his flashlight, blood was gushing down my arm.

"Oh no," Kai said.

I refused to look down at the gash. If I looked, it would only hurt worse. I gritted my teeth. "Do we have any Band-Aids?"

"I think it's too big for a Band-Aid." Kai's face was pale.

This was bad.

"Here, Tegan," he said, handing me the flashlight. "You stay here and wait for me to come back. I'll run as fast as I can."

"Where are you going?"

"To get help."

In the flashlight's glow, his eyes met mine, and that's when everything hit me. We weren't really going to stay in the lava tubes. We weren't going to escape our fate. The next day, the sun would rise, and I would board an airplane back to the mainland. Kai and I would have to say goodbye. Who knew if we would ever see each other again.

It couldn't have been more than fifteen or twenty minutes before Kai returned, my parents right behind him, along with a medic from the resort. When they found me, I was sobbing. I've never cried harder than I cried that night.

"It's okay," Kai says. "Shhh, it's okay."

I'm not crying, but I'm on the verge. He can tell. Even when we're talking on the phone, just our voices, and he can't see my face, he can always tell when I'm upset.

"Do you have your phone?" Theo asks. "You could check your call log. Maybe it will jog your memory."

I pat the various pockets of my shorts, but they're all empty except for the pointy sliver of rock I slipped into my front pocket earlier. No purse. No wallet, no money. No phone. No ID.

How did I fly here without my ID? How did I end up in the lava tubes?

"No, I don't have it. Can I borrow yours?" I ask. Tears are definitely welling up in my voice now. "Maybe I can try calling my mom."

"Of course." Kai unlocks the screen and hands me his phone.

I dial the ten digits as familiar as my own heartbeat. My hand is shaking a little as I lift the phone to my ear. I listen to it ring.

And ring. And ring. And ring.

No answer. The call doesn't click over to voice mail like it usually does.

I listen to five, six, seven more hollow rings, and then I sigh and hang up.

When I try my dad's number, the same thing happens. Ring, ring, ring, ring. No voice mail. Only endless ringing.

Frustrated, I hang up and hand the phone back to Kai. "I don't know where my parents are. Can I try calling them again later?"

"Sure," Kai says. "Maybe they put their phones on silent and then forgot. My mom does that all the time."

Still, there is worry in his face, a question in his eyes.

"Tegan, what's the last thing you remember?"

I close my eyes, trying to concentrate. "I was home, studying for finals. I was really stressed out. You and I made plans."

"What plans?"

"That I was going to visit you." I smile, remembering the joy in Kai's voice when I said I would come to Hawaii. He's been trying to get me to return ever since my last trip with my parents three years ago.

Kai's smile doesn't reach his eyes. "And that's the last thing you remember?"

"Well, it's the last time I remember talking to you. The next few days were really busy with finals and graduation. My parents insisted on throwing two separate graduation parties, which annoyed me. I wanted to talk to you about it because I knew that you would understand how I was feeling. But I don't remember talking with you again. Then I woke up in the lava tubes."

"Our place?"

I nod. I explain how I thought I saw him and followed him out of the lava tubes and up the path—and how it turned out to be Theo.

Kai focuses on his brother. "What were you doing there?"

"I told you," Theo murmurs. "I had to make *a delivery*."

Kai frowns. "And you didn't see anyone else around there?"

"No. No one. That place is tucked away—hardly anyone knows about it."

My attention is snagged by a calendar hanging on the wall behind the Christmas tree, wedged between a poster for a community luau and a flyer about a surfing competition. The calendar is turned to July. Which is funny, because it's June.

I point to the calendar. "What's today's date?"

"July 8th," Kai says.

No. No. The last thing I remember is graduation, and that was June 16th. I've lost nearly a month? Where has my memory gone?

Theo meets my eyes, a strange intensity in his voice. "Are you sure you're okay, Tegan? You don't—you don't have any bruises or scrapes, or, um—blood?"

Kai shoots him a look. All of a sudden, I understand what they are worried about.

"No," I say, feeling numb. "No, nothing bad happened. I mean, if I was attacked or something, I would remember, right?"

Kai and Theo don't say anything.

"I would," I repeat. "I would remember."

A look crosses Kai's face, and he seems to make a decision. "Hang on," he says, jogging toward the back of the store.

Ten minutes later, I'm in the passenger seat of Kai's Jeep. He drives; Theo's in the back seat. Before long, we pull up to a squat beige building with a big sign: MEDICAL CLINIC + URGENT CARE. The same place my parents took me the night Kai and I tried to run away as kids, when I split my arm open and needed stitches.

"Don't you think this is overreacting?" I ask.

"I know this isn't top on your list of Hawaiian destinations," Kai says. "But we need to get you checked out, T."

"But I don't have my ID or my insurance card or anything!"

"It's okay. This is a neighborhood clinic. My aunt works here. It'll be fine."

The clinic is exactly the same as I remember: small and empty, with light-blue walls and nubby gray carpet. It smells of antiseptic and pineapple air freshener. At least the room is air-conditioned. I collapse into a plastic chair beside a potted palm tree while Kai and Theo deal with the front desk.

I feel exhausted and embarrassed. *Why can't I remember anything?* Trying to reach beyond my memory of that last phone conversation with Kai is like staring and staring at a blank piece of paper. Nothing.

The plastic chair is hard and uncomfortable. My nerves are on edge. *I would remember*, I keep repeating to myself. *If I was attacked, I would definitely remember.* But, considering everything since graduation is an utter blank in my memory, I'm not able to reassure myself very well.

After a few minutes, Kai and Theo join me. "It's all taken care of," Kai says, handing me a few forms to fill out. "Aunt Sarah is going to see you soon. Luckily, it's a slow day, so we shouldn't have to wait long."

"Thanks, guys. For doing this. For worrying about me."

Theo gives me a thumbs-up and flips through a surfing magazine. Kai reaches his arm around my shoulders protectively. "You okay?" he asks.

"Yeah, I'm fine."

"Are you sure?"

I nod and bite my lip.

"Hey," Kai says after a few moments, smiling at me. "I like your necklace. Someone with extremely good taste must have picked it out."

"What?" I reach a hand up to my breastbone.

"I noticed it when I first saw you. It looks really nice."

My fingers slide down a thin chain until they reach a smooth, small shell. *My puka shell necklace! But how ... ? I'd lost it months ago.*

I try to mask my surprise—I don't want Kai to know I lost, or thought I lost, the gift he gave me. "This is my favorite necklace," I tell him.

The door opens, and a nurse pokes her head out. "Tegan?" she says. "We're ready to see you now."

Kai squeezes my shoulder, and Theo gives me another thumbs-up. I stand and follow the nurse into the exam room. *I would remember. I would remember. Please, please, please ...*

I'm grateful the nurse isn't chatty as she leads me back into an exam room. She weighs me, takes my blood pressure, checks my temperature. All normal. Then she tells me she's going to leave the room and asks me to undress from the waist down. "There's a paper gown, to cover yourself with," she says, pointing to a papery white sheet folded on the exam table.

She shuts the door behind her, and I peel off my jean shorts and underwear, folding them and placing them on a chair. I sit on the paper-covered exam table, pulling the paper gown over me like a shield. The paper is scratchy, and my bare legs are cold from the air conditioning.

Instinctively, my fingers feel for the scar on my right knee, circa fifth-grade recess. I used to love playing basketball with the boys ... until sore loser Tom LaRusa shoved me on a fast break layup. I fell hard, splitting my knee open on a jagged rock. I needed three stitches. Whenever I'm anxious, my hand gravitates toward the scar, rubbing its smoothness. It's a small dimple—nobody else would notice it—but it comforts me. It reminds me of the power within all of us to heal.

Only right now ... I don't feel the scar. I lift up the papery cloth, looking down at my right knee. A normal, average knee. Identical to the left one.

Where is my scar?

I'm pulling my knee up to my face, to study it more closely, when there are two brisk raps on the door. I let my knee fall back down and arrange the cloth over my legs. "Come in!"

The door opens, and a middle-aged woman with Kai's crinkle-eyed smile enters. Curly hair is piled on top of her head in a messy bun. She's wearing a white lab coat and bright, crazy-patterned socks. I like her immediately.

"Hi there. My name's Sarah," she says. "And you must be Tegan?"

"Yep, that's me."

"It's nice to finally meet you, Tegan. I've heard a lot about you from my nephew." Her eyes twinkle.

She reminds me of my mom, whom I miss with a sudden and fierce ache. *Where is my mom? Where is my dad? How did I get here?*

Sarah must notice the panic on my face. She places a gentle hand on my shoulder and squeezes it. "We've tried calling your parents, but we can't get through to them. We'll keep trying, and in the meantime I'd like to do a quick examination, if that's all right with you?"

I nod.

"Don't you worry one bit, honey. Everything is going to be okay."

I let myself believe her. *I would remember. I would remember.* For the first time since I walked through the doors of this clinic, my anxiety eases its grip a little.

Sarah does a thorough examination of my entire body, her fingers gently prodding my bare skin. She doesn't find any cuts, scrapes, bruises, or, as she puts it, "anything that would signal physical distress." She also doesn't find any evidence of head trauma, which would have explained my amnesia.

"Sometimes we can have selective amnesia," Sarah says. "The brain blocks out what it doesn't want to deal with. Has anything happened lately to upset you?"

Well, Kai and I had an argument, but I don't want to talk about that with his aunt. Plus, he and I seem fine now. I don't remember anything happening between my parents that would have upset me. I shake my head. "Sorry, I ... I can't think of anything."

"That's okay, hon. Here, let me listen to your heart." She slips her stethoscope under my tank top. The metal is cold against my skin, and I shiver.

After a few moments, Sarah pulls away. "Good. You sound perfectly healthy," she says. "I'm sure you hear this all the time, but I really like your tattoo. What does it mean?"

My tattoo? I don't have a tattoo. My expression is undoubtedly pure confusion, because Sarah taps my chest and says, "This one.

Over your heart."

I look down and push aside my tank top. Right where Sarah had placed her stethoscope, there is a simple black ink drawing of an hourglass. Most of the sand is up in the top half, but a few grains have slipped down into the bottom.

What the hell? I have no memory of getting this tattoo and no clue what it means.

"It's, um, just a reminder, you know," I fumble. "Time is always ticking away, and you better make the most of every second."

Sarah nods. "You are a wise young lady, Tegan Rossi. I can see why my nephew is so infatuated with you. Oh, and one more thing." She gives me a white paper bag, the top folded over twice.

"What's this?"

She smiles. "A little something we give to all the young women who visit the clinic. I call it our 'women's health packet.' Listen, sweetheart—" She glances meaningfully at the door. "Never let anyone, including my nephew, pressure you into doing something you don't want to do, okay?"

Understanding dawns. I blush deeply. "Oh, we're not—"

"Sex is a perfectly wonderful and healthy part of the human experience. Just make sure it is consensual and make sure you're safe about it." She hands me the bag. I feel so embarrassed that I take it without a fight. I just want this conversation to be over.

Sarah leaves the room so I can get dressed. When I return to the waiting room, Kai immediately stands up, worry painted over his features. "Hey," he says, his voice hesitant. "Are you ... is everything ... all right?"

I am flooded with this overwhelming desire to protect him. To wipe that worry from his face and bask in the warmth of his smile.

Which is why I do what I do next.

"Yes—everything's perfect! Sorry for freaking you out. I'm totally fine." It's as if by saying the words out loud, I can force them into truth. And once I begin, the lies keep coming. "Sarah said it's likely that I was disoriented from the jet lag, and I also got a little dehydrated, which can make anyone confused. But I'm much better now."

Relief lights up Kai's face. "So your memory came back? Are you here with your parents, or … ?"

"No, I'm, um—I came to surprise you. After graduation. I lost my phone at the airport, so I couldn't call you."

"How did you lose your phone?"

"My purse was stolen. I mean, I forgot it on the plane, and when I went back, it was gone. My wallet and phone were inside."

"That's terrible! Let's head back to the airport—they must have a lost and found."

Already my lie is becoming unwieldy. "I, um, checked the lost and found when I first realized, but my purse wasn't there."

"What about your suitcase?" Kai asks.

"What?"

"Where's your suitcase?"

"Oh, I, um—it didn't make the connection. I waited and waited at Baggage Claim, but it never came down the conveyor belt. So I left my name with the airport. I gave them your phone number. I hope that's okay. They'll call if they find anything."

"Of course that's okay, T." I can't tell if he believes me or not. "I'm sure your suitcase will turn up soon. And your purse too. We can go shopping to get you new clothes."

"That would be great! Thanks. Anyway, that's why I went to the lava tubes—I was hoping to find you there. Then I fell asleep, and when I woke up I was jet-lagged and dehydrated, and it made me super disoriented. But everything's fine now!"

I'm overdoing it. My voice sounds too cheerful. Too forced. There's no way Kai is going to swallow this load of crap. He's going to see right through me.

For a long moment, he stares into my face. Then he beams, pulling me into a hug. "I can't believe you surprised me like this! Best present ever!"

Maybe it's easy to hear what we want to hear, to believe what we want to believe. For the past three years, Kai has been trying to get me on a plane to Hawaii. Now that I'm here, he must desperately want to accept my explanation without question.

I do too. I almost believe my hastily cobbled-together story. I want to believe it so badly.

"So how long are you here?" Kai asks.

"Until Sunday." I don't know where the answer comes from. But these feel like the truest words I've spoken all day.

"Great!" Kai says. "We have a whole week!"

On the drive down the two-lane road with Kai and Theo, away from the clinic, the mood in the Jeep is buoyant. I hate lying to Kai, but it was the right thing to do. Soon, I'll talk to my parents and figure out what happened. For now, I want to enjoy being here in Hawaii with my best friend. Windows down, warm breeze blowing. Palm trees nodding their heads along the roadside. Off in the distance, sparkling turquoise water blurs into blue horizon.

We drop Theo off at his friend's and continue down the road to Kai's house. He tells me his parents will still be at work—his mom's working in the tourism office, and his dad's leading a dolphin snorkel group—and his kid brother Paulo is at soccer practice. I am grateful. This day has been such a whirlwind that having some quiet time with Kai sounds perfect.

His neighborhood is peaceful. Unassuming houses, grassy lawns studded with palm trees and hibiscus bushes. He pulls into the driveway of a house painted sunflower yellow with teal trim.

"Here we are," Kai says, cutting the engine.

"Wow. I like it!"

"My mom has a thing for bright colors. Wait till you see the inside. My room is the only one with white walls—my form of rebellion, I guess."

"I can't wait to see your room," I say. "In person, I mean." I've glimpsed his bedroom when we video-chat, but my mental image is composed of puzzle pieces that don't quite fit together.

I follow Kai up the concrete path, lined with blue stones and white seashells, to the glass-paned front door. A furry head lifts up from the floor and gazes at us through the glass.

"Oh my gosh! Olina!" In all the craziness, I'd forgotten about Kai's family dog.

"That's her," Kai says, unlocking the door.

Olina gets up, tail wagging. She is a Labrador mixed with something else—Kai's family got her at the animal shelter a couple of years ago. Apparently, she loves the water and swims in the ocean when Kai goes surfing. When I talk to her on FaceTime, she always barks at the sound of my voice.

"Hey, Olina. Hey, sweetheart." I scratch her head. She barks her friendly bark and slobbers all over my hand.

"She likes you," Kai says. "Usually she's kinda scared of new people."

"But I'm not a new person. Leen and I go way back, don't we girl?"

"Leen?"

"It's my nickname for her. Obviously." I bend down to Olina's face and roll my eyes. "Some people just don't understand, do they girl?" Olina wags her tail.

Kai laughs and leads me down the hall, through the kitchen and family room. Olina follows us, her nails clicking on the wooden floors. Kai wasn't joking about the walls. They're painted bright colors: sunset orange, jade green, deep purple. The house reminds me of what my house was like before my parents got divorced. Just the right amount of cozy messiness. Everyone's belongings swirled together. The kind of house that makes you feel comfortable kicking off your shoes and staying awhile. After the divorce, my parents sold our house, and my mom got really into interior decorating. Dad moved into an apartment, and Mom and I moved into a condo. Mom threw herself into fabric samples and color coordination and organization bins, and now it's like we live inside a magazine. It's beautiful, but it doesn't really scream "home" to me. We eat with linen napkins, and Mom dusts the carefully arranged bookshelves every week, and if I make myself scrambled eggs for breakfast, I wash the pan right away instead of leaving it in the sink. My room is the only place in the house that collects any clutter.

"This one's mine," Kai says, opening a door partway down the hall. "Sorry, it's a bit messy." He flicks on the light switch.

After the bright energy of the rest of the house, his room is serene and quiet. White walls, simple wooden furniture. Dresser, desk, bookshelf, nightstand. Comfy-looking bed covered with a blue quilt. Sunlight streams through a big window. On his walls hang a couple of surfing posters and a black-and-white Ansel Adams print of the moon rising over a dark silhouette of mountains.

"I love it," I tell him. "This space is so ... you. It's perfect."

Kai scurries around picking up dirty clothes off the floor. "Well, thanks. It's not anything special, but at least it's my own space."

I think of my bedroom at home: the bulletin board covered with overlapping photos and sketches and ticket stubs, the stuffed animal dolphin I got on my family's first trip to Hawaii that lives deep under my covers, the stacked piles of paper on my desk with a precise organization system that only I understand. "I know exactly what you mean," I say.

Kai tosses his dirty clothes into a laundry basket. "You must be exhausted. Are you hungry?"

"No, not really. But yeah, I am a little tired."

"Why don't you take a nap?"

I sit down on the edge of the bed. Turning back the covers and snuggling up inside sounds heavenly. "Are you sure?"

"Of course! You need to rest up, Rossi. I'm taking you out to dinner later."

"Dinner? Really?"

He winks. "We need to celebrate our reunion!" He turns off the lamp so the only light in the room is the late-afternoon sunlight filtering through the gauzy curtain. "If you need anything, I'll be right down the hall in the family room."

"Okay."

"Don't drool too much on my pillow. C'mon, Olina!" She follows him into the hall. He grins and pulls the door shut behind him.

hey t,

me again. i didn't hear back from you, so i'm assuming you're still mad at me. but i'm gonna write to you anyway. i took a nap and had the most vivid dream about you, and when i woke up, it felt like our fight had never happened because in my dream we were good again. it was like the old days, but better, because we were the ages we are now. you and me, together on the island, savoring the summer. no worries, no curfews, no responsibilities. paradise. just like i always said it would be if you ever came back to visit.

sorry. didn't mean to bring that up, and honestly i don't want to start that whole argument again. what i meant to say was, the dream was really wonderful, and you looked absolutely radiant, and i hope you are as happy as you were in my subconscious. it's crazy that even hanging out with your dream self makes me happy. i woke up smiling, and i can't remember the last time that happened.

write back? please?

—kai

Slamming into something hard. A sharp intake of breath. A scream lodged in a throat.

I wake up clawing at the covers, my heart beating wildly. The room is dim. It takes me a few moments to place where I am: *Hawaii. Kai's bedroom.* The clock on the nightstand reads 5:47.

I clamber out of bed, wishing desperately for a toothbrush, a shower, a change of clothes.

Kai had pointed out the bathroom, Jack and Jill–style between his room and Theo's. Maybe I can rummage around in the drawers and find a new toothbrush. I cautiously open the door.

There, in the middle of the tiled bathroom floor, is a suitcase.

A large floral-print, red-zippered suitcase.

My suitcase.

I got it three years ago when there was a sale online and Mom told me to pick something out because I needed my own suitcase. The subtext being: *to schlep between this place and Dad's apartment,* but neither of us had mentioned that part. I picked this suitcase specifically because it was such a unique pattern. *No one else will have this suitcase,* I thought. And, in all the times I've used it, no one else has.

Gingerly, I approach the suitcase. I'm half-expecting it to disappear or to fly open on its own like something out of Harry

Potter. But when I reach out and touch it, nothing happens. I slowly unzip the red zipper.

My stuffed animal dolphin stares back at me with glassy eyes.

There's also my favorite pair of jeans, my comfy fleece pajamas, and a tank top I got last summer that Andrea always said brings out the flecks of green in my eyes. My two best bathing suits. My toiletry bag. Mom's gray sweater that I always borrow. I bring it to my face and breathe in; it smells like her perfume. Tears fill my eyes.

I can't remember ever missing my mom this much. *Where are you, Mama?* Despite our ups and downs, my mom always has my back—and she always has answers. If she were here, or if I could talk to her, she would explain what's going on. She would be able to fill in the blanks I've forgotten.

Suddenly, I remember my scar—my absence of a scar. I bend down and study my knee. It is smooth and flawless. The scar is gone. *Maybe it's been slowly fading away, and I've been too busy to notice?* I turn my wrist and study my arm, searching for the scar I got from the lava rock the night Kai and I tried to run away as kids. It's a bigger scar, a narrow raised white line—it wouldn't have faded.

But it's gone. My arm is smooth, the skin unblemished.

My stomach flips. Something is going on. *Is this magic? Am I dreaming?*

I dig farther down into the suitcase. Along with my favorite clothes, there are also some items I don't recognize. Brand new, the tags still on. I didn't buy these. Or maybe I did, and I don't remember. A pink surf shirt with a tag that reads "built-in SPF." Shorts made out of athletic, sweat-wicking material. Yellow sandals. And—I pull it out with a little gasp—a gorgeous red sundress, studded with tiny white and yellow flowers.

I check the suitcase pockets, nearly shrieking with joy when my fingers touch smooth pleather, and I pull out my little black purse. Inside are my wallet, keys, and phone. *Yes!* I try calling my mom again, and then my dad. When neither answers, I text them, hoping beyond hope that they will write back, *Glad you're okay, sweetheart! Have fun!* Hoping beyond hope that my lie is actually truth, that I really did hop on a plane to Hawaii to surprise Kai, that soon everything will make sense again.

I search my email for a plane ticket purchase, but nothing comes up. Stalking myself on social media doesn't help jog my memory. My last post is from graduation: a photo of me and my mom, and a separate photo of me and my dad. Kai had commented on the post: *woot woot, congrats t! can't wait to celebrate with you soon!*

That makes it sound like I was indeed coming to visit him in Hawaii. *Okay. So that must be the answer. I came to visit Kai after graduation like we planned.* I try to shrug off my worries, but questions remain: *Why can't I remember the past few weeks? Why can't I find any evidence of my flight to Hawaii? Why was Kai surprised to see me?*

I pull off my dirty shirt and shorts and rummage in my toiletry bag for shampoo and conditioner. In the mirror, I study my new tattoo. *Why did I get an hourglass? The image has zero personal meaning to me. Maybe it's a temporary tattoo?* I turn the shower to Hot and grab a towel from the folded stack under the sink. Stepping under the warm waterfall feels like renewal. I envision all my anxious questions falling away with the water and swirling down the drain. *You're with Kai,* I remind myself. *You're in Hawaii. Enjoy it. There must be some explanation for everything. You'll talk to Mom soon.* I scrub vigorously at the hourglass tattoo, but the ink doesn't fade.

Twenty minutes later, I've towel-dried my hair, brushed my teeth, and slipped on the red sundress. It fits perfectly, hugging my curves in all the right places. Lifting up my hair, I put my puka shell necklace back on. I lean into the mirror and swipe on eye shadow and mascara. Then, I step back and look at myself. I feel more beautiful than I have in a long time. My eyes shine. My hair is damp and wavy and loose. I am ... me, at my purest essence. I open the bathroom door and step out, pulling the floral suitcase behind me.

Kai is stretched out on the bed, reading. Olina is curled up at his feet. They both glance up when I come in. Kai's eyes widen.

"Wow," he says. "You look ... *wow*."

I blush. "Thanks."

"Hey, how did your suitcase get here?"

"Someone from the airport must have dropped it off. My purse was inside!" Which doesn't actually answer his question—*How did someone from the airport get the suitcase inside the bathroom?*—but Kai doesn't seem to notice. He looks stunned.

He shakes his head. "That dress ... *man*."

I wedge my suitcase into a corner of the room, where it will be out of the way. "Well, you said we're going out to dinner. I wanted to look nice."

"You look more than nice. You upped the game, T. I better go change."

"You don't have to do that!"

He runs a hand through his hair, grinning. "Naw, I was going to anyway. I'll take a quick shower, then we'll be off. Sound good?"

"Sounds perfect."

He gets up from the bed, and, for a moment, it seems like he's going to come over to me. But then he gives a little wave and disappears into the bathroom.

I put on Mom's gray sweater and the yellow sandals and wander over to Kai's bookcase. His shelves hold a wide mix of literature: *To Kill a Mockingbird. Strawberries in Wintertime. The Particular Sadness of Lemon Cake. Chronicles of a Death Foretold.* There are also surfing trophies and a carved wooden box. *Did Kai carve this?* A crisscross pattern covers the lid, with flowers adorning the corners. Along the sides creep ornate vines. My fingers itch to open the box, but of course I don't. I'm not *that* much of a snoop.

Framed photographs are displayed on his bookshelves. One of him, Theo, and a small boy I'm assuming is Paulo. They are smiling proudly and holding up three large fish; Paulo's is the biggest. Another photo features a group of young people—Kai's friends from school. It's a beach shot, and everyone is wearing swimsuits. I pick out Kai in the back, laughing. And there, in the front, is the girl I bumped into earlier. The girl with the flyers for the art show. Suddenly, I remember why she was familiar: she was Kai's prom date. He sent me a couple of photos, after I bugged him about it a million times. He insisted they went as friends, but they sure looked cozy in the pictures. She's really pretty. Nadia. I think that's her name.

Stepping back from the bookshelf, my stomach sinks in disappointment. I was hoping there would be a photo of us. Which is silly—we don't have any photos together. Well, except for the one I found of us as kids that I mailed to him last year. But that one was a little blurry and off-center, taken by a disposable camera my mom bought for the trip. It's not really the kind of photo you frame and display. Besides, I don't need some framed photograph as proof of Kai's friendship. I know how much he cares about me.

I sit down on the bed. The shower has stopped running; Kai will be out soon. My stomach grumbles. Olina flops onto her side, and I stroke her soft belly.

On the nightstand, there's another photo frame—only this one is facedown. *Maybe it fell over?* Tentatively, I lift up its face.

A photo of me. I'm looking away from the camera, laughing at something my friend Mel said. Andrea had snapped the photo—she was in her photography phase at the time, taking photos constantly with the fancy camera her parents bought her for her birthday. I've always liked this photo of myself. Sometimes in posed photos I look guarded, the edges of my smile too tight. In this photo, my walls are down.

Kai keeps this photo of me on his nightstand? That means he sees my face every night, right before he goes to sleep, and every morning when he first wakes up. My heart soars. But in the next breath, it deflates. *Why did Kai have my photo facedown?* I know the possibility is slim that the frame fell over by accident. He must have purposely laid it facedown. He did not want to see me. Our fight must have been a big one, whatever it was about.

Carefully, I place the photo back where I found it, glass kissing the wood surface of the nightstand. A few moments later, the bathroom door opens, and Kai emerges, wearing khaki slacks and a button-down dark-gray shirt. His floppy hair is slicked back, and his stubble is clean-shaven. He looks so handsome.

I clamber up from the bed. "You clean up nice," I say, attempting lightness. But I wonder if he can tell from my expression that he is lightning, and I've been struck.

"Thanks," he says, grabbing his wallet and keys from the dresser. "Are you ready? Let's try to sneak out before my mom gets home."

"Are you trying to hide me from your parents?"

"No, exactly the opposite—I'm trying to hide *them* from you. Once everyone gets home, this place becomes a madhouse."

As he opens his bedroom door, there's a rumbling mechanical sound, and he freezes. "Shit. The garage. They're home."

The door to the garage bangs open, and a boy emerges in soccer gear, running down the hallway toward us. His face lights up when he sees Kai. "Guess what! Guess what!" he exclaims.

"Hey, little man." Kai tousles his hair. "You're sweaty."

"*Guess what!*"

"What?"

"I scored a goal! In the scrimmage!"

Kai throws his hands up into the air. "GOOOOAAAALLLL!!" he shouts.

The boy laughs, his eyes crinkling shut. It's like seeing Kai as a little kid again. When the boy stops laughing, he notices me hovering in the doorway to Kai's room. "Who are *you*?" he asks.

"Paulo, this is my friend Tegan. Remember? I told you about her."

"You live on the mainland?" Paulo asks me, in the tone you might use to ask someone if they live on the moon.

"Yep. But I love Hawaii. You guys are pretty lucky to live here, huh? It's paradise."

Paulo beams as if I have paid him a big compliment. "That's what Kai always says. *Hawaii would be total paradise if only—*"

"Hey, little man," Kai interrupts. "Why don't you introduce yourself to Tegan the way I taught you?"

Paulo's expression becomes serious. He holds out his hand. "Hello, my name is Paulo. What is your name?" He speaks slowly, overenunciating each word.

"I'm Tegan," I say, placing my hand in his. His palm is slightly sticky.

He pumps my arm vigorously. "It is a pleasure to meet you."

"It's a pleasure to meet you too."

"Great job, Paulo!" Kai says, grinning. "That was very professional."

The garage door bangs open again, and a round-faced, pretty woman comes in. "Boys! Come out here and help me carry in these groceries!"

"Mom!" Paulo shouts. "Should Tegan help too?"

Their mother stops, peering down the hallway at us. "Tegan? Kai's Tegan?"

I smile weakly and give a little wave. *Is she going to be upset? I mean, what kind of person visits unannounced like this? Maybe Kai's parents won't want me to stay here. Maybe they'll say they don't have room for me. Then what will I do?*

But as Kai's mother moves toward us, her face breaks into a broader and broader smile. She drops her bags of groceries onto the carpet, stepping past Olina, and pulls me in for a hug. Her skin is soft, and she smells like jasmine. "My goodness, the last time I saw you, you were a little slip of a thing." She pulls back and studies my face. "Now look at you. An absolutely gorgeous young lady."

I blush. "Thank you. It's so nice to see you, Mrs. Kapule. I'm sorry for dropping in like this—"

She waves away my words. "Please, call me Lana. You are always welcome here, my dear. Anytime at all. Whether Kai is here or not." She gives him a meaningful look.

What was that about? I try to meet his eyes, but he is studying the carpet.

Mrs. Kapule picks up one of the grocery bags. "Tegan, can you carry that other bag for me? Thanks, dear. Boys, go out to the car and bring in the rest of the groceries, please! I'm making a feast tonight, now that we have a special guest with us."

Kai runs a hand over his face. "Mom, you know how much I love your cooking, but Tegan and I are going out to dinner tonight. I've already made reservations."

She raises her eyebrows. "Reservations, huh? Someone's getting fancy." She leans in close to my ear and whispers loudly, "He's never made reservations for anyone before."

"Is that so?" Now I raise my eyebrows at Kai.

Mrs. Kapule picks up one of the grocery bags; I grab the other. "I'm taking Tegan into the kitchen to help me unload these groceries," she says, a twinkle in her eye. "Don't worry, baby, I won't interfere with your reservations."

"Don't get sucked in, Tegan! Don't get sucked in!" Kai says, as Paulo pulls him off to the garage.

I shrug in a teasingly helpless gesture before following Mrs. Kapule into the kitchen.

"How are your parents doing?" she asks, opening the fridge and unloading vegetables into the crisper.

"They're fine. They, um, got divorced? A couple years ago? So I live with my mom now. But I still see my dad pretty often." I remove cans and boxes from the grocery bag and stack them on the counter.

Mrs. Kapule straightens up and pushes a wisp of hair out of her eyes. She looks at me with care and concern, but I don't see pity in her expression. Pity is what most adults give me when they learn about the divorce. I don't like pity.

"That must have been tough," she says simply.

Usually, I don't like talking about the divorce. But for some reason, I want to confide in Mrs. Kapule. "Yeah. I mean, they were fighting a lot, so in a way it was a relief. But I was also really sad when they told me. It's complicated, I guess."

She nods. "Life is complicated, huh? Sometimes I wish it came with an instruction manual."

I laugh. "Yeah. Me too."

"Well, I only met your parents a few times, but one thing that was very clear about them was how much they love you."

I'm surprised to feel tears pricking my eyes. I look down, swallowing, tracing the lines of grout on the tile countertop. "Thanks."

"It's the truth. And I need to thank *you* for coming to visit Kai. I'm sure you've been able to tell that he's been having a hard time lately. It means a lot that you traveled all the way here to cheer him up."

Kai, having a hard time? Is this related to our fight—or something bigger?

I'm about to ask her more, but Kai and Paulo burst into the kitchen. Paulo is carrying one grocery bag; Kai swings two in each hand. He settles all the bags onto the counter, then links his arm through mine.

"Okay, Mom, your groceries are here! Now, I hate to run, but I must sweep this charming lady off *immediately* so we aren't late for our very important dinner reservations."

Mrs. Kapule smiles. "Where are you taking her?"

"The hottest place in town."

"Pulling out the big guns, eh?"

"Where is it?" Paulo asks, jumping up and down. "Where are you guys going? Are you going to get shave ice?"

Kai laughs. "Maybe we'll get shave ice tomorrow."

"But shave ice is the best!"

"That's true, buddy. I should've had you plan this date, huh?"

Date. Is that what this is? A date with Kai? Do I want it to be?

The same thoughts must flash through Kai's mind because he quickly shifts gears, releasing my arm and bending down to Paulo's height. "Right now I can't tell you where the restaurant is, because it's a surprise for Tegan. But I'll tell you tomorrow, okay? You've been there before."

"I *have*?"

"Yep. I think you'll approve. Now, we've got to go!" He straightens up and looks at me. "Ready, T?"

I smooth my hands over my dress. It seems like the question is about more than just dinner. Ready or not, I'm here, with Kai, in Hawaii, and this moment has arrived. Here I stand, on the cusp. I can either retreat—run away, give in to fear, and hide—or I can lean into all of the uncertainty and complexity of right here, right now. *Life is complicated*, Mrs. Kapule had said.

"Yep." I smile at Kai and slip my arm through his. "I'm ready."

It is immediately apparent where The Blue Oasis got its name: the entire building is painted a vibrant sky blue. I'm expecting a quirky, laid-back place with a beachy island atmosphere. Kai gives the hostess his name, and she leads us inside, and immediately my perspective shifts. Inside the restaurant, it does feel like … an oasis. A *fancy* oasis. White tablecloths, stylish silverware, bright floral centerpieces. Twinkling lights are strung on the walls, and tea candles flicker around the room. The ceiling is painted to look like a night sky, and one entire wall of the restaurant is open to a patio area, where there is a makeshift wooden stage.

"Wow," I murmur to Kai as we sit down. The hostess hands us menus and flits away. "This place is incredible."

Kai smiles at me across the table. "I've always wanted to take you here. Just wait till you try their food!"

I'm poring over the menu, trying to decide between the pulled-pork tacos and the "living salad"—*What does that mean?*—when Kai says, "Hey, man," and I notice something off in his voice. On edge. I look up, and a guy around our age is standing there with a water pitcher. His dark hair is pulled back into a short ponytail, and he has a stud earring in one ear.

"Welcome to The Blue Oasis," he says in an exaggerated monotone, reaching over to fill our glasses with water. The pitcher sloshes, and ice spills onto the tablecloth. "Whoops. Sorrrry," the guy says. His tone makes clear it was no accident.

"So, is this her?" he asks Kai, smirking at me.

Kai clears his throat. "Tegan, this is R.J.; R.J., meet Tegan. She's visiting for the week."

R.J. leans close to Kai's ear, but his whisper is loud enough for me to hear: "Doesn't look like she's worth it, to me." Then he darts away, heading across the room to another table.

My cheeks burn. "What was that about?" I murmur.

"I'm sorry. He's an asshole. It was nothing." Kai rubs his thumb against the tablecloth. "Just dumb high school stuff. People stirring up drama. You know how it is."

No, I don't, not really. I always stayed the hell away from all that. When I smelled a whiff of drama, I fled in the other direction. That's part of why I've never come down here to visit before.

Kai forces a smile, his tone abruptly cheerful. "But hey, none of that matters anymore. High school is behind us! Cheers to that, right?" He lifts his water glass.

I raise my water glass and clink it against his. After a moment, I say, "Kai, I owe you an apology."

"For what?"

"Our big fight. I know I did something that upset you. But I can't remember any of the details."

His brow furrows in concern. "I thought your memory came back."

"Oh. Um, some of it did. But I still can't remember our fight."

He waves my words away. "It's not important now."

"I'm glad—I mean, I'm grateful that we've moved past it. But still, will you tell me what we fought about? Maybe it will help me remember."

Kai fiddles with his fork. "So the last time you remember us talking is when you promised to come visit me after graduation?"

I nod.

"Well, about a week later, you backed out. You decided to head down to Georgetown early to take summer classes instead. You wouldn't even consider the possibility of doing both. And I—I probably overreacted. I was just so disappointed, T. You laughed like it had been a joke, like it wasn't even a big deal, but your trip was a big deal to me." Pain washes over his face. "It seemed like you didn't even care about me at all."

Wow. I really hurt him.

"And we haven't talked for the past month?" I ask softly.

He shakes his head. "Whenever you called, I would let it go to voice mail. I didn't answer your emails or texts. I needed some time and space to decompress. Like I said before, I was overreacting. I'm sorry."

I reach across the table and touch his hand. "No, I'm the one who's sorry. I can't believe I bailed on you like that. And of course I care about you. More than you know."

He smiles, his thumb brushing mine. "It's okay. None of it matters now. You came to visit after all! Best surprise of my life."

The waiter comes to take our order. Kai chooses the pulled-pork tacos, promising I can try some, so I order the living salad. The waiter seems pleased. "Very good, very good!" he says, tucking his pen back behind his ear. Then he whisks off, and we're alone, and now that my big apology is out of the way, I cannot think of a single thing to say.

Across the table, Kai is golden in the candles' glow. With his faint shadow of stubble and that crisp button-down shirt, he looks so grown-up. This is definitely the closest we've ever come to a date. *Is this a date? Do I want it to be?*

Kai interrupts my thoughts. "I still can't believe you're here!" he says. "What do you want to do this week? Give me the whole list."

"Hmm … maybe hike that waterfall you told me about?"

"Akaka Falls? Yeah, we can easily do that hike—it's only a short drive away."

"Cool. And I'm excited to see the ocean. It's been years since I've been in the waves!"

Kai gives me this *look*, like I said it's been years since I've eaten. "Wait—you haven't been to the ocean since you got here?"

"Nope. I went to the lava tubes, then I came to see you downtown, then we went to the clinic and to your house. No ocean yet."

Kai slaps the table decisively. "Well, that's what we're doing after dinner, then."

I laugh. "At night?"

"The ocean is best at night."

Before I can ask more questions, the waiter appears with our dishes. "For you, miss," he says, setting a tray before me with a flourish. In a little boxlike bowl, a miniature garden of leafy greens is growing. Beside the garden is a dainty pair of scissors, and next to that rests a salad bowl, an array of chopped-up toppings like carrot and jicama, and a carafe of dressing.

"Oh my goodness!" I exclaim.

"The living salad," the waiter says, setting down Kai's plate of tacos. "It is aptly named, yes?"

"It's almost too pretty to eat!" But I'm starving, so as soon as the waiter leaves, I pick up the scissors and begin snipping away at the tiny garden. "This is so much fun!"

"You're like a little kid," Kai says.

"You know you want to try some."

"Okay, let me at it."

I nudge the tray toward him, and he snips off the tallest leaf of lettuce. He takes a bite, chews thoughtfully, and then proclaims, "This is what my pops would call 'rabbit food.'"

"You're not supposed to eat it like that! You're supposed to mix it all up in a salad. It's *de-lect-able*."

"If you're a rabbit."

I stick out my tongue at him, he sticks out his tongue at me, and I'm not nervous anymore about being on my first-ever real date with Kai Kapule (if this is even a date). I forget about trying to act fancy and grown-up. I forget to worry about when I'm going home, or what that R.J. guy was talking about, or whether Kai will find out I lied to him, or if my memory of the past few weeks will ever come back. Instead, I sink into myself, into this moment that feels both familiar and brand new: a warm summer night; a delicious meal in a candlelit restaurant; laughing across the table from the one person in the world who knows me best.

I eat every bite of my living salad, plus a couple bites of Kai's pork tacos. I don't know if the food is fresher in Hawaii or if maybe not being stressed about finals means I can actually slow down and enjoy eating—whatever it is, food tastes better here than in my usual life. Kai is skimming over the bill (I want to split the check, but he stubbornly refuses to take my money) when, from out of nowhere, ukulele music starts to play. As I glance around the restaurant, my gaze settles on an elderly man set up with a microphone and sound equipment on a makeshift stage against the far blue wall. He strums a bit more, then closes his eyes and begins to sing. His sandpapery voice complements the joyful ukulele notes with surprising beauty. The lyrics are something about magic and water and moonlight.

When the song ends, I feel wrung out. I turn my head, and Kai is looking at me with an expression I can't quite read. When our eyes meet, he smiles and says, "Wanna get out of here?"

"Yes."

Kai drives with the windows down. The night air is just cool enough to make goose bumps rise on my legs. I breathe in deeply. Ever since

I woke up in the lava tubes, there's been this strange tightness in my chest, as if I can't get enough oxygen into my lungs.

"Where are we going?" I ask.

He winks. "You'll recognize it when we get there."

I dig my hands into the pockets of my sweater, and in the left one—a pocket I swear was empty before—I discover a package of sweet mint gum.

"Want some?" I ask.

"Sure," he says. I pass him a stick, and we chew in comfortable silence as the road unwinds beneath us. Outside the window, the lava rock could be the dark side of the moon.

He pulls into the parking lot for the resort—the place I used to stay with my parents, the place Kai and I first met as children, the place we bumped into each other again three years ago.

"Perfect choice," I tell him as we climb out of his Jeep. I spit my gum into a trash can, and Kai does the same.

We skirt the edge of the hotel grounds and make our way onto the soft sand. There is a full moon tonight, but otherwise the beach is dark. Kai pulls out his cell phone and turns on the flashlight. I can't see the ocean, but I can hear the waves. A siren song. The pull is magnetic. For the millionth time, I wonder how I was able to stay away for so long. *How did I ever think the lake was the same as this?*

My foot sinks into a hole, and I stumble forward, reaching out for Kai's arm. He is there, steadying me, keeping me from falling.

"Careful," he says. "You okay?"

"Yeah, thanks. It's these sandals—they make me clumsy."

Reluctantly, I release his arm so I can slide the yellow straps off my feet. I hold the sandals in one hand as we continue down the beach. My free hand dangles, close to his, within reach. I think of all the times I heedlessly grabbed his hand when we were kids, pulling him this way or that, wanting to show him something. Back then, I would reach for his hand without thinking. I knew his childhood hands—their scratches and blisters and bitten fingernails—as well as I knew my own.

Our arms brush. *A mistake?* They brush again. Then his calloused palm kisses mine. As our fingers interlace, a wide grin spreads across my face. I'm grateful for the dark. The dark, and the moon, and the crickets, and the waves. His hand is warm and firm. It seems like nothing bad can happen, as long as he is holding my hand.

We trudge through the soft sand, cool against our bare feet. This silence with Kai is a companionable silence, like the silence you experience when you're alone, except without a hint of loneliness. One night in tenth grade, when I was upset about my parents' divorce and Andrea's new boyfriend, who took up all her time, I called Kai and vented about everything. Just totally unloaded. I remember he didn't try to give me advice or tell me that everything would be all right. He didn't try to fill the silence with platitudes, and he didn't need me to fill it either. He stayed there quietly on the phone, breathing softly, and soon I began to feel calmer. I remember closing my eyes, resting my cheek against the pillow, cell phone pressed to my ear. It felt like he was there with me.

At the time, I thought that was good enough. Cell phones and text messages and FaceTime and email. For years, he's existed as a photo on my phone screen, a ringtone blaring from my nightstand, a disembodied voice, and strings of sentences without capitalization because he doesn't believe in email formality. But Kai was right—all that other stuff is better than nothing, but it doesn't come close to being side by side like this in real time.

We reach the more densely packed sand, where a couple of empty chaise lounges, covered with towels, wait for tomorrow's sunbathers. We walk farther in, until the waves sweep over our feet. I jump at the cold. Kai laughs and squeezes my hand, pulling me back out of the waves. He turns off his flashlight and fiddles with his phone, apparently searching for something. His gaze is focused downward, so I take the opportunity to drink him in. The glow from his phone screen lights up his features: his straight nose, long eyelashes, strong cheekbones. The same face of the boy I met all those years ago, yet also a different face—more mature. A man. Maybe that's why I feel weirdly shy around him.

"Aha! Found it," Kai announces with a triumphant smile. He tucks his phone into his shirt pocket, and soon the first notes of music wind their way into the night. It takes me a few seconds, but then I recognize the delicate ukulele melody.

"Is this the song from the restaurant?" I ask.

Kai nods. "One of my all-time favorites. It's called 'Magic by the Water,' written by a Hawaiian musician."

"It's beautiful."

Kai lifts one hand in the air, like a waiter holding an invisible tray. "Miss Rossi," he says in a formal voice, "will you give me the pleasure of this dance?"

"I would be honored, Mr. Kapule." I place my hand in his.

Kai pulls me close, wrapping an arm around my waist. I place my other hand on his shoulder. He smells like laundry soap and coconut. Crazed butterflies flap around in my stomach. Ever since he emerged from his bathroom earlier looking all clean-scrubbed and grown-up, my body has been humming with a constant low-level excitement. It can no longer be contained; now all of my nervous energy is exploding into overdrive.

I let my temple rest against his cheek and close my eyes. Together, we sway to the music, our feet shuffling a circle in the sand. I can hear the waves rolling in and receding, rolling in and receding. A breeze gently lifts the hem of my dress and plays with tendrils of my hair. My heart is beating rapidly—I wonder if Kai can feel it through the thin fabric of my dress. His hand shifts on my back, drawing me closer; his fingers ignite sparks across my bare skin.

Kai leans back slightly, looking down at me. I pride myself on never being afraid of anything, and yet as I lift my gaze to meet his eyes, my nervous energy is tinged with fear. It is like Kai and I are dancing along the edge of that massive precipice we have chosen to ignore for all these years—or, at least, *I* have chosen to ignore—and now, suddenly, we are gazing over the edge, preparing to leap together into the unknown.

Once we cross this line, there will be no way to un-cross it.

It's terrifying. And yet … *I want this.* I want this more than I can ever remember wanting anything. It feels so right, being here with Kai, slow dancing in the sand under an enormous glowing moon. He was right all those years ago, when we sat together in the lava tubes and he tried to kiss me. He was right when he said that being together was worth risking our friendship. All this time I've been telling myself I'm being practical, but really I've just been scared.

Kai's eyes are dark pools. *Does he feel it too—this buzzing electricity between us?*

"I still can't believe it," he says. "You're here. You're really here."

"I'm here."

"Tegan Rossi," he murmurs, smoothing a stray lock of hair away from my eyes. "You dazzle me, you know that?"

I laugh, looking past Kai's shoulder, out to the milky white moon and the dark endless ocean. In the distance, the resort is all lit up like a giant cruise ship. For most of my life, I have felt the furthest thing from dazzling. Gritty, maybe. Stubborn. The girl unafraid to get her hands dirty, to dig in, to patiently put in the long, drudging hours of work.

But dazzling? I don't think I have ever dazzled anyone.

The song emanating from Kai's shirt pocket is winding down, the ukulele melody slowing. Everything feels fragile. I think of a tiny pink seashell. I think of spun glass. The musician is plucking a single string now, notes floating out softly into the hushed, humid night.

"I'm serious," Kai says. He gently lifts my chin so there is nowhere for me to look but his face. "You are a blaze of light."

There is a question in his eyes that I ache to answer. The moment builds, electric, inevitable. The cliff beckons us over the edge.

Time unfolds in slow motion. Kai leans down. I reach up and meet his lips with my own. His mouth is warm and tender, somehow both new and familiar at once. He tastes of sweet mint gum. His hands softly cup the back of my head, thumbs grazing my neck. I clutch his shirt, pressing my body closer to his. I can't get close enough. We are both breathing hard.

"Oh, Tegan," he whispers. "You're really here."

"And I'm not going anywhere."

His smile is contagious. He grabs my waist and scoops me up, carrying me over to one of the chaise lounges and gingerly setting me down on top of an abandoned beach towel. He starts to lie down on top of me, then hesitates.

"Am I squashing you?"

"No!" I laugh. "No. Come here." I pull him down. His weight

is comforting, sturdy—a tether, pressing me to the earth, to here, to now. Soon there is nothing but the ocean waves and the midnight air and his urgent fingers on my skin; everything else melts away.

hey t,
do you like sweet mint gum?
just curious.
—kai

TUESDAY

The sensation of moving very fast. Speed building and building. Out of control. Suddenly, jerking sideways. Slamming into something hard. A sharp intake of breath. A scream lodged in a throat.

I wake up panting, covered in sweat. My vision is blurry; it takes a few seconds for my surroundings to click into focus. I'm lying on a chaise lounge in the middle of a deserted beach at daybreak, waves crashing onto the shore a mere three feet away from my toes. A rainbow-striped beach towel is pulled up to my chin. I sit up and look around, wrapping the towel around my shoulders like a blanket. There is an identical chaise lounge next to mine. Empty. I'm still wearing the red dress from last night. One yellow sandal is wedged beside me in the sand; the other is …

I leap up and dash into the ocean waves that are pulling my rogue sandal out to sea. The cold water laps at my ankles. Lunging for the flash of yellow in the waves, I soak half my dress—but it's worth it when my fingers close around the smooth plastic strap.

I hear laughter and look back at Kai, watching me from the beach. He's holding two to-go cups and raises one to me. "Once you're done with your morning swim, I've got coffee!" he shouts.

I kick an arc of water in his direction, but he's too far away to be splashed. He settles into one of the chaise lounges, nestling my coffee cup into the sand. I am happy to see him but also shy, unsure how I'm supposed to act now that we've crossed that invisible line. Remembering his lips on mine makes me blush. I turn and gaze out at the expanse of ocean. Sunrise spreads across the morning sky like watercolors on a wet canvas. It's stunningly beautiful—somehow the sky seems bigger here than it is back home.

I can sense Kai's eyes on me. I wonder what he's thinking.

The hem of my dress drags back and forth in the waves.

What are we supposed to do now? What if he acts like nothing happened? What if he thinks last night was a mistake?

Eventually, I wade back to shore, my dress clinging to my damp legs. Kai's expression is inscrutable behind his sunglasses.

I plop onto the chaise lounge beside him and reach for my coffee. It tastes hot and strong. "Thanks for this."

"No problem."

"I forgot how good the coffee is here."

"It's the only coffee I'll drink."

"Such a snob. Hey, guess what? It's my first time actually drinking this coffee here, in Hawaii." Kai sends me bags of Kona coffee for my birthday and Christmas, and sometimes just because, so I've brewed it at home many times. But the last time I was in Hawaii, I hadn't started drinking coffee yet.

"I think that calls for a toast," Kai says, bumping his cup against mine. Our fingers brush. "Tegan Rossi, good morning, and welcome to the first day of the rest of your life. May you never go back to second-rate coffee ever again."

I raise my cup. "Here's to being coffee snobs together."

We sip in silence for a little while, listening to the waves roll in and out, in and out, an unending rhythm. Then Kai turns to me. "So what do you want to do today?"

The way he says it: like we're a unit. My heart lifts to know that no matter what today brings, we'll be spending it together.

"Don't you have work?" I ask.

"I told my boss I have a friend visiting, and he gave me the day off. Actually, he gave me the whole week off."

"Really? Was he upset?"

"Naw. I told you, he's chill. Besides, I have vacation time saved up."

"Well, that's awesome! As long as you're sure you won't get in trouble."

"I'm sure." Suddenly, Kai leaps up from his chair and crunches his empty coffee cup in his fist. "I am *the Hulk*!" he growls, waggling his eyebrows.

I laugh so hard I nearly choke on my coffee. As kids, we would rent inflatable water wings from the pool desk and strap them to our arms, crushing cups of water and stomping on seaweed, pretending to be the Hulk and the She-Hulk. "I can't believe you still remember that!"

"I remember everything about us," he says.

Us.

I look down at my feet, digging my toes into the sand. "Maybe today, we could … go snorkeling?" I suggest.

Kai grins. "That is an excellent idea, Miss Rossi." He reaches down and pulls me up from my lounge chair. I want him to keep holding my hand, but he lets it drop. We trudge side by side through the sand, toward the fancy resort, toward the parking lot where Kai's Jeep rests, toward a future that somehow also seems like our past.

"Do you think it's like riding a bike?" I ask.

"What?" Kai looks up at me, his nose adorably scrunched in confusion. He's sitting on the floor of his parents' garage, trying to reattach an ancient snorkel spout to an equally weathered mask.

"Snorkeling." I twist my hair into a rope and coil it into a bun, wrap a tie around it once, twice, three times. "I didn't go snorkeling the last time I was here. I haven't snorkeled since we were kids. And that was, like, a lifetime ago."

"It hasn't been *that* long."

"Ten years! That's almost a decade of snorkel-less existence for yours truly."

"That just means we've got a lot of lost time to make up for."

"Do you think my body will remember what to do?"

Kai nods assuredly. "Our bodies always remember."

I glance at him, then down at the floor, a hot blush creeping across my neck and chest when I think about last night on the beach, how his lips were soft and warm, and how he gently cupped the back of my head in his hands as if I was something valuable, something worth holding onto. Now I can feel his eyes on my face, but I stare at the gray concrete floor, too nervous to meet his gaze. I take out my hair tie and release my bun, letting my messy waves fall around my shoulders.

Kai clears his throat. "I think I've almost got this thing fixed. Could you grab those flippers, and we'll head out?"

It is another gorgeous day in paradise. Cloudless blue sky, warm breeze. We roll down the windows to let in the sea air. The terrain is aridly beautiful, tufts of green-brown grass and spindly trees sticking up from the black waves of lava rock. Both times I came to Hawaii before, my parents and I barely left the resort at all—only to go shopping in downtown Kona and manta ray snorkeling.

"You're gonna love this place," Kai says. "Best snorkeling on the island. It's a local spot, off the beaten path."

"Sounds awesome. Do you think we'll see any turtles?"

Kai grins. "I haven't seen one in months. But you're my lucky charm, Rossi. So I say chances are high."

"Should we follow it around the world this time?"

"If you want to. I'll follow wherever you want to go."

We're both wearing sunglasses, so I can't see Kai's eyes, but I can imagine their intensity—the same expression he had that long-ago night in the lava tubes, brazenness mixed with vulnerability. He is one of the only people I know whose emotions are so apparent on their face and in their voice. I used to think he was that way with everyone—an open book—but now, after seeing him interact with his family and that guy at the restaurant last night, I'm beginning to wonder if maybe he only lets down his guard around certain people. Namely, me.

Which is why I can't keep up this cheerful façade much longer. If my memory doesn't come back soon, I have to tell Kai the truth: that I don't remember planning to surprise him, that the flight here remains a giant blank in my mind, that I can't even find evidence of a plane ticket. Earlier this morning, I called both of my parents again, shoving away the panic rising inside me with each empty ring. No replies to my text messages. No new emails. When I tried to upload a photo of my living salad to social media, it stubbornly refused to load. Maybe something is glitchy with the Wi-Fi here.

Kai turns off the main road down a small paved street that winds through the lava rock, toward the ocean. Eventually, we reach a tucked-away parking lot shaded by a cluster of trees. Outside the Jeep, I vigorously spray myself with sunscreen. Kai studies me with a half-smile.

"What?" I ask.

"Nothing," Kai says. "Just remembering."

Remembering what? I want to ask, but instead I twirl my finger through the air. "Turn around," I tell him. "Let me get your back."

"Want me to get yours?" he asks.

"Nope." I pull the pink surf shirt out of my bag and yank it down over my head. "This baby has SPF included. No way I'm trusting you with my back again, Kapule."

"C'mon, that was years ago! I've apologized a hundred times!"

"Worst sunburn of my life." Which is the truth. But I'm smiling, and Kai's smiling, and all these years later, I don't care anymore about the strip of skin on my lower back that is perpetually three shades lighter than all the rest—it healed that way after the epically bad sunburn I got when we went snorkeling as kids. Eight-year-old me trusted eight-year-old Kai to put sunscreen on her back. He missed a spot.

Now, Kai takes off his shirt and turns to look out at the distant waves. I spray the sunscreen, being extra careful not to miss any spots. Then I press my palms against his warm skin and rub it in. His muscles are firm under my fingers. I want to lean forward and make a trail of kisses down his spine.

Kai clears his throat.

"Sorry if my hands are cold," I say.

"It's okay," he murmurs. "That feels really nice."

I spray some more on his lower back and reach down to rub it in, my fingers brushing the waistband of his swim trunks. Then I'm blushing, thinking about what's underneath his swim trunks. We didn't go any further than making out last night. I wonder if Kai knows that I've never had sex before. Has he had sex before? It seems strange not to know this about your best friend, but this is one topic we studiously avoid. I know he's dated a few girls—"casual, nothing serious," he would always tell me—but I'm not exactly sure what "casual" means. If my school is any indication, you can definitely be in a casual relationship with someone and have sex. That just never sounded appealing to me. Giving up control of your body and your emotions like that, with someone you hardly know? The situation never felt safe enough. Maybe all this time I've been subconsciously waiting for Kai. Wanting my first time to be with him.

I imagine him turning around and taking me into his arms, like he did last night. I imagine us climbing into the back seat of his Jeep. I imagine tugging down his swim trunks and taking off my own swimsuit. Letting him see my nakedness. Being vulnerable enough to share every bare inch of myself with him.

I've zoned out; Kai's sunscreen is definitely rubbed in. I drop my hands from his back and busy myself with putting the sunscreen away, trying to calm down. *Take a chill pill, Tegan. This is Kai. Just Kai. Nothing's changed.*

79

Only that's a lie. Everything has changed. Even though we haven't talked about what happened last night, and even though Kai hasn't tried to kiss me again, I can tell we're not going back to where we were before. Last night shifted something between us. The energy is different now. I used to be able to push aside my flickering feelings for him, pretending they didn't exist. Now that my feelings have been uncaged, they're all I can think about. He's all I can think about. He'll never be *just Kai* again.

But what about him? Was kissing me what he expected it to be? Ever since the phone conversation when Kai tried to talk honestly about our relationship—if I'm real with myself, ever since that night in the lava tubes three years ago—I've known that his feelings for me were more than strictly platonic. Does he still feel that way? Or am I *just Tegan* to him now that his curiosity has been satisfied?

"You okay, T?" Kai asks, peeking around the open door of the Jeep.

"Yeah, I'm ready." I tuck my bag under the seat and slam the door closed.

Kai hands over my snorkel gear, and our fingers brush. I spend the entire walk across the parking lot, through the scrub, and into the soft sand trying to figure out how I can subtly get him to hold my hand again. I switch my bag of snorkel gear to my other shoulder. It's like I'm back in middle school with an all-consuming crush. Like I'm trying to figure out a tricky logic problem in math. If only relationships were as easy as solving for x.

Kai's talking about this snorkel spot, how he used to come here all the time with Theo and some other friends but hasn't been here in a while. "Snorkeling is still fun, but it's not the same as when you're a kid, you know? Back then everything was so exciting. Now I guess some of the magic's gone."

"Maybe that's just part of growing up," I offer.

"Maybe. I don't know. Does it have to be?"

"I hope not. Being here in Hawaii with you makes me feel like a little kid again. The world seems filled with adventure and surprises."

"It makes me really happy to hear you say that," Kai says, his eyes locking onto mine.

Suddenly, I don't care anymore about innuendos or logistics or solving for *x*. I've always prided myself on being fearless—I'm tired of being scared in this one area of my life. I boldly reach over and grab Kai's hand. Nothing subtle about it.

For one heartbeat, two heartbeats, panic swells within me. *What have I done?*

Then Kai looks at me with a giddy smile. He threads his fingers through mine and squeezes my hand.

A giddy smile spreads across my own face. So I'm not *just Tegan* to him, like he isn't *just Kai* to me. And I'm pretty sure mine wasn't the only world that shifted last night with that first kiss.

Other than us, the beach is deserted. It's that timeless time of day when it seems like the sunshine might stretch on forever. The light has a magical quality. Kai leads me across the soft sand to the edge of a precipice overlooking the ocean. Below, a coral reef juts out, forming a shallow cove of clear blue water.

"Wow," I murmur. "It's beautiful. How do we get down there?"

"We jump," Kai says.

I stare at him. He stares back. After a few seconds, he laughs.

"Just kidding! Follow me."

We walk along the cliff edge thirty feet or so, until it naturally starts to curve. Kai points down. Carved into the rock of the sea cliff are steps leading down to the cove.

"Who made these?" I ask in awe—and gratitude.

Kai shrugs. "The island is full of little gifts like these steps. Some people say the gods made them for us."

"Do you believe that?"

"I think humans made them, a long time ago. I bet they would be glad to know others are using them. C'mon!" He tugs me forward. "Be careful—might be slippery."

We slowly make our way down the narrow, uneven steps. Kai keeps his hand in mine, even though it's an awkward angle for him to stretch his arm backward. When we reach the sand below, I revel in its cool softness between my toes. Kai strips off his T-shirt, and I try not to stare. I duck behind a giant rock to take off my shorts. Once we're in the water, I'll forget that I'm in bikini bottoms, but right now I feel so exposed. I pull out my snorkel gear and fit the goggles over my eyes and nose. The salty plastic smell takes me back to the last time I went snorkeling, years and years ago, with Kai. The lenses are a little smeary, exactly the way I remember. I carefully fold my shorts and place them high on the rocks, away from the waves, along with the snorkel gear bag. Then I grab my fins, take a deep breath, and step out from behind my cover.

Kai is facing away from me, putting on his fins. A memory flashes through my mind of his little-boy self spraying me with water through his snorkel. I run up and kick the waves, splashing him. He turns toward me, laughing. His mask is up on his forehead.

"Be careful, Rossi. Remember who you're messing with!"

"And who is that?"

"The Splash Ninja! I'll get you when you least expect it! Consider yourself warned." He winks, then adjusts his mask down over his eyes and nose.

"So how do we do the fins? I forget."

"Put them on here, in the shallow water," Kai suggests. "Then walk backward out into the waves. It's awkward at first, but once the water gets deep enough to swim, you'll be great."

After a bit of struggle—one flipper almost gets carried away by a wave—I manage to fit the rubbery fins over my feet. Together, Kai and I take big steps backward into the ocean. The water is a cool bath. When we're in deep enough, Kai says, "Ready?"

I nod and bite onto my salty-tasting mouthpiece. Nerves flutter in my stomach. *I hope I remember how to do this.*

Kai turns and dives into the water, his snorkel tube popping up above sea level. I practice taking one, two, three breaths through the breathing tube, and then I follow suit.

Through my goggles, an expanse of turquoise. Shafts of light filter down through the water. The world condenses to the sound of my breathing. My lungs still have that weird can't-get-enough-oxygen tightness. I remind myself to take even, slow breaths. When I first tried snorkeling as a girl, I got anxious and began to hyperventilate. I remember swallowing water and popping my head above the surface, sputtering with frustration, on the verge of tears. My dad calmed me down and taught me to count in my head as I got acclimated to breathing through the tube.

One, two, three, in. One, two, three, out. Before long, I get the hang of it again, and I don't need to think about breathing anymore. It comes naturally.

I swim after Kai, toward the coral reef. My fin-feet propel me forward. My hair trails out behind me. I am a mermaid. Underwater, Kai turns and gives me a thumbs-up, looking adorable in his snorkel mask. He prides himself on being the suave local, but snorkeling is one activity that levels the field. Everyone, even Kai, looks like a tourist in a snorkel mask. And maybe we are all tourists in this underwater world—snorkels are our temporary visas, allowing us to visit this mysterious country for brief slices of time.

Kai waves me closer. I swim forward slowly, careful not to get too close to the jagged coral. I learned as a kid that while it looks soft, coral is actually quite sharp. It's easy to get too close, brush it accidentally, and cut yourself. From a safe distance, I look down at a living, breathing painting of colorful fish in all shapes and sizes. Later, Kai will tell me the names of the different creatures we saw. For now, I mentally give them silly names: princess shiny-fin, silver glitterfish, rainbow delight. I recognize a couple of poky purple urchins and tranquil starfish, and—Kai grabs my arm excitedly and points—a seahorse! I've never seen a seahorse in the wild before. It looks like a tiny dragon, speeding around the branches of coral.

Out of the corner of my eye, something catches my attention. Movement, shadows flickering through the watery sunlight. And then, I see him.

Our sea turtle.

He swims around the bend in the coral reef, right toward us.

Ten years ago ...

I was in the shallow water, my feet touching the sand, practicing my steady breathing through the snorkel tube. I was able to do it pretty well within the safety of the shallow waters. But I wasn't ready to venture out much farther.

Kai swam over, gesturing wildly. He bobbed his head above the surface, so I did too. My mouth hurt from clenching around the mouthpiece.

He spit out his snorkel tube. "Tegan, follow me!"

"Where? What's going on?"

"There's a sea turtle! C'mon, quick, before he swims away! You've got to see him!"

I hesitated, for only a second, but Kai noticed.

"Don't be scared," he said. "It's not that far out."

My defenses rose. "I'm not scared. I just don't get what the big deal is."

"Legend has it, you can follow a sea turtle to the end of the world. Let's do it!"

Kai's excitement was contagious. "Okay," I relented. "I'm ready."

I popped in my mouthpiece and dove into the water. Kai swam ahead, waving at me to follow him.

After what seemed like a long time, but was probably only a couple minutes of swimming, the sea turtle came into view. He seemed so friendly, smiling lazily at us. A barnacle clung to his shell. I wanted to reach out and hug him. I wanted to hang on to his shell just like that barnacle. I wanted him to take me on a ride.

Together, Kai and I swam after the sea turtle. But we didn't get very far. A wave swept over us and filled my snorkel tube. Panicking, breathing in salt water, I burst up above the ocean's surface, sputtering and coughing. The shore was so far away—I wished desperately for something to hold on to, to steady myself.

Kai popped up beside me. I clung to his arm. "It's okay; you're okay,"
he said, pulling me gently back to shore.

Safely on the beach, I felt embarrassment eclipsing my distress. "I'm
sorry," I told Kai.

"What do you mean?"

"We lost the turtle because of me."

Kai shrugged. "Naw, my arms were getting tired. I would have
turned back soon."

I dug my toes into the sand. "Thanks for showing him to me."

"He was pretty awesome, right?"

"Very awesome."

"We're lucky that we saw him. My dad says people used to find turtles
a lot, but not as much anymore. I've only seen, like, five, in all the times
I've been snorkeling."

"Wow." And I did feel lucky, sitting there on the beach with my
new friend Kai. For the first time in my life, I believed there was magic
swirling around in the world, and it had settled onto my shoulders.
The magic had chosen me. In that moment, I was so confident that the
magic would continue on and on, that it would keep choosing me and
choosing me.

This sea turtle is almost certainly not the same sea turtle we saw all
those years ago.

But it could be. It looks exactly like him.

I yank on Kai's arm and point. The sea turtle glides unhurriedly
through the water, a calm expression on his face. He approaches

us steadily, getting close enough for me to glimpse a few barnacles clinging to his massive, beautiful shell. Then he turns and heads into the deeper water.

Like an instinct or a muscle memory, I follow.

Kai swims beside me. His eyes behind his mask are wide with excitement. Time has circled around and swept us back into its orbit. We've caught up to something that previously slipped away, something I thought was gone forever. It seems possible to keep swimming and swimming forever. Maybe we *can* follow this sea turtle to the end of the world.

The water gets colder the farther we swim out. I've never swum this far from shore before. But I don't feel afraid.

What nobody tells you about sea turtles is that they look graceful and calm, even lazy, as they move smoothly through the water—but don't mistake this for slowness. They are speedy. Gradually, steadily, our sea turtle pulls away from us.

I try to swim faster, but my arms are heavy and tired. Even though I'm wearing fins, my legs are spaghetti from kicking and kicking.

Our sea turtle's shell becomes smaller and smaller, receding into the expanse of clear blue water, until he is a faint glimmer.

Kai touches my arm, gesturing toward the shore. I gaze out toward the ocean's depths a little longer, searching. I think I might see him. But maybe not. Maybe that's a distant shadow in the water.

I nod at Kai. Wordlessly, we turn around and swim back. *Goodbye-for-now, sea turtle.*

As we approach the shore, the pull of the waves grows stronger. I was so swept up in the exhilaration of following our sea turtle that I hadn't noticed the goose bumps on my arms and legs. Now I'm cold. And exhausted. As soon as we are close enough to touch the ground,

I pop my head above water and let my fins rest on the sandy floor. Kai does the same.

I take off my snorkel mask and wipe water from my eyes. It is strange to take in gulps of air after breathing through the tube. When Kai pulls off his mask, there are red marks on his face from the suction. I bet there are twin marks on my face.

"That was incredible!" Kai exclaims, pumping a fist in the air. "Our sea turtle! We found him!"

"Do you think that was really the same one? From so long ago?"

"Could have been. Did you know that sea turtles can live for a hundred years? So our childhood is a small blip in time, to a sea turtle."

The sand shifts beneath my feet. "Those memories were a lifetime ago. Does it seem that way to you, too?"

Kai shrugs. His face is guarded all of a sudden, as if he's bracing himself for what I might say next.

I step nearer to him. "But now that I'm back here with you, everything seems so much ... closer. Like I could reach out and touch the past. Like its heart is still beating, if that makes any sense."

Kai's face relaxes. "I know what you mean," he says.

The waves sweep into us. Their unending rhythm comforts me. These waves were here when we were kids. They were here during my last visit. They were here during all the years I was somewhere else. The waves are here whether I am thinking about them or not. They simply exist. Here before we were born. Here after we die. These waves, rolling in and receding out. Constant.

I look into Kai's eyes. There's so much I want to tell him— emotions and thoughts jumbled up inside me like tangled knots— but I don't know where to begin. So we stand there silently for a few moments, holding our snorkel masks, our finned feet touching the ocean floor. Gazing at each other.

Involuntarily, I shiver.

"You cold?" Kai steps forward and wraps his arms around me. "You've got goose bumps!"

"You're not cold?"

"Naw. I'm used to being in the water forever. After a while you develop a tolerance."

Another wave hits us. Kai tightens his arms around me. Our floating snorkel masks bump into each other.

"We should head in," Kai says. "Get you a towel."

"Yeah, that sounds nice."

But neither of us moves.

"Thank you," I say softly.

"For what?"

"For yesterday, for today. For everything. I'm having the best time here with you."

Kai beams. "I'm so glad. This was all I wanted for graduation, remember? It's paradise, having you here."

At that word—*paradise*—something flashes into my mind from yesterday. Something Paulo said. *Kai always says, "Hawaii would be total paradise if only—"* But then Kai interrupted him. *What was Paulo going to say? Did it have anything to do with me?*

Kai's fingers trace circles on my back. "I've been thinking about yesterday," he murmurs.

My heart beats, beats, beats. "You have?" I ask.

"About last night. About … "

His eyes search mine: asking permission. I lean closer and tilt my face up: granting it.

"About how I've been dying to do this again," he says, his mouth meeting mine.

"Me too," I whisper against his lips.

We kiss, and it's not awkward at all, and I wonder what I was so worried about. He tastes like the ocean. He runs his hands along my arms, rubbing away the goose bumps. We sway with the waves. I wrap my legs around his waist, barnacling myself to him. His hands cup my bottom: a perfect seat.

Eventually, reluctantly, we pull apart. My lips tingle with salt. One of my fins and both of our snorkel masks have floated away. Kai swims over to retrieve them. I follow him to shore, splashing in the waves.

I always thought the magic in my childhood memories with Kai stemmed from what we did together here: snorkeling, lounging in the pool, building sandcastles, claiming our secret hideout. But the magic of those memories doesn't live in the activities we did. The magic comes from the person I did them with. I would feel just as much magic if Kai and I were sitting side by side studying for finals in some bland coffee shop.

Studying for finals. I wish that Kai and I were going to the same college. *Is he going to college at all? Or is he still planning to work at the shop? It would be a waste of his talents to not even try college.*

Ahead on the swath of beach, Kai holds open my striped beach towel. "It was baking in the sun for you!" he shouts.

I don't want to think about college or the future or anything else but this moment.

I run into Kai's arms, and he hugs me with the towel. How glorious it is to be warm and dry after swimming in the ocean. It's way different from the lake back home. It feels much more satisfying to come out of the ocean, to stumble back onto dry land. To turn around and look at the vast expanse of blue you were just a part of, mysterious and everlasting.

On the way back to the Jeep, Kai grabs my hand and squeezes it. "We have to do something before we go home."

I arch an eyebrow. "Oh really?"

Kai blushes. "Not anything like that. I mean, um, unless you wanted … "

"I was joking!" I pinch his side. "I mean, I *barely know you*."

He laughs, and I laugh, and the awkwardness dissipates.

"Besides," I continue, "I'm not in a rush. We've got all the time in the world."

He squeezes my hand again, and we walk in silence for a little bit. I savor the sun warming my bare shoulders and the comfort of Kai's fingers interlaced with mine.

"Wait!" I say when we reach the Jeep. "What do we have to do before we go home?"

"Oh yeah." Kai loads our snorkel gear into the back. "If we don't do this, Paulo will be extremely disappointed in us."

I trace a smiley face into the dust on Kai's side window. "Let me guess. Just give me a minute … " *Aha!* I point my finger at Kai. "Shave ice."

He points at me. "You up for it?"

"Is the same place still there, from when we were kids?"

"Halo-Halo Island Breeze. You bet. The best shave ice in town."

I climb into the front seat. "I think there's a halo-halo with my name on it. Let's go!"

Shave ice is something I've only encountered in Hawaii. It's like ice cream mixed with a snow cone. Sounds weird, but it's delicious. My favorite flavor is the halo-halo—a flavor I never would have tried without Kai's influence. My little-kid self gravitated toward the traditional offerings: strawberry shortcake, chocolate fudge. Kai ordered the halo-halo and insisted that I try it before I ordered. I was skeptical. His ice cream was purple, and I've never liked grape-flavored things. But Kai assured me it was not grape, so I tentatively took a bite. The taste was like nothing I'd ever tried before. Sweet, but not too sweet. Creamy, savory richness that made me immediately want more. It tasted like … sunshine, if sunshine had a taste.

"What *is* that?" I remember asking Kai, my voice filled with wonder.

"Ube. It's a form of purple potato. There's azuki beans in there too. And boba."

I did not know what ube or boba or azuki beans were. I only knew I wanted more. So, I ordered my own halo-halo, and the rest is history.

Kai pulls into the parking lot of Halo-Halo Island Breeze. Actually, it's the parking lot for the local fish market, and Halo-Halo Island Breeze is a food truck that has taken up permanent residence in the far corner. Sometimes, Kai tells me, the line for shave ice stretches all the way around the parking lot. Today, we're lucky; there are only a handful of people in front of us. The line moves slowly, but nobody seems to mind. The late-afternoon sun is warm, the sky a cloudless blue. I study the menu posted on the side of the truck. The caramel volcano sounds intriguing. So does the Kona coffee crème. But when it's our turn to order, and Kai looks at me expectantly, I say: "The regular, please."

"We'd like two halo-halos."

Kai pulls out his wallet, but I beat him to it, pushing a handful of bills through the window.

"This one's on me!" I say, dropping my change into the tip jar.

A few minutes later, the man calls our number and hands our plastic bowls through the food truck window. Kai and I sit on a bench shaded by mango trees. Closing my eyes, I taste the creamy, deliciously cold shave ice.

When I open my eyes, Kai is smiling at me. "As good as you remember?" he asks.

"Even better!" I slowly savor another bite.

We sit in silence for a little while, enjoying our shave ice. Occasionally, our elbows brush. I rest my knee against his.

"Hey, Kai. Can I ask you a question?"

"Of course. Shoot."

"What was that R.J. guy talking about? In the restaurant last night?" My mind keeps circling back to that strange, tense encounter.

Kai sighs. "Oh, Tegan—he's a jerk. It wasn't really about you. He was just trying to get under my skin."

I slide my spoon around the rim of my bowl. "What does he have against you?"

"He's angry. We used to be friends, but then ... there was a misunderstanding, I guess you'd say."

Kai is holding something back. I don't want to push him, but I also wish he would confide in me. His mom said he's been depressed lately. Does this "misunderstanding" have something to do with it?

"I heard what R.J. said about me," I murmur. "I heard him say, 'Doesn't look like she's worth it.' What does that even mean?"

Kai crunches an azuki bean. He looks uncomfortable. "Okay, here's the story. It's really not a big deal. I went to prom with this girl Nadia—"

I nod. "I remember. You sent me photos."

"Yeah. We went as friends. At least, it was clear to *me* that we were going as friends. But I guess Nadia wanted to be ... more."

In the photos Kai sent me, Nadia's body was pressed against his. Her smile was huge. The two of them fit so well together. And Kai looked happy. It would have been easy for her to think ... to hope ...

"Anyway," Kai continues. "I never felt that way about her. I always liked her as a friend. We've been in the same group since middle school. R.J.'s her twin brother. He's a decent guy, actually. Just protective. After prom went down, he got all over me for 'breaking Nadia's heart.' He claimed I was purposely leading her on and that the only reason I didn't want to be with Nadia was because I was holding onto a stupid pipe dream ... "

He glances over sheepishly, as if suddenly remembering that he's talking to *me*.

I tuck a loose strand of hair behind my ear. "Was I the pipe dream?"

Kai nods. "My friends all knew about you. They liked to give me crap for being in love with this mainland girl who barely even knew I existed."

"Hey—that's not true! You're my best friend."

A corner of Kai's mouth lifts in a half smile. "I would insist that you and I were just friends, but they always knew I was lying. R.J. and the other guys could tell I had a crush on you. And when I let down Nadia, everything boiled over."

I'm not used to Kai talking so blatantly about his feelings for me. My entire body is buzzing. "What do you mean, 'boiled over'?"

"R.J. ambushed me after school and punched me in the face. I had a black eye for a week. None of the other guys came to my defense. The girls all took Nadia's side and stopped talking to me. I pretty much lost my group of friends."

I touch his arm. "Kai, that's terrible. I'm so sorry."

He shrugs. "It was only the last few weeks of school. Then we all graduated. I guess they weren't really my friends after all."

I think of the photo on his bookcase. All of them leaning in close together, laughing. I find it hard to believe they weren't really friends.

"Did you try to apologize?" I ask.

"Apologize? What for? I did *nothing* wrong."

Sometimes I forget about this aspect of Kai's personality: his stubbornness. It only rears its head very occasionally—but when it does, watch out. Kai's stubbornness is like lava barreling down a mountainside. Impossible to change its course.

I lean my head on his shoulder. "You must have felt so alone. Why didn't you tell me about this when it happened?"

"It was too complicated. I didn't want to bore you with my stupid friendship drama."

"You never bore me! You know that."

Kai wipes a smear of whipped cream off my cheek. "Okay, the real reason? I didn't want to bring up something that hinted at my feelings for you. I thought it would scare you away. You're too important to lose. I couldn't risk it."

And then we had our big argument, and stopped talking to each other, and you put my photo facedown on your nightstand. Did you think that you lost me? I take his hand, bring it up to my lips, and kiss it. "I'm sorry."

"It's not your fault."

"I mean, I'm sorry it took me so long. To stop being afraid. To let myself fall. To admit my feelings for you."

Kai kisses me. He tastes of ube and sugar.

"You're worth the wait," he says. "I always knew you would be worth the wait. That's why I kept waiting."

He stands up and gathers our empty bowls and sticky plastic spoons for the trash can. When he comes back, he's smiling. "Besides," he says. "I was never alone. I had you."

It's a sweet thing to say, and I nod and tell him, "Of course. You'll always have me." But I wonder: *Is that enough? Am I enough?*

As if in response to my thoughts, he reaches down and pulls me up, wrapping his strong arms around me. He smells of the ocean and sunscreen and something else—his own Kai scent. I breathe him in. For years I've seen his face on a screen and heard his voice through my phone speakers, but I didn't realize all that I was missing: the smell of his sweat, the feel of his warm skin against mine, the taste of his lips. Now my senses can't get enough of his body occupying the same physical space as mine.

A few minutes later, as we walk across the parking lot to his Jeep, I tell Kai about *literally* bumping into Nadia yesterday, when I was following Theo to the Tiki Room. I leave out the part about how cold she was, because I understand that now. At the time, I had thought she looked familiar; she must have immediately known who I was. She must have felt ambushed. The same way I felt when Kai emailed me photos of the two of them all dressed up for prom. I had asked and asked for the photos, because I was trying so hard to force Kai into the friendship box. Yet a lump had formed in my throat as I clicked through the images, a brittle smile cracking across my face. I had tried to push away and ignore the ache in my chest, telling myself that he and Nadia made a cute couple, even though a deeper part of me was sick at the thought.

I feel for Nadia. And I feel for Kai. He needs his friends back. As much as I would like to forget about my life outside of Hawaii, I'm not able to stay here forever. I'm starting college in a couple of months.

College. A memory half-surfaces, like a split second of déjà vu. *I sit down, pull out my phone, and open a new text to type a message to Kai. But I can't find the words. So, I close the screen without sending and shove my phone back into my coat pocket.*

Kai nudges my hip. "You okay, T? You look freaked out."

My mouth is dry. "I'm fine. Just a sugar rush." The flash of memory fades away, like a dream that only gets hazier the more you try to pin it down.

The interior of the Jeep is dense with heat. Kai rolls down the windows, and a timid breeze sweeps in as we pull out of the parking lot.

"Anyway," I say, changing the subject back to Nadia. "She had these flyers for an art exhibit in town."

"Yeah, it's on Thursday. The gallery is down the block from where I work. I have a piece there."

"Wait—what?" I smack my palm against the dashboard. "You have a piece of art? In an exhibit? And I'm *just now* learning about this?"

Kai flushes. "I guess it happened when we, um, weren't talking. But it's not a big deal."

"Don't be silly! This is a *huge* deal! We are totally going to the exhibit on Thursday."

"No, we're not."

"What are you talking about? You've been trying to get your art into exhibits for ages. Why are you not more excited about this?"

Kai looks out the window. I follow his gaze. In the distance beyond the arid landscape, bright-blue ocean glimmers like a mirage.

"It's because Nadia works at the gallery. They're all gonna be there. My old friends. It's all messed up now, you know? It doesn't seem worth the bother to go."

"Kai, pull over."

"What?"

I point to the side of the road. "Can you pull over for a minute?"

He guides the Jeep over to a patch of scrub at the side of the road and cuts the engine. The late-afternoon sun slants into our eyes. Without the breeze, the air quickly grows warm.

I maneuver my body in the bucket seat so I'm facing Kai as best I can. I stay quiet for a few seconds, looking into his eyes. I want him to know that I'm serious. That this is serious.

"You deserve to be there," I say. My voice is quiet, but my tone is fierce. "This is your exhibition too. This is your artwork. This is a big deal. You deserve to be celebrated, Kai."

He looks down at his lap, fiddling with his keys. Silence settles into the space between us. *Is he upset with me? Have I stepped out of bounds?*

"It's really good to have you here, Tegan," he says finally. His voice is like sandpaper. He clears his throat. "I forgot what it was like to have someone on my side, fighting for me."

The moment seems delicate, like any wrong move can shatter it. I reach across the center console and quietly hold his hand. I rub my thumb against his, hoping touch can convey what I'm feeling right now: tenderness and regret, sadness and comfort. I'm so relieved to be here with Kai—to finally be together like this—but at the same time, I ache to think of the struggles he's been going through lately, without me. I wasn't there for him when he needed me. And I can't go back in time and change that. I can't undo our argument. All I can do is try to be here for him from now on.

"I'll always fight for you," I say. "And never forget—you're a fighter too."

Kai gives me a little smile. He turns the keys in the ignition, and we pull back out onto the road.

"So tell me about this exhibition piece," I say, talking loudly over the breeze flapping through the open windows.

"It's a wood carving," Kai says.

"Cool. What's it about?"

Kai winks, back to his usual self. "That part is a surprise. You'll just have to wait and see."

Wait and see. Happiness bubbles up inside me. Although the stubborn part of Kai doesn't want to admit I changed his mind, we're definitely going to the art exhibition on Thursday.

"So Tegan, how are you enjoying island life so far?" Kai's dad asks.

"I love it here! It's so beautiful, and peaceful, and relaxing … I wish I could stay forever!" As the words leave my mouth, I hear how they might sound to people who are letting me crash in their home, and I hurry to add, "Not that I actually *will* be staying forever; don't worry."

"You are welcome in our home as long as you like, sweetheart," Kai's mom says, passing the basket of warm rolls around the table. She has made a feast of grilled fish and vegetables, fresh pineapple, poi, and baked sweet potatoes. Even though Kai and I devoured shave ice just a couple of hours ago, the smell of dinner makes my stomach growl. As each dish is passed around, I fill my plate.

I am grateful to be sitting at this crowded dinner table, welcomed as part of this beautifully chaotic family. Growing up, I always wished for siblings, and the wish only intensified after my parents' divorce. To have a brother or sister to share everything with—rolling our eyes at Dad's series of girlfriends, binge-watching Netflix when Mom works late—to laugh together and cry together and *understand* each other, like no one else truly could. My whole life, I've yearned for a family like this one. I would gladly settle for even one more filled seat at the small dining table in my mom's kitchen. Kai doesn't realize how lucky he is.

Paulo looks at me with wide, excited eyes, like I'm a celebrity. His behavior toward me oscillates between adorable shyness and friendly openness. "How long is Tegan staying?" he asks.

"Until Sunday," I say. I have no idea where that answer comes from. It's not like I have a return plane ticket, even though I've scoured my email a hundred times. Weirdly, I haven't received any new emails since I arrived in Hawaii, not even spam. When we got home this afternoon, I tried calling my mom again—four separate times—but all I heard was that same hollow ringing. Not even the chance to leave a message asking her to call me back. Her work number gave me the same result. I don't know what is going on. If this keeps up, I'm going to have to tell Kai the truth soon.

Paulo frowns, digging a fork through his poi. "I don't want her to leave."

Kai reaches over and ruffles Paulo's hair. "I know, buddy. Me neither."

Mrs. Kapule lifts the basket of rolls to pass around the table again. "But she won't be gone forever. You'll come back to visit again, right Tegan?"

I smile with a lump in my throat. "Yes, of course I will."

After dinner, I try calling my parents again—no answer—while Kai and his siblings wash the dishes. Then we all pile into the family room to watch a movie. All except Theo, who tells his parents he's going to a friend's house. He and Kai exchange a look, but I can't tell what's behind it. Paulo has saved me a seat on the amazingly comfortable couch, the kind your body sinks into so it's impossible to get back up. Olina, clearly an equal member of the family, is wedged beside him, her large head resting comfortably on the couch arm. Kai sits on my other side, and his parents take the love seat. The movie's just started when Theo waves goodbye and heads out, the door banging shut behind him. Kai sighs.

"You okay?" I murmur.

"Yeah. I'm gonna get some juice. You want anything from the kitchen?"

I can't move—don't want to move—because Paulo is cuddled up against me.

"Juice would be great, thanks!" I'm usually not much of a juice drinker, but I can't get enough of the flavors here. Pineapple, guava, passion fruit. Kai likes to mix them all together.

One tall glass of juice, one pee break, and two hours later, the movie has ended, and Paulo has fallen asleep against my shoulder. His mom gently wakes him up and leads him off to bed. We say goodnight to Kai's dad. Olina is stretched out on the rug, snoring, her legs twitching as she chases after seagulls in her dreams. Theo hasn't arrived home yet. Kai glances at the front door before he turns off the lamp in the family room.

Once we're safely in his bedroom with the door closed, I ask him point-blank. "Are you worried about Theo?"

Kai runs a hand down his face. "I don't like the people he's hanging out with. Theo's just a kid, but some of those guys are dealing drugs, like, seriously. I keep telling Theo that a little extra pocket money isn't worth the risk. But he won't listen."

"Do your parents know?"

He shakes his head. "They have no idea. Telling them would be breaking Theo's trust in me. I keep hoping he'll decide on his own to stop."

"You should tell your parents, Kai."

"You think so?" His eyes search mine.

My opinion matters to him. "I do. Theo might be angry with you initially, but in the long run, he'll thank you."

Kai sighs. "You're probably right." He looks at his closed bedroom door, as if expecting Theo to burst in at any moment. "But I don't want to set off a bomb of family drama when you're here. How about I give Theo the rest of the week to get his act together, and if he doesn't, then I'll tell my parents?"

I sit on the bed. "That sounds like a good plan."

I expect Kai to sit next to me, but he remains standing. He shifts from one foot to the other. "So, um, I'm gonna grab a pillow, and then I'll get out of your hair."

"What are you talking about?"

He gestures to the door. "You can take my bed, and I'll, um, crash on the couch."

Oh. After last night, I wasn't expecting this. "You don't have to do that, Kai."

"It's not a big deal."

"Do your parents want us sleeping in separate rooms?"

He chuckles. "No, they don't care. When I turned eighteen, they sat me down and explained that I'm an adult now, and I get to make my own choices. They pretty much let me do what I want. Plus, they like you."

"I like them too." I pick at a loose thread on my shorts. "So, um, are you saying that you *want* to sleep on the couch? If anyone sleeps on the couch, it should be me. I'm the one who showed up here unannounced."

"No! You are not sleeping on the couch. I mean, I'm fine sleeping there. I want you to have my bed for yourself if that's, you know, what you want. Your own space. Some privacy. I totally understand ... "

He is so adorably flustered that I can't even bring myself to tease him. I stand up, pull him toward me, and kiss his lips.

"I was hoping you'd stay here with me," I whisper.

Kai's face relaxes. "Really? I mean, I didn't want to assume ... there is no pressure to, like, do anything ... "

I interrupt his words with kisses. Soon our breathing becomes more urgent, and he's tugging off my sweater. His hands feel so good on my bare skin, and his lips electrify me. I can imagine going all the way with him—I *want* to; my body wants to—but I don't feel ready. Not yet. I force myself to pull back.

His hair is rumpled, and his cheeks are pink. "You all right?" he asks, concern in his eyes.

I nod. "Is it okay if we just ... make out? And cuddle?" I feel lame, but Kai smiles and says, "Of course!" and I know it's the right thing because relief washes through me. We change into our pajamas, dropping our eyes away from each other for privacy. Then we crawl under the covers. Our bodies face each other like two halves of the same whole.

"I've never slept with anyone before," Kai says softly.

"Do you mean, slept together in the same bed? Or ... had sex?"

"I mean both. Er, neither. I've done neither."

This new knowledge nestles within me. *So we weren't keeping anything from each other. I do know him. Has he been waiting for me, like I've been secretly waiting for him all this time?*

"Me too," I say. "Er, me neither. Unless you factor in slumber parties with Andrea where we slept in the same bed. But that doesn't really count."

Kai grins. "So, you and Andrea, huh? Tell me more."

I hit him with my pillow.

He laughs. Then his face grows serious. His dark eyes find mine and hold my gaze. "Listen, T. You know how I feel about you. In my opinion you are the sexiest, most beautiful girl on this planet. But I am perfectly content just hanging out with you—even just being in the same *room* with you. Anything else is a bonus. There is no pressure, *ever*, from me. All right?"

"I know," I tell him. "But thank you for saying it."

We lie there in silence, looking at each other. Our bent knees touch. My fingers are cold, and Kai cups them in his hands, warming them beneath the blankets.

I scoot toward him, even though we can't really get much closer. "You're the best; did you know that?"

In response, he kisses me—sweetly, gently. We kiss for a while longer, until my lips are numb, and my eyelids droop. Then Kai turns out the bedside lamp. I shift onto my other side, and he wraps his arms around me, spooning me, and it feels natural. Normal. As I drift off to sleep, the word echoing through my mind is *safe*.

I never realized that falling in love could feel so effortlessly, completely safe.

dear tegan,

i don't even know what to say. i don't know why i'm writing this, because you won't ever read it. maybe there's some part of me that still thinks you will. i can't believe it, t. it's not real. you're not really gone. you can't be.

i had another dream about you last night. that's three times in a row, if you're keeping track. we went snorkeling and saw that same sea turtle from all those years ago. we tried to follow him, but then we got distracted ... the best kind of distracted, if you know what i mean. god, i'm too chicken to type the words even though i know you're never going to read this. i can't believe the only chance i'll ever have to kiss you will be in my dreams. my idiotic, yearning, hopeless dreams.

when i woke up this morning, the dream was so real in my mind i could swear it actually happened, and you still hadn't replied to my emails. so i caved in and looked at your Instagram, which as a rule i never do because i don't like to feed the jealous part of myself. i don't like to click through photos of you with other guys, driving myself crazy wondering if you're hooking up with them or not. i don't like spending twenty minutes typing and deleting, typing and deleting, trying to decide if i should attempt to write some witty banter or inside joke as a comment, or if it would just look like i'm trying too hard. ever since that night on the phone—you know the one i mean—ever since then, i never wanted to seem like i care too much and scare you away.

but when i clicked onto your profile, my heart stopped. all these comments from people saying how much they loved you and how much they would miss you and what an amazing person you were. WERE, past tense.

you can't be in the past tense, tegan. you just can't. you're the most real person out of everyone i've ever met.

you know what i realized in my dream last night? the whole point all those years ago wasn't to follow the sea turtle all the way around the world. no, the point of it was simply to be swimming by your side. to be heading somewhere, you and me, together.

maybe i should join you, wherever you are now.

—kai

PART TWO

WEDNESDAY

A gentle rocking motion. *The mundane chatter of voices. Out the window, a blur of tree branches. The sensation of moving very fast. Speed building and building. Out of control. Suddenly, jerking sideways. Slamming into something hard. A sharp intake of breath. A scream lodged in a throat.*

I jolt awake. My vision is blurry again, and it takes longer than it did yesterday for my surroundings to solidify into focus. I blink into the bright morning light streaming through Kai's bedroom curtains. Yawning, I rub my eyes and turn around in the sheets. The bed is empty. Cozy breakfast smells waft in from the kitchen.

I pull on one of Kai's sweatshirts, breathing in his scent. Thinking about last night makes my whole body glow. *Me and Kai. Kai and me.* I can't believe it's really happening. And I also can't believe it took us so long.

I brush my teeth, wash my face, and pad into the kitchen. Kai is at the stove, his back to me. The countertops are stacked with dirty dishes—from his family's breakfast this morning, I assume. The clock on the wall reads 9:23.

"Good morning." I slip onto one of the barstools.

"Hey," Kai says, a smile in his voice. "Give me one sec. I want to make sure these babies don't burn."

"What are you making?"

"Macadamia nut pancakes."

"Wow! Like they serve at the resort!" When I was a kid, I ate so many macadamia nut pancakes that I got a stomachache. But I didn't care—I ordered the same thing the next day when my parents and I went down to breakfast.

Kai flips a pancake; it sizzles when it hits the pan. "Well, keep your expectations low. Mine aren't as fancy as those. I'm not exactly a five-star chef."

"I'm still impressed. These smell like heaven."

He turns off the burner and spatulas the final pancake onto a plate stacked high. He slides it onto the counter in front of me. "Chef Kai, at your service."

I love getting to see his adorable bed head and his plaid pajama bottoms. I love getting to fall asleep beside him at night and eat breakfast with him in the morning. I love getting to play house like this—no school, no worries, no chores. Just summer, sunshine, and each other. Shyly, I hook my leg around his and draw him closer. He grins and buries his fingers in my hair. He tastes like Kona coffee.

Eventually, my stomach grumbles, and Kai laughs and pulls away. "Let's get you fed," he says, reaching into cabinets and drawers for clean plates and silverware. He rummages in the pantry. "I know we have syrup in here somewhere … *aha!*" He holds the bottle aloft like a trophy and plunks it down on the counter next to the pancakes.

"Wait a minute … you don't have homemade coconut syrup?" I tease. "At the resort they always served them with homemade coconut syrup."

"What the heck is homemade coconut syrup?"

"I don't know. But it's delicious."

"Well, Rossi, regular syrup is all we got here at Kai's Pancake Kitchen Café."

I divvy up the pancakes onto two plates. "Wait—is it Pancake Kitchen or Pancake Café?"

"It's both."

"How can it be both?"

"Two is better than one."

I sigh dramatically and pick up the slightly sticky syrup bottle. "I guess this will have to do, then."

Kai playfully pinches my side, and I lean into him, kissing his neck. I grab my phone and take a selfie of us—I want to try sending a picture to Andrea—and then snap a photo of my syrup-drenched stack of pancakes.

"Does the Wi-Fi act up for you sometimes?" I ask, opening Instagram.

"Not really," Kai says. "Did I give you the password?"

"Yeah. Maybe it's an issue with my phone." I try to post the pancake photo, but all I get is a frozen screen.

As I stare at the screen, my vision blurs. When I blink, there's a new photo on my Instagram profile. It's me, beaming, holding a suitcase and standing in front of a train. The caption reads, *Philly –> DC <3 Georgetown, here I come!* It was posted on Monday. As in, two days ago.

Wait … that's not possible. Three days ago, I woke up here. In Hawaii. My heart races, and my stomach heaves. My body knows something. All of a sudden, I remember my dream from last night—such a vivid dream.

I told Kai that I didn't have time to visit him in Hawaii after all. Instead, I chose to head down to campus a couple of months before the semester began so I could move into my new apartment and take summer courses and find a job and and and …

I was filled with excuses and fear. So I took the easy path. College was my convenient pretext to run away from him. From us. I told myself that I didn't have room in my life for complications; I had to focus on my future. I couldn't get caught up in that long-ago idyllic summer. Summer doesn't last.

So, I bought a train ticket. Philadelphia to DC isn't very far, and it was way cheaper than a plane ticket. I told myself it would be fun—arriving to college on a train, just like an old-fashioned character in a novel.

Mom snapped a photo of me standing outside the train with a ginormous fake smile on my face. I hugged her goodbye and stepped aboard. Wrestled my suitcase onto the luggage rack. Sat down and pulled out my phone, opening a new text to type out a message to Kai. But I couldn't find the words. So instead I posted a photo to Instagram, trying to plaster over my misgivings with a string of cheerful emojis, before shoving the phone back into my coat pocket.

My eyes are blurry again. I stare at my phone screen, willing them to focus.

"Tegan?" Kai says. His voice sounds faraway. "Are you okay?"

"Look at this." I shove my phone at him. "What do you see?"

"Um, your Instagram. Is the Wi-Fi still not working? I'll go reset the router—"

I grab his sleeve. "No, Kai, wait. Look at my profile. What's the last photo you see?"

He peers down at my phone. "You at graduation."

My head is spinning. I close my eyes. I'm being pulled back into my dream from last night—more like a nightmare.

A gentle rocking motion. The mundane chatter of voices. Out the window, a blur of tree branches. The sensation of moving very fast. Speed building and building. Out of control. Suddenly, jerking sideways. Slamming into something hard. A sharp intake of breath. A scream lodged in a throat.

I wrench open my eyes, stifling a scream. My skin is clammy. I look down at my phone again. There I am, grinning in front of a train. I scroll down. Below the photo are dozens of comments from people saying how much they love me and how much they will miss me and what an amazing person I was. *Was.* Past tense.

This must be some sick joke. It has to be.

I open a new browser window to do a quick search: *train from philadelphia to dc.*

The screen floods with news stories from the past few days.

DEADLY TRAIN ACCIDENT IN VIRGINIA

Sixty-eight people were killed and hundreds wounded in a commuter train accident on the Northeast Corridor from Philadelphia to Washington, DC, on Monday. The train unaccountably derailed, and the first two cars careened into

```
the mountainside, killing sixty-
seven passengers along with the
train conductor. Eight passengers
remain missing.

     Authorities have not announced
the cause of the accident and
are withholding further details
pending further investigation
by the National Transportation
Safety Board.

     Vigils are being held for
the victims in Philadelphia and
Washington.
```

Kai rests his hand on my back. "Tegan? You're freaking me out a little. Are you okay? You're white as a sheet."

I try to gulp in a lungful of air, but my breathing comes in shallow gasps. Pain radiates from my heart, down my arms and up my jaw.

The knowledge surges within me. I try to ignore it, but I can't. My body remembers. My legs are shaking, and the hair rises on my arms.

I was on that train.

I was in that train accident.

"Tegan?"

Kai's voice reaches me through a long, hollow tunnel. My vision blurs again, and then the world goes black.

Kai and I are driving down the highway. Instead of an arid desert, our surroundings are lush and green. Tucked into a cliff, I spot a small waterfall—a stream of water dissolving into mist. We turn off the highway onto a dirt road. After a few minutes, the dirt road ends, eaten up by grass and shrubs. Kai parks the Jeep, and we climb out, walking down a worn path toward the waterfall. Soon, the path opens up into a clearing. There is a small wooden house, painted a deep green with sky-blue trim. We hurry toward it. The house seems magical, like it grew up out of the land itself. We climb the creaky steps of the porch, and I reach out my hand to open the door …

My fingers grasp a warm, firm hand. It takes an enormous effort to lift open my eyelids. The room seems exceedingly bright. I have a pounding headache, and my mouth is dry.

"Tegan? Tegan, wake up," Kai says, alarm in his voice.

Slowly, my eyes adjust, and the blurriness recedes. I'm lying on the couch in Kai's family room. He's crouched down beside me, holding my hand, wiping a cold washcloth across my forehead. Our eyes meet, and I smile weakly.

"Sorry about that," I tell him. "I got really dizzy all of a sudden."

"You fainted. Scared the crap out of me, T. Has that ever happened to you before? We should go back to the clinic and see Aunt Sarah—"

"No, it's fine. I'm fine." I'm definitely not fine. My mind zooms back to the picture on my Instagram and the article about the train accident and my all-too-real nightmare. I try to push away the dread eating up my insides. But a persistent little voice in the back of my mind keeps insisting, *That was you. You were on that train.*

"It's just hunger," I tell Kai. "Sometimes I get light-headed when I go too long without eating."

Kai hurries into the kitchen and microwaves the pancakes, then brings me a plate stacked high along with a huge glass of juice.

I force down bite after bite, despite the knot in my gut. "Wow, these are delicious," I say, smiling at him, even though I feel like throwing up. Kai keeps looking at me like I'm an extremely fragile glass vase and he's afraid I'm going to shatter. After we finish eating, I insist on helping him wash and dry the dishes.

As I rub the towel over the grooves of a plate, panic begins to overtake me again. My thoughts are a whirled mess. I can't pretend that everything is normal. I need to confide in Kai. Maybe he can help me figure out what is going on.

"Kai," I say softly. My voice is croaky. "I need to tell you something."

He hands me a couple of dripping forks. "What is it?"

"I lied to you. I didn't come here to surprise you."

He laughs. "What are you talking about?"

I reach for his hand. "I'm so sorry, Kai. I lied to you. I still don't remember what happened or how I got here."

Kai's forehead crinkles in concern. "Wait, what? But I thought . . . then what are you doing here?"

"I don't know."

"You don't know? Tegan, that's—that's ridiculous. You've been acting so normal this whole time. Haven't you been, like, freaked out?"

"I forced myself not to think about it. I kept believing it was only a matter of time before all my memory flooded back."

"But it hasn't come back?"

"No. The last thing I remember is graduation."

Kai steps back, away from me. "So why did you make up that whole story, about coming here to surprise me?"

I squeeze his hand. "I was hoping so desperately that it was the truth. I just wanted … I just wanted to enjoy being here in Hawaii with you. It seemed best to pretend that everything was normal."

Kai sighs and pulls away from me. He runs a hand over his face. The silence lengthens between us; with every second ticking away, the distance between us lengthens too. *Is this going to be another big argument? What if he wants me to leave? What will I do then?* I yearn to fill this silence with words, with excuses and explanations and promises, but I bite my lip and make myself be still. Finally, Kai looks at me.

"I guess I understand," he says. "I'm glad you told me the truth now. What I'm worried about is your memory. That's not normal, T. Let's go back to the clinic, and maybe they can run more tests or something—"

"Wait, Kai. There's more." I gaze directly into his deep-brown eyes. "This is going to sound crazy, but I need you to hear me out, okay?"

"Okay … "

I hand him my phone, pulled up to the news article. His eyes dart back and forth across the screen as he reads. When he finishes, he looks at me in confusion. "I don't get it. What does this train accident have to do with you?"

I take a deep breath. "I think I was on that train."

He laughs. "What?"

"I think I was in that accident."

"Tegan, are you trying to mess with me? You couldn't have been on that train. You're here with me."

"I know, but—just look." I pull up my Instagram account to show him, but the photo of me in front of the train has disappeared. Now the last photo features me, in my grad cap and gown, hugging my mom.

Maybe I should feel relieved. Instead, I am mostly frustrated, because I need Kai to see what I see—what I *saw*. The photo was there. I swear it was. I can't shake this eerie feeling washing over me in waves. My body *remembers* boarding that train.

I click on the graduation photo and swipe right. The screen fills with a matching photo of me with my dad. The wind is blowing my tassel into his face.

I remember taking these photos. I remember that day.

And I remember another day too. Misty glimmers of half-veiled memory.

The sensation of moving very fast. Speed building and building. Out of control. Suddenly, jerking sideways. Slamming into something hard. A sharp intake of breath. A scream lodged in a throat. My last thought was a wish: that I could see Kai's face one more time.

I try again. "I know it sounds crazy … but I swear I was in that train accident. There was a picture on my Instagram of me standing in front of a train. *That* train. Monday morning, Philadelphia to DC. I was on my way to Georgetown for the summer."

Kai taps his knuckles against the countertop. "Like you were planning to do, before you changed your mind and came here?"

"Exactly. I had this really vivid dream last night—although maybe it wasn't a dream; maybe it was a memory—of getting on that train to Georgetown and pulling out my phone to text you. But I didn't know what to say because we were still locked in that stupid fight, so instead I posted a photo on Instagram with a caption about how excited I was for college."

Kai looks down at his phone. "But what happened to the photo? It's not on your Instagram now."

"I know. It was there, but then it ... disappeared." The words sound ridiculous as they leave my mouth.

Kai places a hand on my forehead, as if to check for a fever. "T, I'm seriously concerned right now. You can't remember how you got here. You're seeing things. You fainted—don't try to act like you were just hungry. What else is going on with you? I want to get it all out in the open. Tell me everything."

I swallow. "Okay ... well ... remember my scars?"

"The one on your arm, from when you fell in the lava tubes?"

"Yep, and I had another scar from a fifth-grade basketball accident." I thrust my wrist at him and step my leg up onto a chair, to show him my knee. "They're both gone. See?"

Kai leans close, studying my smooth skin. "That's really weird," he murmurs, turning my arm over and back in the light. His fingertips delicately brush my arm. "I remember your scar so clearly, from when you showed it to me. But that was three years ago. Scars fade, right?"

"Not like this. Not overnight." I pull the V-neck of my sleep shirt farther down. "And I have this strange tattoo."

Kai's eyes widen. "Wait—what tattoo? You don't have a tattoo."

"I do now. I don't remember getting it. But look." I show him the hourglass etched over my heart.

Kai runs his fingers over it. "Wow. I never expected you to get a tattoo. It's cool, though. I like it. What does it mean?"

"I have no idea."

He raises his eyebrows.

"And," I continue, "the creepy part is that it's changing."

"What?"

I look down at my chest. "See the amount of sand in the top half of the hourglass? How much would you say is there?"

"It's about equal. Half in the bottom, half in the top."

"Exactly. But when I first noticed the tattoo, on Monday, there was way more sand in the top than in the bottom. Don't give me that look—I'm serious. It's like the tattoo is a message from the universe. My time is running out."

"*Message from the universe?* T, do you even hear yourself? You're the most logical person I know. You never talk all *woo-woo* like this."

"Maybe because I've never died before." I say it as a joke, but as soon as the words leave my lips, my chest constricts, and my whole body turns ice-cold.

I died. I died in that train accident.

"That's not funny, Tegan," Kai says.

I grab my phone and do another internet search. It doesn't take long to find a memorial tribute to all the accident victims. I quickly scan through the list of names. And there—right in the middle— my eyes lock onto the familiar combination of letters. My stomach heaves with the knowledge I somehow already knew.

TEGAN ROSSI

The edges of my vision begin to blur again, and I wonder vaguely if I might faint. I grip Kai's arm tightly to steady myself and hand him the phone. I watch him read the list of names.

"Tegan," he breathes. "Oh my god, Tegan." When he looks at me, there are tears in his eyes.

Those tears rocket up my fear to an entirely new level. Never have I seen Kai cry.

"But how is this possible?" he says. "This can't be possible. You can't have been on that train. You're here. There must be some mistake."

I lean my head against his shoulder, trying to focus on steadying my breathing. *In and out. In and out.*

"Maybe you got off the train at the last minute, and you flew here instead. You changed your mind. I'm sure that's what happened, T. You decided to come visit me instead." Kai's voice has taken on a manic edge. His tear-filled eyes are wild. "We need to contact them and tell them that you're okay. You're not dead. You're here, and you're fine … "

In and out. In and out.

"We need to call your parents. There's been some mix-up. There must have been another Tegan Rossi on that train … "

I clench my fists so my fingernails dig sharply into my palms. The pain is proof that I am here, in this moment, alive. "I've tried calling them, Kai. I've called them and called them. The phone just rings endlessly."

"I'm going to try," he says, pulling his own phone out of his pocket. I recite the numbers for him, seeds of hope sprouting in my chest as he holds the phone to his ear and waits … and waits … and waits. My hope withers. He tries calling my mom, and then my dad, and then he tries my mom again. He waits a long time before hanging up.

"It can't be true, T," he says softly. The crazed fire in his eyes has dimmed. "You came to visit me. You came to visit, just like you promised."

I bury my face in his T-shirt and mumble the words against his chest. "Am I dead? Is this … Heaven?"

Kai strokes my hair quietly for a few moments. Then he says, "No. That's not possible. If this is Heaven, wouldn't that mean I'm dead too? But I still have my memory. I still have my scars. I'm not dead. And Theo, and Paulo, and my parents and Aunt Sarah, and everyone else we've run into? We're not all dead. We can't be. So no. You're not dead either."

I tilt my head back and look up at him. "I want this to be real. I want this to be real so badly."

"This is real." He squeezes me against him. Solid. Safe. "We're here, together, right now in this moment. What could be more real than this?"

Kai wants to take me back to the clinic, but I resist. Whatever answers I'm searching for, they are not at the clinic. I am certain of that.

"Well," Kai says, crossing his arms. "Then what do you want to do? You can't brush this off, T. This is a big deal. This problem is not going to solve itself."

"I know." I keep compulsively checking my phone, refreshing Instagram over and over, but the photo of me on the train is gone. I'm starting to doubt myself. *Did I imagine it?*

I thought that once I regained my memory, all my problems would be solved. I never fathomed that fragments of my memory returning would make me more confused than ever.

Closing my eyes to center myself, I breathe in and out, in and out. Suddenly, I recall the vision I had earlier this morning, when I fainted. I describe it to Kai, attempting to capture the details before they fade away. The lush landscape … the waterfall flowing down a cliff … the little wooden house, painted green with sky-blue trim.

"Wait," Kai says. "Where did you see this house?"

"In my dream—er, vision—or whatever it was when I passed out."

"That's so weird. I guess I must have shown you my painting. I didn't think I showed it to anyone. It wasn't my best work. I ended up painting over it. I could never capture the house quite right."

I jump up from my seat. "No, you never showed me that painting. So you're saying it's a real place? The little green house with blue trim, at the base of a waterfall?"

"Yeah, it's my grandpa's house," Kai says. "Or, it *was* his house. He passed away last year."

"Oh no—I remember when it happened. I'm so sorry, Kai. I know you were close."

Kai traces the grout between tiles on the kitchen counter. "We were. Thanks. You would have loved him." He looks up at me and shakes his head, as if shaking off a memory. "Anyway, I haven't been back there since he died."

"Is anyone living there now?" I ask.

"No, the house is empty. My parents keep talking about fixing it up and selling it, but they haven't done anything yet."

"Can you take me there?"

Kai scrunches up his nose. "To my grandpa's house? Why? We have more pressing issues to deal with. I really think we should go back to the clinic—"

"No, Kai, listen. I had a vision about your grandpa's house. It must be a sign from the universe. Maybe the house has answers. We need to go there."

"I never thought I would hear Tegan Rossi talking about *the universe* like this." One corner of his mouth lifts in a half smile. "Okay, T. But promise me this: if we don't find any answers there, then we head back to the clinic and get you checked out again."

I lean in and kiss his cheek. "It's a deal."

The sun seems especially bright today. We're driving toward Hilo, on the "wet side" of the island. I've never been away from the "dry side." Kai says that his home is a contradiction: a desert and a jungle, smooshed together on one small island. I gaze out at the arid landscape, black lava rock stretching as far as the eye can see. Seagulls wheel through the empty sky. I close my eyes and focus on the touch of the sun's rays warming my bare arm through the cracked-open window. I focus on the solidity of Kai's hand in mine, resting on the center console. The hum of the Jeep tires on the asphalt. The gentle breeze lifting and dropping tendrils of my hair.

All of these things exist. They must exist. Because this is too real to be a dream.

Gradually, the landscape becomes more lush with life. Tangled green trees dot the mountainside. Bushes erupt with bright-pink and yellow flowers. Tucked into a cliff, I spot a small waterfall—a stream of water dissolving into mist.

"Almost there." Kai turns onto a narrow dirt lane.

I grip the door handle for balance as the Jeep bumps over ruts in the road. We're heading toward the cliff. Toward the waterfall.

After a few minutes, the dirt road ends, eaten up by grass and shrubs. Kai parks the Jeep, and we climb out. The air is humid. We're surrounded by green—eucalyptus and jacaranda trees, creeping vines, bushes and ferns as tall as my shoulders. A narrow pebbled path leads into the underbrush. Kai takes my hand, and I follow him, remembering that long-ago night when we crept along a similar path toward our hideout. Right now, it feels like we're running away all over again. Like we're trying to escape the inescapable.

A neon-green gecko darts in front of us. Dragonflies buzz past our ears. I squeeze Kai's hand. *Please, let this all be real.*

My face is sweaty, and my legs are tired. The path opens up into a clearing; we have reached the base of the waterfall. A small wooden house is nestled there, surrounded by mist. The house is painted a deep green to blend in with its surroundings. It looks like something out of a fairy tale.

"Here we are," Kai says.

I am suddenly nervous. *What are we going to find here? What am I hoping to find?*

The porch stairs creak under our weight. Up close, I notice the green paint is peeling, and a corner of the porch has rotted away. It is as if the house is sinking down into the earth, resigning itself to becoming part of the wild land surrounding it. The doorframe is painted a vivid blue, and, above us, a wind chime tinkles in the breeze.

Kai lifts his hand to fit the key in the lock, but a second before he does, the door opens wide. We both jump back. An old man stands there. His hair is a thick shock of white, and his eyebrows are gray caterpillars. He is wearing a plain white tank top, and, for an old man, his arms are surprisingly muscular. He smiles at us as if he has been waiting all day for our arrival.

"Welcome," he says. "We've been expecting you today." His voice makes me think of the ocean depths, infinite and mysterious.

Is this Kai's grandfather? I glance at Kai. His eyes narrow in suspicion.

"Who are you?" he says. "What are you doing in my grandpa's house?"

"You may call me Okalani," the old man says. "I live here with my wife. And I knew your grandfather."

"You did?"

"Akamai Kapule. He was a good man. And he was very proud of you. He talked about you often, always with a big smile on his face."

"Really?" Kai says. The tension in his shoulders drains away. "I'm, um, sorry to intrude on you like this. I didn't realize my parents had sold his house already."

"No need to apologize. Come in, come in. My wife is eager to see you." He opens the door fully and gestures for us to enter.

I look at Kai, and he looks at me. *Is there a reason I dreamed of this house? Can these people help us?* Likely not, but it's worth a shot. I nod my assent.

Kai slips off his sandals in the entryway, and I follow suit. The interior of the little house is dim and smells of lavender and jasmine. Potted plants and flowers abound. Okalani leads us through sparsely furnished rooms. Everything in the house is clean and simple.

We enter a room filled with books. On the floor, an old woman is seated on a cushion. She is wearing a bright flowered dress, and her silver hair erupts in curls. Her face is warm with smile-wrinkles.

"Hello," she says. "Welcome. It is so good to see you both."

"Hi," I say uncertainly. "I'm Tegan, and this is Kai."

"You may call me Keone."

"Please, sit," Okalani says, opening his arms. There is a tattoo of a small fish on the inside of his left wrist.

Kai and I lower ourselves to the cushions on the floor. Okalani sits down beside us. He seems as limber as a young boy. The cushion is surprisingly comfortable, and I cross my legs beneath me, my body relaxing a little.

"What are your worries, child?" the old woman asks, looking directly at me. Maybe she senses that I need help. I bet she can read the confusion and fear on my face.

"Oh ... nothing," I say unconvincingly. "I'm fine."

Keone narrows her eyes at me. Her expression is exactly the same one that my mom gives me sometimes—the look that says, *Don't you dare try to bullshit me, Tegan Rossi*. As she leans forward to take a sip of her tea, her necklace dangles and catches the light. I gasp.

"Your necklace!" I say, pointing. "I have the same one!" I've never seen anyone else with a puka shell necklace like mine. It must be a sign.

A second later, I feel foolish. Of course she has the same necklace as I do. Kai got it for me here in Hawaii. Probably lots of people wear this same necklace.

Keone smiles. "My husband got this for me," she says, her fingers delicately brushing the shell. "A long, long time ago. Back when we were teenagers, like you two."

"Wow," Kai says. "You've been together a long time."

"Oh, we were only friends when I gave her that necklace," Okalani puts in. "Believe me, I wanted to date her. I wanted to marry her. I was completely in love with her, from the moment we met as little kids. But she kept me at arm's length. She only wanted to be my friend."

"I was afraid," Keone says. She takes Okalani's wrinkled hand in her own and kisses it. "Falling in love can be terrifying. By opening yourself up to love, you open yourself up to loss as well. But I sense you two already know that."

"It's worth it, though," Kai says. His tone is fierce. "It's a million times worth it."

"You are wiser than I was," Keone tells him. "It took me a little while to trust enough to make the leap."

"So how did you convince her to date you?" I ask Okalani, not caring if I sound nosy. I am strangely invested in this couple. I want to hear their story.

"I got her to spend time with me," he says. "Quality time, just the two of us. I took her to all the places I loved. I let down my guard and held my heart out for her to take, if she wanted it." Okalani smiles. "And it turns out, she did want it after all."

There are so many more questions I want to ask, but Keone interrupts my thoughts. "Tegan," she says. "You still haven't told us. What are your worries, child?" She resolutely sets down her mug and brushes a curl away from her face. *Is this a random question she asks all her guests, even strangers? Maybe it's her idea of deep conversation?* But then she leans closer and whispers, "Be honest. We can only help you if you trust us."

My arms break out in goose bumps. *Can this couple give me answers? Is that why my vision brought us here?*

I clear my throat. "I, um ... well, this is going to sound ridiculous," I begin. Kai reaches over and squeezes my hand.

Okalani and Keone gaze at me with patient eyes. How far does their patience stretch? If I tell them what I remembered—or *think* I remembered—will they conclude I'm completely insane? I picture

Keone urging us out of the house, sweeping at our legs with a broom, but the image doesn't hold. Even though I only met Keone and Okalani moments ago, I can tell they aren't the type to chase people away.

"It's okay, T," Kai urges me on.

I look at Keone, who is smiling at me with gentle, authentic warmth. She makes me think of my grandma, who died when I was five. I hardly remember my grandma at all ... and yet, here in Keone's presence, I am reminded of her somehow.

I decide to take the plunge and put it all out there. "I woke up in Hawaii two days ago. I didn't remember how I got here. But I've been having recurring nightmares about an accident ... and then, this morning, I started to remember." I tell them how, weeks ago, I made plans to visit Kai here in Hawaii but then canceled those plans and decided to move to college early. How Kai and I got into a huge argument because of it. I describe the disappearing photo on Instagram, the news article about the accident, and my name on the list of victims. I show them my hourglass tattoo and the smooth skin where my scars used to be. I tell them about my fragmented memory of boarding the train, settling into my seat ... and then the sudden violent chaos of the accident. How my last wish was that I could see Kai again.

The entire time I'm speaking, Okalani and Keone are silent. It is obvious when someone is waiting for you to stop talking so they can start talking, versus when someone is truly listening to what you are saying. I can tell Okalani and Keone are deeply listening to me. It is as if they hear not only the words I speak but also the words I *don't* speak—the complicated emotions and jumbled-up questions racing through my mind and my heart.

When I'm done, silence settles into the corners of the room. Time stretches and compresses. Kai, still holding my hand, rubs his thumb against mine. High up in the sky above us, the clouds must shift, because a ray of sunlight spills through the window. The beam of light illuminates Keone.

Keone presses her palms together and gazes into my eyes. Her eyes are startlingly familiar. She looks into my face as if searching for something.

"Have you heard of the *o'opu alamo'o*?" she asks finally.

I shake my head.

"At Akaka Falls, there is a fish called the *o'opu alamo'o*."

"We're going there!" Excitement fills me at the mention of a familiar place. Is what I need at Akaka Falls? "Kai's going to take me there."

Keone nods. "I know he is. On Friday, yes?"

Kai and I look at each other and shrug. "Or maybe tomorrow," I say. If the answer is at Akaka Falls, why wait until Friday to go there? "It's not far, is it?"

"No, it is not far," Okalani puts in. "Nothing is too far." I'm not sure if he's talking about the island or if he's speaking in more general terms. But he doesn't elaborate.

"We'll go there tomorrow. Today, even," Kai tells me.

Keone smiles at us like we have told an amusing joke. "These fish," she continues, "the *o'opu alamo'o*, they are born in the waters above Akaka Falls. Their offspring drift in the current all the way down the falls, down the river, and out to the Pacific Ocean. There, they grow into adult fish. When it is time, they swim back from whence they came, up the freshwater streams, up to the base of the waterfall. Then, they climb."

Kai's eyes are wide. "How do they climb? They're fish. And Akaka Falls is, like, hundreds of feet high."

Keone nods. "Yes. Four hundred and forty-two feet tall."

Okalani stretches his left arm out to the side, showing us the fish tattoo on his wrist. "The *o'opu alamo'o* climb using a special sucker on their bellies," he explains. "Slowly, painstakingly, they climb up the sheer cliff wall, up and up and up, until they reach the top of the waterfall." As he speaks, something strange happens. Each time I blink, the fish tattoo moves a little higher up his arm. Forearm. Elbow. Bicep. Shoulder.

"There, at the top of Akaka Falls," he says, "the *o'opu alamo'o* hatch the eggs of the next generation of *o'opu alamo'o*, new fish that will make the same journey." Yes, the fish tattoo is definitely on his shoulder now—his wrist is clear and smooth.

What is going on? Maybe it's a trick of the light.

I shake my head and close my eyes, taking a couple of deep breaths before opening them again. "Okay ... but how do these fish relate to me?"

Keone leans closer. "The *o'opu alamo'o*, you see, understand that life is a cycle," she says. "Sometimes we must hoist ourselves up waterfalls in our own lives, back to our origins, back to where we began."

"Is that what I need to do?" I ask. "Hike to the top of Akaka Falls?"

Okalani chuckles. "Oh, no," he says. "You are not the *o'opu alamo'o*. You are Tegan Rossi."

How does he know my last name? I didn't tell them my last name, did I?

"Tegan Rossi," he continues, "you have been given a special gift. When we die, each of us gets to relive the Best Week of Our Lives. This reliving period is what you are experiencing now."

My brain tries to take in his words, but one word keeps hitting my consciousness like a sucker punch. Kai must feel the same way, because he leans forward, pain on his face. "Die?" he says. "What do you mean, *when we die?*"

My heart is being squeezed in a vise. My throat is dry, but I manage to get out the words in a whisper: "So I really died in the train accident?"

Keone's eyes contain eons of sadness. "We do not have all the answers, my child. We do not know why things happen. But from what you tell us, yes. I think that is what happened."

I focus on the cushion beneath me, solid and real. Kai's hand in mine, his palm damp with sweat. The pattern of sunlight dancing on the wooden floor beneath the window. Artifacts of this world. Proof of this life.

"But I'm not reliving anything," I protest. "This week has never happened before. I haven't been to Hawaii since the summer I was fifteen, and I only saw Kai for a couple hours that trip. What's happening now … all of this is brand new."

Keone pats my knee. "It seems, dear one, that when you died, the Best Week of Your Life had not happened yet. So you are getting to live it now."

"Wait," Kai says. "So, you're saying this week is what *would* have happened if Tegan had come to Hawaii instead of boarding the train?"

Keone and Okalani both nod.

"But what if she got off the train, at the last minute, and she's safe here now?"

Okalani smiles sadly. "It is a beautiful wish, but wishes are not always enough."

Kai's voice plows on. "Then we've got to change what happened! There must be some way to fix things."

Okalani puts his palms together like a prayer. "The *o'opu alamo'o* must climb up the waterfall they have been given. None of us can change the past. I urge both of you, do not try to change what has already happened."

"Instead, enjoy the time you have left together," Keone says. She taps her own heart. "The hourglass shows your remaining time, Tegan. When the final grain of sand runs out, your Best Week will be over."

I try to swallow, but my throat is sandpaper. "And what happens then?" I ask.

"No one knows for sure, dear one. But your journey here will end."

My mind wants to resist what they are telling me. *I died in the train accident? All I have left are a few more days, here in Hawaii with Kai?*

"What about my parents—my mom—am I never going to see her again? Or even talk to her again? Why can't I reach her on the phone?"

Keone runs her fingers over her puka shell necklace—the same gesture I do sometimes, when I am deep in thought. "You are meant to be savoring this time in Hawaii with Kai," she says. "Your Best Week is lived when you are fully present here. Does that make sense?"

"I guess so." If I *had* visited Kai instead of boarding that train, it's not like I'd be on the phone with my parents all the time. That must be why my calls are not going through. Whatever this reality is, my parents aren't a part of it.

"How do you know all this?" Kai interjects, flinging out his arms. "I've never even heard of a Best Week. Why should we believe you?

This is just a wild story you're making up."

Okalani leans back in his chair, crossing his arms over his stomach. The fish tattoo has moved back to his wrist. "No one is forcing you to believe anything. But if I could give one word of advice, it would be this: trust."

I think back to what Keone said earlier, about falling in love. *I had to trust enough to make the leap.* This moment is similar. My brain doesn't want to make the leap Okalani and Keone are suggesting, but my heart trusts what they are telling me.

"So what is this place?" I ask. "Am I in Heaven? Am I dreaming? Is none of this actually real?" I think of all that's happened with Kai in the past two days, and there is a sharp pain in my gut to realize everything has been a dream—a last wish, a fantasy. Not something that counts.

"Reality is a matter of perception," Okalani says. "You perceive this to be real, so yes, it is real. And no, you are not controlling what happens here. You are living it, and Kai is living it, as if you had come here instead of boarding that train. You are making decisions, and those decisions have consequences. You feel hunger here, yes?"

I nod.

"You feel tired here?"

I nod.

"If you cut yourself, you will bleed. If you run into the ocean, you will feel the waves against your skin. This is reality, is it not?"

I don't nod. I don't know what to say. I think about my first kiss with Kai, how my entire body felt aglow with light.

"No," I murmur, shaking my head. "No, no." *How can this be true? How can this be The End? I'm only eighteen. I have so much more living to do. I have so much more to figure out.*

A strange raspy sound escapes my throat, as if I am choking on my own panicked dread. I want to push away everything they have told me, but, despite myself, deep down I believe their words. The strange gap in my memory was only related to the train accident. My flower-patterned suitcase is filled with everything I would have packed if I actually had taken this trip to Hawaii to visit Kai. The scar on my knee is still gone. So is the one on my wrist. It's as if my body has been wiped clean, except for the hourglass tattoo: an ever-present reminder of time ticking away.

Even though my mind doesn't want to believe what all of these things point to, my soul recognizes the truth.

"This is not the news you were hoping for," Keone says gently. "But you must try to delight in these days as best you can. This week is a gift to you, Tegan, from the universe."

She captures my gaze and holds it. Her eyes are filled with such raw emotion, such kindness and empathy and understanding, that it is almost as if she knows exactly how it feels to be me in this moment. Unbidden, a memory surfaces. I'm four or five years old, bending over a dead bird at the park. I poke it with a stick, and then I start to cry when I realize it's dead. My grandma is there. She hugs me and smooths my hair. Together, we pick flowers and sprinkle them over the lifeless bird. "Let us pay tribute," Nonna says, "to the beautiful life of this beautiful creature, who spread its wings and soared and now has returned to where it came from." I am uplifted, even though I am too young to articulate the feeling—and even though I am still sad the bird had died.

I break Keone's gaze, and the memory recedes. Tears roll down my cheeks as I am flooded with somber acceptance. It is almost a relief, to shift from not knowing to fully knowing. Maybe Keone is right; maybe this is a gift. A painful gift, but a gift all the same. To be able to spend time with Kai like this. To taste what could have been—what *should* have been.

I risk a glance at Kai. His face is a stone statue. His eyes are hard obsidian.

He catches me looking at him and abruptly stands from his cushion on the floor. "C'mon, Tegan," he says, and his voice is gruff. "We should go. We've heard all we need to." He nods at Okalani and Keone. "Thank you both for your time."

I rise uncertainly from the cushion. *Do we need to rush off like this?* But Keone and Okalani are standing as well. Our visit appears to be over. As Kai and I follow them back through the house, I rack my brain for any other questions I want to ask.

I keep returning to the same one.

In the doorway, I grab Keone's wrinkled hand. "Are you sure there's nothing I can do? To fix this?" More tears spring to my eyes. "I really don't want to die."

Her eyes are oceans of compassion. "I know, my child. And I am not certain of anything. Life is a mystery, just as death is a mystery. The best answers come from listening to the murmurs of your heart. Your heart is wise. Your heart is strong. Let yourself love, dear one. Let yourself love, hugely and bravely. That is all any of us can do."

Kai and I are quiet as we walk along the narrow pebbled path through the underbrush, back to where the dirt road ends, back to where his Jeep is parked. It seems like we have been gone a very long time, even though the sun is still high in the sky. We climb in, and Kai turns the Jeep around. We bump over the ruts in the dirt road, back to the main highway. I roll down my window. The breeze is fresh and clean, and I close my eyes, savoring the soft air brushing against my face.

Kai breaks the silence. "So, do you want to head to the clinic now, or should we get lunch first? Are you starving?"

I cross my arms. "We're not going to the clinic. There's no reason to go there."

"You promised to get checked out."

"Only if we didn't find any answers. But Okalani and Keone gave us answers. I believe them. I sense in my gut that what they told us is true."

"It's not true, Tegan! It's completely ridiculous. So what are you—a ghost? A zombie? Should I be worried that you're going to eat my brains?"

"This isn't a joke, Kai. It's real. You know I'm not a zombie or a ghost. I'm alive—for the rest of this week, at least."

"Don't say it like that."

"Why not? We have to accept the truth. This is the Best Week of My Life, and I'm getting to live it now."

"It doesn't make any sense. How can you be alive if you—" He clears his throat. "How can you be alive like this, if you were in the train accident?"

"It's like Schrödinger's cat paradox. Remember, when we talked about it that night in the lava tubes?"

"Yeah, I remember. But I didn't understand that trippy cat riddle back then, and I still don't get it."

I shift in my seat, turning to face him more fully. "Until you open the box, the cat is both alive and dead at the same time. Until you answer the phone and hear the results, you both have cancer and you don't have cancer. Until Sunday, I'm both alive and—"

Kai interrupts me. "So you're willing to bet your life on what those random old people said?"

"They didn't seem random to me. I think we were guided to that house for a reason. Something about them was so ... familiar."

Kai's hands clench the steering wheel. He doesn't respond.

"The clinic would be a waste of time," I add. "I'm fine."

"You're not fine, Tegan."

I try to smile. "I mean, I'm fine other than being technically dead."

Wordlessly, Kai pulls over to the shoulder of the road. It seems we're destined to have deep conversations inside this Jeep. I think back to yesterday, driving home after eating shave ice, when I told Kai to pull over and we talked about the art show and Nadia and his friends. That seems like a million years ago.

Kai looks over at me, and his eyes are not hard obsidian any longer. His eyes are filled with life, scared and pleading. "Don't say that, Tegan."

I swallow. "But it's true. I died."

Suddenly, Kai punches the steering wheel. I flinch. I've never seen him hit anything before.

"I'm sorry," he says, burying his face in his hands. He's breathing hard. I can't tell if he's going to cry or scream. Tentatively, I reach over and place my palm on his back. I can feel the warmth of his skin through his T-shirt.

"I'm grateful for this time with you," I murmur. "I'm grateful for every moment with you. That's what I'm choosing to focus on. Aren't you happy that the Best Week of My Entire Life is with you?"

Kai raises his head and looks at me. Tears pool in his eyes. "Of course I am. I treasure every moment with you. These past few days together have been amazing. But they aren't enough. One week isn't nearly enough."

"I know. I feel the same way. But our only option—"

"No. There must be something we can do." Kai takes my hand. "How about this? We don't have to go to the clinic right now. But let's go to Akaka Falls."

"Now?"

"Tomorrow. It's a two-hour drive, and it's already past noon, so it makes the most sense to wait. I'm thinking we get an early start and head there first thing in the morning."

"That sounds good to me." I don't really care what we do—I just want us to feel normal again. I want to pretend that this week is the beginning of something, instead of the end.

"We can spend all day there," Kai continues. "Looking for clues."

Wait ... what? "Clues?" I repeat.

"Yeah—clues, signs, whatever you want to call them. Information about how to fix this. There must be a reason that Keone and Okalani put so much emphasis on Akaka Falls."

"Kai, they were using a metaphor. They specifically said that we shouldn't try to change what has happened. We need to accept it. I *died* in that train accident."

Kai grimaces, looking down at the floor. "Please, Tegan," he pleads. "Please let me take you to Akaka Falls tomorrow. I bet there's something there that can help us."

I want him to accept my fate. The sooner he does, the sooner we can focus on squeezing out the very most of the time we have left.

"Kai," I say gently. "There's nothing for us to find at Akaka Falls.

There are no clues there. No secret portals or medicines or spells that are going to make me all better. Okalani and Keone were using a metaphor about the fish going back to where they began."

He stares down at the steering wheel, and I'm not sure if my words are making an impact at all. But then, he looks up, and his eyes sparkle.

"Tegan, that's it!" He leans over and kisses my hair. "You're a genius." He starts up the Jeep and pulls back out onto the highway.

"Um, thanks. Where are we going?"

"Back to where we began. Back to our place."

The lava tubes. Of course he would want to go there.

He smiles his sly Kai smile, and I can't even be frustrated with him. Maybe he needs to work through this denial at his own pace.

"Okay." I sigh. "But can we stop on the way there and get lunch?"

Over a lunch of grilled fish tacos, the mood between us shifts. Kai and I both make an effort to talk about everything *except* what we've learned in the past few hours. We're emotionally wrung out. We want to focus on the silly surface stuff—inside jokes, random memories, childhood stories we've already shared with each other a dozen times. I'm thankful, because I don't know if I can handle any more deep talks at the moment. I want easy and familiar and *normal*. If life were a TV show, right now I'd prefer to watch a comforting rerun of an episode I've already seen. I don't want to venture into a new episode, where anything could happen—and beloved characters might be killed off.

I eat every last bite of my fresh fish tacos, trying to savor every detail of my final days here. But I don't really taste the food. My stomach is unsettled, and I'm worried about Kai. Fear and despair lurk in his eyes. I know that searching the lava tubes for clues will be fruitless. I think, deep down, he knows it too.

We ball up our lunch wrappers, throw them into the trash can, and climb back into Kai's Jeep. As we head down the highway, the breeze whipping my hair all around, I wonder what would happen if we just kept driving and driving and driving. I'd imagine there are worse ways to spend your last days on Earth.

Kai parks in the lot for the golf course. We follow, in reverse, my footsteps from two days ago when I chased after Theo. The same path I walked in the moonlight to meet Kai when we were fifteen. The same path his eight-year-old self raced down to get help when I needed stitches. Now, in the heat of midafternoon, the asphalt is hot beneath my sandals. Eventually, it turns to pebbled dirt. We are getting close.

Trees arch over the path, lush with foliage. I'm grateful for their shade. Everywhere, the buzzing of insects and calling of birds. The air is damp and swollen with heat. A bead of sweat rolls down my forehead. We round the bend, and there it is—the entrance to our place.

Cigarette butts are scattered in the dirt, and a plastic soda bottle lounges against a hibiscus bush. Kai mutters to himself, bending down and untangling it from the flowery branches. He picks up the cigarette butts and drops them into the plastic bottle. I help him, even though cigarettes are probably the grossest things on the planet, and I hate touching them. Before long, we've cleaned it all up. Kai leans the bottle against the lava rock, to pick up on our way out later.

"Do you think Theo's friends did this?" I ask, wiping my fingers on my shorts.

Kai nods. His jaw is set in a hard line. "Those guys don't have respect for anything. I can't believe Theo would bring them here."

I wrap my arms around his waist and kiss his cheek, then his lips. It is the first time we have kissed since Okalani and Keone told us the painful truth. Kai's mouth meets mine gently at first, as if he is afraid to break me. But soon we are kissing urgently, ravenously, like we can't get enough of each other and time is running out. Which, of course, it is. Time is slipping through our fingers, and this knowledge only makes me want more of him. It feels so good to kiss Kai. He can't protect me from fate … yet I still feel safe in his arms.

When we eventually break apart, my hair has come free of its braid, and Kai's shirt is rumpled. His cheeks are flushed, and I'm sure mine are too. His eyes are alight with new hope.

"C'mon!" he says, grabbing my hand.

Entering the lava tubes is like crossing the threshold from day into evening. Kai uses the flashlight app on his phone to scan the shadows as we venture into the dim, cool cavern.

"What are you looking for?" I whisper. I don't need to whisper, but something about the atmosphere of the lava tubes makes whispering feel appropriate.

"I'm not sure, exactly," Kai says. "I'll know it when I see it."

Before long, my eyes adjust to the dimness. As Kai sweeps the walls with his flashlight, I release his hand and venture deeper into the cave. Up ahead, a shaft of light filters down through an opening in the ceiling. It's hauntingly beautiful. It reminds me of photographs of the Pantheon in Rome, which I've always dreamed of seeing in person. I walk toward the stream of light, my sandals slipping a little on the loose lava rock. I was planning to study abroad during college, to spend an entire summer backpacking through Europe. *It's not going to happen now. None of it.*

I try my best to hide the fright away. Focusing on all that I've lost won't do any good. What I do have is this moment. Right here, right now. The lava tubes. Kai. This is the gift I have been given. I reach my arm forward, into the dusky beam of light. My skin is striped with daytime and shadow.

I think about when I first woke up here a few days ago. I was so groggy and confused, like I was half-asleep. When Theo had stepped into this shaft of light, he'd looked like an actor standing onstage in a spotlight.

Now, I let myself imagine what things might be like at the end of the week, when I move on from this place. I definitely don't believe in Hell, and I'm not sure if I believe in Heaven either. But maybe there is some sort of afterlife, and I'll get to see my grandma again. Maybe I will look down on those still alive, and it will be like when I first saw Theo step into this spotlight. Maybe the afterlife will be like watching actors bumble around onstage, making their way through the drama of being human, and I will care what happens to them but in the detached way you care about characters in a movie or a book. When it doesn't quite seem real.

I hug myself, feeling my stomach move as I breathe in and out. I place a palm on my chest and feel the steady beating of my heart. I stand on my tiptoes. I clench and unclench the muscles in my legs. My animal body. Its vivid realness. I don't want to ever forget what this is like. The aching, exuberant, messy beauty of being human.

I step fully into the beam of light, tilting back my head. High above, there is a round hole in the ceiling of the lava tubes, and through it I glimpse a perfect circle of blue sky.

I close my eyes. I try to imagine what's next, but all I'm met with is blank openness.

When I open my eyes, I sense that someone is watching me. I look over, and in the shadows I can perceive Kai, standing a few feet away. I leave the shaft of light and walk toward him. When I reach him, my chest constricts. Tears are running down his face. He doesn't even bother wiping them away.

"I knew it when I saw it," he says.

I reach up and wipe his cheeks with my fingers. "What are you talking about?"

"I didn't exactly know what I was looking for here—but I had this overwhelming sense that I would know it when I saw it. And that's what happened. When I saw you—standing there, surrounded by that beautiful light—it was like you were already outside of this world, Tegan. You were already away from here and entering the next place. And in that moment, I knew. I *really* knew."

He hugs me, and I nestle my face against his warm neck.

"I'm going to miss you," he says. "I'm going to miss you so much." His voice breaks, and then he's sobbing, and I am too. All the tears I've been trying to rein in since this morning break through, a dam being flooded. We clutch at each other, our shoulders shaking and our sobs hiccupping, in the frantic unrestrained way you cry as a child when you can't catch your breath.

Eventually, we run out of tears. I'm not sure how much time has passed. Kai wipes his face with his T-shirt. "I keep thinking about the last time we talked—before this week, I mean," he says. "I was such a jerk to you."

"What do you mean, 'the last time we talked'? Our argument?"

Kai nods. "You called and told me you weren't coming to visit after all, and I got so upset ... " He punches his fist into his palm. "I want to go back and shake myself. Why was I being such a stubborn asshole? Why did I try to push you away?"

I grab his hand, bring it up to my lips and kiss his palm. "You weren't the jerk, Kai. I was. I can't believe I canceled on you like that, at the last minute. I was just ... scared."

"I know," he says. "You think I wasn't?"

"You were scared?"

"Of course. I mean, yeah, I've had a massive crush on you forever. Ever since that night we met up here, when I tried to kiss you, and you turned me down."

We've never talked about this before. "I'm sorry about that."

"No need to apologize. Our actual first kiss was much better." He smiles. "But yeah, I was worried—that things would be awkward between us, that you wouldn't have a good time, that your purely platonic feelings for me would be readily apparent and I would have to pack up my hopes into a box and shove them under my bed forever. Move on, as my friends kept telling me to do. Let you go."

It's painful to hear him say these words. Painful to think of how close I came to losing him, this—us.

"Is that what you did?" I ask in a small voice. "After our fight? Did you let me go?"

Kai sighs. "I tried to, T. I really tried. You seemed so cold on the phone—so aloof. Like I didn't matter to you all that much."

"Oh, Kai. I'm so sorry. You're the most important person to me. You've always been that person." I lick my lips and taste salt, as if I am part of the ocean. "Did I tell you the first thing I did, after I boarded the train? I pulled out my phone to text you. I didn't send it because

I didn't know what to say."

"I can't tell you how many times I almost texted you," Kai says. "I would write out a message but then delete it. Everything I wrote sounded stupid."

"You could never be stupid. I love you." The words slip out, effortlessly, like three fish slipping from a stream into the big, wide ocean. Like an ancient sea turtle returning home.

I see the words in Kai's eyes before he says them. "I love you, Tegan Rossi."

Then his lips are on mine, and his hands are holding me, and my hands are grabbing his shirt, and my cheeks are wet with fresh tears. *I love you*, I think. *I love you, I love you, I love you.* It's so completely simple and obvious—so completely right—that I don't know how I was able to ignore it for so long.

Kai kisses my earlobe. "I love you," he whispers. "God, it feels good to say that."

I kiss his chin. "I love you."

"God, it feels amazing to hear you say that."

"And to think, you almost let me go."

He links his arms around my back. "But I obviously didn't do a very good job of it. Because by some magic, you ended up here."

"Here with you."

"Here with me."

I lean my forehead against his, and we stay like that for a little while. When we pull apart, the pained resignation in Kai's eyes breaks my heart. Part of me wants him to keep questioning, keep arguing, keep searching for a way out of this bittersweet, dead-end reality. But a larger part of me knows that denial will only waste time. And we have precious little time left together.

"Do you think it hurts?" I ask softly. "To die?"

Kai kisses my hair. "No. I don't think it hurts. I think it will be ... calm."

I squeeze my eyes shut. "I hope so."

"When we had to put our old dog Makana to sleep, he was in a lot of pain. But in that moment when he crossed over, he looked at peace."

Will I ever feel at peace? Will I ever accept this fate? It seems impossible.

We pick our way back across the loose rock and the smooth floor of hardened lava. As we step out of the lava tubes and into the slanting afternoon sunlight, I can't explain it, but a single thought fills my consciousness. Clear and unmistakable. *It's all going to be okay.*

Which doesn't make any sense, because things are definitely *not* going to be okay. I died, and in four days I will be gone from even this liminal existence, and it's not fair. My life wasn't supposed to end like this. I had so much more living to do.

But the thought persists, resounding through my brain. The voice, while not my own, is familiar. *It's all going to be okay.*

I don't understand how these words can possibly be true, but I cling to them all the same. Just as I will cling to every last second I am given of this existence. Just as I cling to Kai's hand as we walk back up the dirt path toward the golf course. The plastic bottle filled with cigarette butts dangles from his other hand, bumping a rhythm against his leg. *Okay, okay, okay, okay. It's all going to be okay.*

Later that night, before bed, I pull out my phone. Even though I know what to expect, I call my mom. The phone rings and rings and rings. I call my dad. The same. I call Andrea and Mel. The hollow, steady ringing fills my ears.

I let myself fall backward onto the bed and close my eyes. In my mind, I picture each person one by one. *Goodbye, Andrea. Goodbye, Mel. Goodbye, Dad. Goodbye-for-now.*

Last of all, I picture my mom's face. Her serious eyes. Her small, straight nose that I inherited. Her childlike smile when something catches her off guard and delights her. *I love you, Mom*, I think. But I can't bring myself to say goodbye to her yet.

hi t,

i'm sure you're not surprised that i had another dream about you last night. we visited an elderly couple who lived in my grandpa's house, and they told us you had died. this will sound trippy, but they were us. you and me, sixty years into the future. they went by different names, but they were clearly us. i would know your smile anywhere. even as an old lady, your smile is the same. dazzling.

anyway, they said we should focus on enjoying the time we had left together, in the dream. but i was shaking my head. no, no, no. i didn't believe you were dead. i mean, you were too real. you were right there, next to me.

and when I woke up, the feeling persisted. i grabbed my phone and checked your Instagram. there was an update from your mom, writing from the hospital, asking for prayers. the doctors originally declared you brain-dead, but now one neurologist has said there might be signs of life. you're still in a coma. but there's a sliver of hope.

c'mon, t. you're a fighter. you can do this.

i don't want to settle for dreams about you. i want the real thing.

please wake up, t. please. please.

let's become that old couple in sixty years. let this dream be a premonition.

—kai

THURSDAY

*D*arkness. *Deep, pillowy darkness. Like being underwater, so far down below the surface that no light reaches you. A steady beeping. Voices. Where am I? I try to move my arms, but I can't—*

"Tegan! Tegan, it's all right."

I open my eyes to find Kai gently shaking me awake, his features etched with concern. Sunlight is streaming cheerfully through his bedroom window. I'm wrapped up in the covers like a caterpillar in a cocoon. I am flooded with such joy to see him that, for a flicker of a moment, I forget everything that happened yesterday. Everything we learned. But then, of course, it all comes back. The heavy stone returns to my gut.

We both tried valiantly to stay up all night, not wanting to miss a second of our remaining time together. But at some point, we must have drifted off. And I actually think it's good that we did. I've never done well on little sleep, and I don't want to pass through my final days like a bleary-eyed robot on autopilot. I want to feel fresh and awake, able to soak in everything fully. Plus, there's something necessary about the oblivion of sleep. Both of us need a break from the constant pressure of the ticking-down clock.

"You were shaking and making noises," Kai says, wrapping his arms around the bedcovers and me. "Were you having a nightmare?"

"Yeah, I was. Thanks for waking me up." I kiss his nose. "Sorry if I was a cover-hog last night."

He touches my hair, my cheek. "I don't mind."

"So you're saying I *was* a cover-hog?"

"Oh, most definitely. You have mastered the tuck-and-roll."

"The what?"

"The tuck-and-roll. It's your signature move. Here, let me demonstrate." Kai tucks the covers around his body with his arms. Then, he rolls to the side away from me. The covers slide with him.

"See?" he asks, rolling back to face me. "Very effective."

"I'm sorry!" I laugh, and he does too, and it feels so good to be like this. Normal. Us.

But then Kai breaks the mood. "So," he says, "do you still want to go to Akaka Falls today?"

I frown. "Kai, I thought we agreed that we're not going to waste the time we have left looking for clues that don't exist. I thought—"

He holds up a hand. "You're right, you're right. I don't want to look for clues. But do you still want to go to Akaka Falls, just to see it?"

"Oh." I feel relieved. "Yes. In that case, I would love to go there."

"Okay, we'll do it."

"Okay."

"Okay."

But neither of us moves. Lying here like this, the warm covers cocooned around us and the bright sunlight streaming in through the window, my face inches away from my favorite face in the universe … this feels like the closest thing to Heaven that I can imagine. I wonder, despite what Okalani and Keone said, if maybe this is it. *This week, here in Hawaii with Kai—maybe this is all I get. Maybe this is Heaven. Maybe after the clock strikes midnight on Sunday, and the last grain of sand falls through the hourglass, everything will simply melt away to nothing, and it will all be over.*

"Whatcha thinking?" Kai asks, brushing a strand of hair away from my forehead.

I shake my thoughts away and smile. "How happy I am to be here with you," I say. *If this is it—if this is all the Heaven I get—I'm going to soak up every last drop of it. I'll make this week enough to last a lifetime.*

On the nightstand, Kai's cell phone buzzes, and he untangles his arm from the covers to reach for it. The framed photo of me is upright again, my laughter aimed directly at his pillow. I imagine this photo of me, living on for months and years after I'm gone, and suddenly that heavy rock is back in my gut. Actually it's not a rock anymore—it's molten lava, throbbing. I kick my way out of the covers and sit up.

"Slow down, slow down," Kai says into the phone. He glances at me with a worried expression—*Mom? Is that my mom on the phone?* I force myself not to grab it out of his hand. I raise my eyebrows in a question.

"It's Theo," he says to me. My disappointment is sharp, even though I didn't *really* think it was my mom. I'm in some other world, outside of regular time and space, and logically I understand that I'm never going to be able to talk to my mom or my dad or anyone back home again. I need to inwardly say my goodbyes and face reality. Still, there's a stubborn little part of me, tucked away deep in my heart, that refuses to give up hope.

"Okay," Kai says into the phone. "Okay, just sit tight."

He hangs up, setting the phone down on his nightstand. He runs a hand over his face. When he looks at me again, he seems much older than he did five minutes ago. Weary, even though he just woke up.

"Is everything okay?" I ask, even though the answer is clearly *no*.

"Theo's in trouble."

"What happened?"

"I don't know much. He was making a delivery. Something went wrong."

I pull my hair back into a ponytail and slip out of bed. "We need to go to him."

"But this is your last week, T! Our remaining time is precious. Theo can figure it out on his own."

"Kai, I know you. You would do anything for your brothers, and Theo needs you. If I weren't here, you would already be out the door on your way to him."

Kai sighs. "You're right. But what about Akaka Falls? What about our plans for the day? I don't want to let you down."

"Of course you're not letting me down! This isn't your fault. Life happens. Besides, we wouldn't enjoy doing anything else. We'd be too worried about Theo the entire time."

Kai reaches over and gently pulls me down onto the bed beside him. He looks me right in the eyes. "Tegan, are you sure about this?

This is supposed to be your Best Week. We only have four days left. I doubt you imagined rescuing my dumb brother as part of your week."

"Don't you get it, babe? It doesn't matter *what* we're doing," I tell him. "It's that we're doing it together. My Best Week could be anything, as long as I'm with you."

Ten minutes later, we're driving away from the house into another beautiful summer morning.

"I'm gonna kill Theo," Kai mutters, hands clenched on the wheel. "How many times have I warned him about those guys? But he never listens."

"Maybe he'll listen now," I venture, reaching across the center console and resting my hand on Kai's thigh. "You're a good brother."

Kai shakes his head. "I'm the oldest. I'm supposed to protect him."

"You couldn't protect him forever. Eventually, he needed to get out in the world and make his own mistakes. You can't protect him from everything, Kai."

He sighs. "I know. But right now—" His brow furrows as if he is in physical pain. He stares off at the road before us. "Right now, I feel like I can't protect anyone from anything."

We're not only talking about Theo. I leave my hand on Kai's leg, proof of my physicality. Of my okay-ness. My younger self might have crossed her arms and tilted her chin up. *You don't need to protect me! I don't need protecting!* But now, after all we've been through the past few days, I understand that what Kai is feeling has nothing to do with my ability to take care of myself and everything to do with his own grief.

"You can't protect someone from bad luck," I say softly. "It was nobody's fault. Just terrible, terrible luck."

He glances over and meets my eyes for a moment before turning his gaze back to the road. His right hand drops from the steering wheel and finds mine.

"I'm here now," I say. "I'm here with you."

I'm telling myself as much as Kai. He squeezes my hand. Out my window, the clouds are darkening quickly. We brace ourselves for an oncoming storm.

I follow Kai down the paved path toward the lava tubes. When we reach the cave entrance, he continues striding forward down the gravel path, past the dark, yawning mouth of our hideout.

"Where are you going?" I ask.

Kai waves me forward. "Theo's not at the lava tubes. He's at the swimming hole. It's down a little farther."

The swimming hole? "How come you've never taken me there?" I ask.

Kai pauses for me to catch up. When I reach him, he slips his hand into mine. "It's only a couple years old. A housing development sprung up nearby, and they built this man-made swimming hole. It's tucked away like some big secret, but even the tourists know about it." His tone is disdainful.

"Hey!" I elbow his ribs. "I'm a tourist!"

"Naw, you're different. You're a local by association."

"Well, thanks." I don't really feel like a local. But I don't quite feel like a tourist either. Not this visit. Not anymore.

"So I take it you're not a fan of the swimming hole?" I ask him.

"The ocean is a million times better."

We round a bend in the path, duck under a clutch of trees, and there is the swimming hole. It is smaller than I imagined, barely larger than a hot tub. It's made out of granite that is obviously intended to look like "natural" rock, but you can tell that the slabs have been carefully fitted together, and the rough parts have been smoothed away, so as not to hurt swimmers' feet. Bright blue water bubbles up from some hidden fountain source. Unkempt grass grows all around, but a few spots have been conquered by large, shiny slabs of rock—prime sunbathing locations, I assume. Other than us, the place is deserted.

"Theo!" Kai calls out. "Theo!"

"Where could he be?" There aren't many places to hide in this open clearing. "Theo!"

"He told me this was where he was," Kai says, scratching his neck. I glimpse that same half-wild look in his eyes from yesterday in the lava tubes, when he was so desperate to find a way to save me.

I'm worried about Theo too. I call out his name again. The wind picks up, whipping my hair into my face.

After another minute of shouting and pacing, the trees behind us rustle, and Theo emerges. I gasp at the sight of him. His nose is crusted with blood, and one eye is already purple with bruising. He's holding his left arm strangely.

Kai rushes over to him. "Theo! What happened?"

Theo opens his mouth to answer, but then his stoic expression evaporates, and he turns away from us. His shoulders shake. Kai wraps his arms around his brother, and Theo lets him. When I glimpse Theo's face again, it is like he has morphed into a little boy, tears running rivers down his cheeks.

"It's okay," Kai says. "It's okay. Let's get you home, buddy."

Theo talks the entire drive back to the house, explaining how he slipped out early this morning to deliver some marijuana. "It was a normal drop," he insists. "Really, not a big deal." Kai raises his eyebrows but doesn't interrupt. Theo goes on, explaining that when he got to the swimming hole, three guys jumped him and stole his stash. They left him shaken, but not too beaten up. That came later, after he called his boss and told him what had happened. "I assumed he'd be understanding," Theo says, wiping his nose and wincing. "I mean, I thought he was my friend, you know?" But his boss made Theo pay for the money he'd lost out on. Left him in the overgrown grass by the swimming hole, curled up in the fetal position as if still trying to protect his head from the blows.

"I didn't know what else to do but call you," Theo says.

"I'm glad you did," Kai replies. "It was the right thing to do."

A few raindrops splatter against the windshield, and Kai turns the wipers on. We lapse into silence, gazing out at the ominous clouds. The wipers swish back and forth, like twin dancers. Soon, the raindrops become steady streams of water, and the wipers' dance becomes more fast-paced, frantic.

"We have to tell Mom and Dad, you know," Kai murmurs quietly.

At first I think that Theo didn't hear him. But after a few

moments, he bites his lip. Nods. "I know," he says. His voice sounds almost relieved.

The rest of the day we spend quietly indoors, avoiding the storm. Kai's parents are at work, and Paulo is at soccer camp all day, and Kai and I are reluctant to leave Theo by himself.

"Are you sure, T?" Kai asks. "I feel terrible. This is so *not* how I imagined us spending the day."

"I'm sure. I don't want to abandon Theo after what happened. Besides, it's raining buckets out there. It wouldn't have been a good day to hike Akaka Falls anyway."

"But there are so many other things we could be doing … "

I stop him with a kiss. "This is exactly where I want to be."

"Seriously?"

"Yes. I'm grateful that I get to be here and support you through this."

We make elaborate grilled-cheese sandwiches for lunch and whittle away the hours playing board games, sprawled out on our stomachs on the living room carpet. Theo's left wrist is swollen and bruised, and he holds a bag of frozen peas against it. He managed to clean himself up, but his black eye is still noticeable. When Mrs. Kapule arrives home from work with Paulo in tow, rain-drenched from soccer camp, there's no hiding anything. She gasps, hugs Theo, and sends Paulo off to the shower and his room. "What happened?" she asks. "Actually, wait—don't tell me. Don't say anything yet. Your father will be home any minute. You can tell us both together."

A few minutes later, while Kai and Theo talk to their parents in the kitchen, I slip out the sliding glass door to the backyard and tuck myself into the hammock. The rain has passed and the air is warm. Olina looks up from the yard, where she is chewing on her indestructible rubber bone. She gets up and trots over, then licks my hand. I pet her soft head and pull out the notepaper I folded into my pocket yesterday morning. I've been trying to write a goodbye letter to Kai, but no words will appear. Everything I come up with sounds corny or clichéd. *How do you say goodbye to your best friend? How do you end a story that is only just beginning?*

"He's my person," I whisper to Olina, who flops down beside the hammock. "He knows parts of me that I haven't shared with anyone else. He should be able to mind-read everything I want to say." But real life doesn't work that way. Maybe that's why I've always hated goodbyes. No words can ever live up to the emotion you feel in those moments. No matter what you say, your words will fall short.

But I need to try. I owe Kai at least that much. He deserves a really good goodbye.

> Dear Kai,
> I want to say

That's all I have written so far.

I chew on my pen, staring off into the yard at the first tendrils of sunset streaming out across the sky. What sweeps into my mind isn't a memory of Kai, exactly. It's more a memory of my mom.

Three years ago …

When we returned from our second Hawaii trip—the one that failed to save my parents' marriage—and Kai, remarkably, continued to text me rather than drop off the face of the planet, I kept him a secret from my mom. I kept him a secret from everyone, even from Andrea. He seemed more special that way. More real somehow. I didn't think anyone else would understand the genuine closeness of our friendship. Even I didn't fully understand it—how a seed we'd planted as kids and then neglected for years could suddenly spring up to life the minute we began giving it sunlight and water. Part of me worried that our relationship, whatever it was, would die just as abruptly. Even though our communication had already lasted longer than I'd expected, I felt sure that it would drop off eventually. And I worried that, if I told anyone about Kai, my feelings for him would bubble to the surface, embarrassingly apparent, and I wouldn't be able to play nonchalant when he inevitably started dating some girl from his school and had no time for me anymore.

Keeping him a secret was easy. Mom was swept up in all of the divorce stuff and then the tasks of moving and decorating our new place. She went on a diet and exercise kick; she cut her hair and bought new clothes. It wasn't that she didn't have time for me—I always knew I could talk to her if I wanted to—but when she saw me, I think she saw me through the lens of her expectations. Initially, she had been concerned about how I was taking the divorce and the accompanying changes; we had a couple of heart-to-hearts in my new room after dinner, when she sat on the edge of my bed and peered into my face, asking how things were going. I told her that I was doing okay. Which wasn't a lie. Yes, we'd moved out of our house, but only five minutes away; I was still going to the same school with my familiar friends and teachers and classes. And yes, I missed my dad, but I still saw him on the weekends. We did more activities together *than we used to—before the divorce, he often worked or went biking on weekends. Plus, he and my mom had been arguing so much the past few years, both of them so clearly miserable, that it was a relief not to be surrounded by screaming matches and tense silences all the time.*

Whenever I did feel sad about my parents' split, I had a perfect distraction at my fingertips. I would text Kai some corny joke or "Would you rather?" scenario, and he would respond with a bizarre answer and equally outlandish question, or he'd tell me something funny that had happened at school that day. I knew so many details about his life that it was easy to forget we lived 4,880 miles apart. We began emailing when we wanted to talk, but the time zones made it difficult. Hawaii is six hours behind Pennsylvania, so when I woke up in the morning, Kai would still be asleep, and when I went to bed at night, he would be having an after-school snack. Sometimes I would actually smile as my alarm went off in the morning, reaching for my phone and anticipating an email from Kai. Occasionally, he'd call me as he skateboarded home from school, and I could hear the rush of wind in the background. On the phone, it was the same as when we texted or emailed: easy and natural. So different from any of the guys I tried talking to at school, where conversation would typically flare out after a minute or so. Either that or they'd ask if I'd done the homework or if I knew the answer to the bonus question on the test. At school, I was a two-dimensional stick-figure drawing, labeled and filed in one specific folder. But Kai saw me in 3-D. To Kai, I was interesting and nuanced, fun and serious, smart and silly. He saw and appreciated all of my components. He really knew me. At least, that was what it felt like.

Our first fight happened because of trigonometry. He was nervous about a big test coming up and asked if I could help him study. "A genius like you needs to help us mere mortals," he said, a smile in his voice. But

I did not smile. I was angry. My deep-seated insecurities came rushing back—all the times people had tried to copy off me, all the guys who only struck up conversations to ask about the homework, all the kids who were nice to me during group projects but then ignored me when we passed each other in the quad. Andrea had recently started dating this water polo player, and she only had time for me during study sessions at the library.

"I can't," I told Kai, my tone cold, even though I had plenty of time and could easily have tutored him. "I guess you'll have to find someone else."

Kai didn't say anything. Disappointment squeezed my rib cage. After all we'd shared, he was turning out to be exactly like everyone else. "I've gotta go," I said abruptly, and hung up without a goodbye—something I never did.

The rest of the day, I kept checking my phone, expecting to hear from him. He would text an apology, or maybe he'd joke about something completely random and pretend that our fight hadn't happened, and we could go back to where we'd been before. I was already starting to feel a little embarrassed about my response. He'd unknowingly struck a nerve, and I'd overreacted.

But I didn't hear from him. Nothing. There was no email waiting for me when I woke up the next morning. No text messages when I checked my phone between classes. No phone calls. Nothing.

That night, I picked at my dinner. Mom noticed.

"Sweetie, what's wrong?" she asked.

I shrugged, opening my mouth to make some excuse, like, "I'm just tired," or, "I'm not that hungry." But I couldn't even get the first syllable out before tears engulfed my voice.

I swallowed and wiped my eyes. I was not and never had been a crier.

Crying was messy and ugly and needy, and I did not want to be any of those things. No. I was self-contained and self-reliant. Even as a baby, my parents said, I had cried so rarely that they would often check on me during the night. But I would be sleeping peacefully, or if I was awake, I'd be staring up at the crib mobile or chewing on my foot or something, and when they'd come into the room, I'd just blink up at them with a gummy smile. "The perfect baby," Mom used to say. "If everyone had babies like you, we'd all have ten kids." I often wondered why they didn't. Have ten kids, I mean. Or at least one more. As a little girl, "brother or sister" was always at the top of my wish list, until I eventually became resigned to our family of three. I'd never asked if they tried having more kids—and it just wasn't in the cards—or if it was a conscious choice.

"Oh, honey," Mom said, getting up out of her chair and hurrying around the table. She put her arms around me, which made things worse. I was unable to clamp down on the tears—they were a fountain, overflowing. I ducked my head, hiding my face against her shirt like a child.

"It's okay." Mom stroked my hair. "Let it out. I know all this change has been tough on you."

Part of me was tempted to let her think this was about the divorce. I wasn't technically lying. She had jumped to her own conclusions. But I thought of Kai's face, and my silent phone, and an unbearable ache flared inside of me. I wanted—needed—to talk to her about it. I needed my mom.

I straightened in the chair and looked up at her. She reached down and wiped my cheeks with her thumbs. She smiled at me with sad eyes. I was hit with a wave of love for her. My mom. Her hair was shorter, with new auburn highlights, and her face was a little thinner from her all-veggie-all-the-time diet, but her eyes were the same eyes I'd been looking into my entire life. They were full of understanding. I thought of how she'd held my hand on the plane ride home from Hawaii that first time, when my little-girl heart had never before felt such pain to leave a place—to leave a person. Kai and I were only kids, and some parents might have swept my sadness aside as "silly" or "cute." But my mom had held me, and she had held my pain too. She had listened without condescension or judgment. She hadn't tried to trivialize my feelings. It was the same way she always listened to me, for my entire life. Suddenly, I felt bad that I had kept my new friendship with Kai a secret from her.

"It's actually—this isn't about the divorce. It's something else."

Mom looked surprised, then immediately tried to hide her surprise. She pulled out the chair next to me and sat down, hands on her knees, leaning forward expectantly. "What is it, Teacup? I'm here."

Where should I even start? "Well ... remember when we went to Hawaii the first time, and I became friends with that boy Kai?"

She nodded.

"I bumped into him again, the last time we were there. On the beach." I decided to skip the part about me sneaking out and meeting him in the lava tubes in the middle of the night. "We, um, exchanged numbers, and we've been texting and stuff. He's actually become one of my best friends."

Mom smiled, her brown eyes dancing. "That explains a lot. I've been wondering why you've been glued to your phone lately. I thought maybe you met a new boy at school."

"Mom! No. It's not like that, with Kai." I could feel myself blushing. "We're friends."

"Okay, okay," Mom said, holding up her hands, but I could tell she didn't fully believe me. "I'm glad you've reconnected with Kai. He was such a nice kid. I always wondered what happened to him."

"He's great." That lump was back in my throat. "Really great."

"Then what's the problem? Why the tears, hon?"

"We had a fight. I ruined everything." I told her about the stupid trigonometry fiasco and why I'd gotten so upset. How everyone at school labeled me. How I thought Kai saw me differently—more fully—than that.

"I think you're right," Mom said. "I think Kai does see the real you—all of you. Just like Andrea does, and just like your father and I do. Don't let the kids at school make you feel boxed in, Tegan. And don't box yourself in either."

I nodded, playing with the strings on my hoodie. We'd had this conversation before. I wasn't boxing myself in. Even though the kids at school annoyed me sometimes, overall I felt comfortable with who I was. Now was not the time to veer off-topic.

"But what about Kai?" I asked. "What should I do?" There was a whiny pleading in my voice. Ugh. When had I started caring this much? Get it together, I told myself.

"You should call him and apologize," Mom said gently, standing up from the table.

I gathered the dirty dishes to bring to the sink. "But what do I say?"

"Tell him what you just told me."

So, after I helped her wash the dishes, I climbed the stairs to my room, flopped backward onto my bed, and pressed the green phone icon next to his name. My heart was pounding. He answered on the second ring.

"I'm sorry," I blurted out. "I miss you."

"I'm sorry too," he said. "It's been so weird not talking to you. I thought I should give you some space. I didn't mean to impose or anything."

"No, no—you never impose." But I didn't want to explain to Kai *what it was like at my school. How the other kids saw me. What if their impression of me tainted his impression of me? Sometimes it seemed he was the only person in the world who truly understood me. I couldn't risk changing that. "I was in a weird mood yesterday," I said. "I'm sorry I snapped. I'm happy to help. So, what questions do you have about trig?"*

"Oh, it's fine. No big deal. This girl in class is going to tutor me."

"Oh." This girl in class. "Okay."

The conversation meandered on, and after that things pretty much went back to normal. But something shifted inside me. I realized how fragile our foundation was. How Kai could disappear from my life if he wanted, and there would be nothing I could do. And that scared me. I realized I had let him in too far. I had been vulnerable and surrendered control. No more. From then on, I vowed not to be dependent on him. Not to need him too much. There was no way I would ever let myself feel more than friendship. I needed to play it safe. Keeping him at arm's length would mean that I could keep him in my life. No messiness and no complications.

In the months and years that followed, Mom asked about Kai occasionally. A few times she waved hello when we were FaceTiming. Mostly, she let me bring him up when I wanted, and she didn't push for more. I couldn't tell if she was happy about my friendship with him or if she was indifferent. All I knew was that she didn't want him to distract me from my studies—from my future. College had always been her dream for me too.

So I thought Mom would be happy with my decision not to visit Kai over the summer. I expected her to applaud my resolve to get ahead on my college courses. But when I told her the news, she looked ... sad. "Are you sure that's what you want?" she asked. "You've worked so hard, Teacup. You deserve a little vacation."

"I'm sure. This is what I want."

She nodded and said, "I bet Kai is disappointed."

Was that blame in her voice? I bristled.

"I haven't told him yet," I admitted. "I'm going to call him tomorrow. I'm sure he'll understand. He'll want what's best for me."

The next day, when I did call him, and when it caused the biggest argument of our entire friendship, I didn't tell my mom. I had a feeling she wouldn't be surprised, and I couldn't bear to see that on her face. I didn't want her to try to change my mind or attempt to "fix" things. I told myself that I had made my decision and that it was the best decision for me, for my future. Kai would come around eventually. I could always visit him next summer.

"Hey," Kai says. I hear him step out onto the patio and close the sliding glass door. "Whatcha doing out here?"

Olina lifts her head. Quickly, I fold up the notepaper and stuff it into my pocket.

"Resting," I say. "I wanted to give you guys some privacy."

Kai steps in front of the hammock. At the sight of him, a goofy grin spreads across my face. *Yes, I held him at arm's length for the past three years—and I almost lost him because of it—but I didn't lose him, and now he loves me, and I love him.* I reach up and grab his shirt, pull him down toward me, and kiss him like it's our first kiss all over again.

When we pull away, his eyes are hazy. "Whoa," he says.

"Whoa," I say.

"Can I join you in there?"

"Of course!" I scoot over as best I can, and Kai folds himself in beside me. The hammock presses our bodies together like we are two caterpillars sharing a single cocoon. He wraps his arm around me, and I rest my cheek against his chest.

"How did things go with your parents?" I ask softly.

"It was a hard conversation, but good. Dad is taking Theo to the doctor right now to get checked out. His wrist is still hurting, and it's pretty swollen. Dad thinks it might be broken."

"Poor Theo." I shift in the hammock, running my hand down Kai's arm until it finds his hand. Our fingers weave together. "Are they going to file a police report?"

"I don't know. Theo doesn't want to. It's complicated because he was wrapped up in the drug stuff, you know? So he could get in trouble himself."

"Yeah. At least your parents are involved now. They'll know what's best."

Kai sighs, but it's a different sigh than earlier. Not a sigh of frustration but a sigh of relief. "It feels so good to have told them. To have this whole thing off my chest. No more secrets." He kisses my forehead. "Sort of like when I confessed my feelings for you, this last time."

I tilt my chin and look up at him. "What do you mean, 'this last time'?"

"Well, the first two times I tried didn't work out so well."

"Two times? What else besides that phone conversation? Which wasn't your fault, by the way. I wasn't ready to hear it. I was too scared."

He grins. "Tegan Rossi, I thought you weren't scared of anything."

"Falling in love with you. That was the only thing that scared me."

Olina grunts and gets up, as if our sappiness is too much for her. She trots over to the grass a few yards away and settles down beneath a mango tree.

"What was the other time?" I prompt Kai. "That you confessed your feelings? I don't remember any other time."

"The first night we reconnected, when you met me in the lava tubes. I was totally trying to put the moves on you."

I laugh. "That was different! You barely knew me! I was some random girl you were hoping to make out with!"

"It wasn't like that, Tegan," Kai says, his voice serious. "You were never some random girl. I hadn't stopped thinking about you since you left."

"Really?"

"Really. I loved you when we were kids. I loved you when we met again three years ago. I love you now." His arm tightens around me. "I'll always love you."

I nestle against him, my bare feet tucked against his calves. We lie there in silence for a while, the hammock swaying gently in the breeze. Birds flutter in the trees and call out to each other. My ear is pressed against Kai's chest, and I can hear the steady beating of his heart.

When the sun sinks fully beyond the horizon, the breeze turns cooler, and goose bumps spring up on my skin. It's time to go inside, but I burrow closer to Kai, trying to hold on to this moment a little longer. *How is another day over already?* A pit yawns open in my stomach, so wide it could swallow me whole.

"We better head in," Kai murmurs. His lips brush my forehead. His breath is warm. "Get ready to go."

"Go? Go where?"

"To the art gallery. I mean, um, if you still want to … "

I sit up. "Oh my god—yes! Of course I want to! With everything that's happened today, I forgot what day it is." Carefully, I roll sideways and swing my legs down out of the hammock. "What time is it? Are we late?"

Kai checks his watch. "It's a little after seven. Let's eat dinner here and then head over. The gallery opens at eight, but we don't need to get there right on time."

"Sounds perfect." I reach down and help him up. "I'm so glad you're taking me to your show, Kai. I know it's a complicated situation, but it's important to me. Thank you."

"No, thank you, T." His hair is adorably rumpled, and one cheek is creased with lines from the hammock. "I wanted to go. Of course I did. This is a big deal—my first piece in a real art gallery! I've been dreaming about this forever. I was just—nervous about it, I guess— and I let myself make excuses. Thanks for calling me on it."

I don't tell Kai, but I'm nervous too. I'm nervous to meet his friends. Will they all be like that guy R.J. was at the restaurant? Looking me up and down, judging me, deeming me not worthy? What if another fight breaks out? What if R.J. tries to punch Kai again?

What if this night is a total disaster, and it's all my fault for forcing Kai to go?

But we need to go. Not only do I want to experience the thrill of seeing Kai's artwork in a gallery for the first time, I also need Kai to make things right with his friends. That's the only way I'll ever be able to let go of him at the end of the week. I need to know he's going to be okay without me.

We head inside, and I duck into Kai's room to change, while he scrounges around for leftovers in the kitchen. In the mirror, I check my hourglass tattoo. I have to force myself not to look at it a thousand times throughout the day, monitoring the infinitesimal trickle of sand. Now, there is definitely more sand in the bottom half than in the top. I run my fingers over the black lines, wishing so desperately I could flip the hourglass back over somehow. Give myself more time.

I take a deep breath, smoothing my hands over a flowing yellow skirt I found in my suitcase. It is also new, and I wonder if in some other life—some alternate past that leads to a future that doesn't end after this week—I bought this skirt thinking of Kai. I always associate him with the color yellow: cheerful, confident, easygoing. Maybe that's why it is so strange to think of him as anything but happy. I remember what his mom said: *He's been having a hard time lately. It means a lot that you traveled all the way here to cheer him up.*

Why was he having a hard time? Was it because of our fight and his falling-out with his friends? Or something else, something more? I need to ask him about it. Tomorrow, I'll ask him.

I pair the skirt with a simple white T-shirt, my yellow sandals, and Mom's gray sweater that still smells like her. Thinking about my mom for too long makes this lion of grief roar up inside of me, and I don't have time for grief. After tonight, I only have three more days here. I need to be present. I need to make the most of the time I have left.

"I'll grieve when I'm dead," I announce to the mirror, mimicking the way Andrea would always say, "I'll sleep when I'm dead" as rationale for her late-night Netflix-bingeing. I almost laugh. Does this mean I'm gradually accepting the fact that I'm going to die at the end of this week—that, in the real world, I am already dead? Or is this funny because it's still so absurd to think of actually dying? Am I still in denial about the truth?

I put on my puka shell necklace and leave my hair loose around my shoulders. Then I leave the bedroom and head into the kitchen, where Kai is heating up some dinner leftovers from last night, pineapple pork and lots of veggies.

"Hey," I say. "Anything I can do to help?"

He looks up, and I wish I could freeze this moment—the expression in his eyes when he sees me. Like he's drinking in every inch of me, and it lights him up inside.

That slow smile spreads across his face, making me blush.

He turns off the burner and sets down his spatula. Then he closes the gap between us and wraps his arms around me. "You're so beautiful," he murmurs in my ear. "I can hardly take it."

Now I'm lit up inside. When Kai calls me beautiful, I know he's talking about more than my appearance. Because he doesn't just see my outside layer, the way the rest of the world does. He peels back all my layers. He knows me, truly and deeply. He loved the little girl I was, who still lives on inside me, at my core. He knows all of me—all my flaws and insecurities and vulnerabilities—and he thinks I am beautiful.

He kisses my earlobe, my forehead, my nose, my lips.

I break away. "Where's your mom?" I would be embarrassed if she came in and saw us like this. Does she even know that we're, like, a couple now? I love spending time with Kai's family and don't want to make anything awkward.

"She's putting Paulo to bed," Kai says. "Little guy's exhausted. Soccer camp always takes it out of him."

He grabs two plates and dishes out dinner. "You ready for this?" he asks.

I'm not sure if he's asking about the meal or the art gallery. Thinking about the latter makes butterflies gather in my stomach. Kai's little-boy voice pops into my head, from our countless games of hide-and-seek as kids. *Ready or not, here I come!*

"Yep," I tell him. "Born ready."

Come and get me, R.J. and Nadia and the rest. I'm not scared of you. I'll be scared when I'm dead. I bite my lip, smiling to myself. I think I've found my new mantra.

The art gallery is wedged into a busy street in downtown Kona, surrounded by shops and restaurants. Kai turns onto a side street to find a parking space. Then we walk together, hand in hand, down the street. Kai's wearing the same button-down shirt from our first date, at The Blue Oasis. I wouldn't be surprised if it's the only collared shirt he owns.

"What?" he asks, and I realize I've been staring. "Do I have something on my shirt?" He looks down.

"No, you look great. I love that shirt. Is that the one you wore the other night?"

"Yeah." He smiles sheepishly. "Don't get me wrong, I have other nice shirts—I'm not *that* much of a beach bum. But this one's my lucky shirt."

"It is? I mean, was it always?"

"Not before that night. But now it's the luckiest shirt ever. It made you finally see me as more than a friend." He smiles, draws in a big breath, releases it. "And I could use a bit of extra luck tonight."

We reach the entrance to the art gallery. The door is propped open with a giant geode; light spills out onto the sidewalk, along with the murmur of voices and laughter. Kai looks at me and raises his eyebrows. *Ready?*

I smile confidently. Fearlessly.

"I can't wait to see your piece," I tell him.

It's the right thing to say, because Kai seems to get a jolt of energy—a reminder of why we're here. This is a celebration! His work is hanging in an art gallery! He leads me across the threshold, into the noise and light.

The gallery has smooth, well-worn hardwood floors and bright-white walls. People mingle around the airy rooms, nibbling on crackers and sipping on wine. I don't see any of Kai's friends. But I'm sure they're here somewhere.

"Look up," Kai tells me, so I tilt my head back. The ceiling is a giant mosaic of seashells and stones, arranged in an undulating wavelike pattern.

"Wow," I breathe. "That's amazing."

"The gallery owner's wife was a mosaic artist," Kai says.

Was. The word niggles at me. *Was* a mosaic artist. Not *is.*

"What happened to her?" I ask.

"She died a few years ago. Cancer. He did the ceiling as a tribute to her. It took him three years to finish."

"It's beautiful," I say. I wonder how her Best Week unfolded, after she died of cancer. Did she spend the week on vacation with her husband? Maybe she went back and got to experience her honeymoon all over again. Or did she relive a week from her childhood? Or perhaps her Best Week was an ordinary week from her life. Making art. Making dinner. Making love.

I wish I could channel this mosaic artist who died. I have so many questions I yearn to ask her. *Does it hurt to cross over? Will I ever stop missing this life, this humanness? Will I ever stop aching for Kai and my parents and my friends—all the people I've left behind?*

Will my life always feel unfinished?

"You okay?" Kai asks. His eyes look pained. I can tell he regrets telling me about the gallery owner's wife. "I'm sorry, I wasn't thinking."

"No, it's fine. I'm fine. Better than fine—I'm excited. Take me to your piece!"

"This way." He grins and leads me through the front room, down a little hallway, and into another room. It's emptier and quieter back here. Then we veer left and head for the far back corner. All I know about Kai's piece is what he told me after shave ice the other day: it's a wood carving. But I have no idea what the subject matter is.

That part is a surprise, Kai had said, winking. *You'll just have to wait and see.*

The first thing I notice about Kai's piece is how large it is—the opposite of his delicate, dainty snowflake ornaments on display at the Tiki Room. It stretches across the wall, the size of a giant flat-screen TV. From across the room, it simply looks like a big, flat piece of wood. I can't tell what the image is.

But as we get closer, shapes begin to emerge. Slowly, I realize what Kai has created. What his hands have brought to life in the grains of this wood. We step up to his piece, close enough to reach out and touch the grooves if we wanted.

"Wow." I let out a long breath I didn't even realize I was holding. "Kai, this is … magnificent."

I look over at him. Instead of studying his artwork, he is studying me. Wanting to see my reaction. He flashes a smile, partly nervous and partly proud.

"Truly," I say. "This is … I have no words to even describe it. I'm speechless."

His wood carving is of manta rays. The giant, magical creatures of the deep, soaring through the water with their graceful fins spread wide. He has captured them so perfectly—it looks as if they are moving. Dancing, twirling, flying. Kelp wavers around the edge, forming a frame around the scene. Tiny fish circle the manta rays like halos around angels. I peer closer, studying the details. It must have taken Kai hours upon hours to meticulously carve these figures into this wood. I am amazed by his talent, his dedication. His vision. That he can look at an ordinary slab of wood and see … this. It's remarkable.

And then, I notice her. On the right side, floating up close to the surface of the water. A girl with wavy hair, wearing snorkel goggles and swim fins.

I glance at Kai. Point to her. "Is that … ?"

"Yep. It's you."

"Oh my gosh." I can't believe it.

"I didn't consciously plan it," Kai says. "It just sort of happened. To be honest, I was angry with you when I made this piece. It was during that period when we weren't talking. But you're always there, in the back of my mind." He grins. "Or the front of my mind. You're in all the art I create, T."

I point at the snorkeling girl. "Not like this. I mean, you've sent me photos of your other art pieces, and I saw your snowflake carvings at the shop. You've never put me into your wood carvings like this before, have you?"

"Not literally," Kai admits. "But the way I feel about you—that love comes through in all of my art."

I squeeze his hand. "I'd say that you're in all the math problems I solve, but it doesn't have quite the same ring to it."

He laughs. I step back, wanting more room to take in the whole breadth of the piece. It really is stunning. I am swept away with this yearning to be there, underwater, with the manta rays and the fish and the swaying kelp.

And suddenly, I know what I want to do on Sunday. On my Last Day. Right before the sand in my hourglass tattoo runs out.

I want Kai to take me on a manta ray snorkel, just like the first time we met, on his parents' boat when I was a little girl. I always wished that we'd gone on a manta snorkel again, when I was here with my parents three years ago. I remember how peaceful and beautiful it was, slipping into the water as day quickened into evening, watching the manta rays glide and dip and twirl. I want to see them again, one more time. One last time.

Acceptance settles within me. I feel truly calm and resolute for the first time since I woke up here in Hawaii. It will be a perfect final memory of this week. Of this life. My time with Kai will come full circle. The mantas brought us together, and they will help us say goodbye.

Before Kai and I wander through the rest of the gallery, I remember that art galleries usually have placards hanging next to the pieces, listing the artists' names. I want to see Kai's name in official gallery lettering. I spot it—a small white card hanging a few feet to the left of his wood carving. I step closer and lean in.

Kai Kapule.
"Homecoming."
Lime wood. Hand-carved original.

I take a photo of the placard, then another photo of him smiling in front of his piece, and one last photo of the piece by itself. Then we walk through the rest of the gallery, taking in the eclectic mishmash of paintings and photographs and sculptures of all different styles, from traditional to abstract. Other than Kai's wood carving, my favorite piece is a detailed, vibrantly colored painting of a starfish sunning itself on a rock, about to be hit by a wave.

"That's Nadia's piece," Kai says.

Of course it is. "Wow. It's wonderful." A surge of jealousy hits me, but I push it away. *Kai needs to reconnect with his friends. Nadia is the keystone.* Plus, I'm curious to meet these people I've only seen in photographs, who have been such a big part of Kai's life. In the framed picture on Kai's bookshelf, they all look so happy together. There must still be fondness there, if only Kai could get past his stubborn pride and reach out to them.

I glance around the room. We haven't bumped into his friends yet; so far, we've mostly encountered older people. A lot of the gallery browsers seem to be tourists, judging from their new-looking Hawaiian shirts and sunburns.

A shadow darkens Kai's face. "They're here," he mutters, nodding across the room. "Over by the snack table. Just like them to take advantage of free food."

I grab his hand. "I'm feeling a bit hungry myself."

"We already had dinner!" Kai says. "We don't need to go over there."

I'm surprised by the genuine alarm in his voice. *He really doesn't want to talk to them,* I realize. *They hurt him. He's scared.*

I take Kai's other hand in mine and gaze up into his brown eyes. Love for him squeezes my insides and wrings me out. *I need to know that he's going to be okay without me. And to be okay, he needs his friends back in his life.*

"Do you remember our very first argument?" I ask.

"You mean when we were kids? Like, about where to build a sandcastle?"

"No—our first real argument, after we reconnected. The trigonometry one."

Kai nods. Looks down at his sandals. "I still don't know what I did to make you upset."

"You didn't do anything wrong. It was my own baggage. I thought—I thought you only wanted to be my friend so you could get help on your homework."

Kai's eyebrows shoot up. "What? That's ridiculous!"

I hold up my hand. "I know it is. That's why I'm so glad I apologized, so we could move past it."

Kai looks wary. "I have an inkling where you're going here, T, and believe me, this situation is completely different. My friendship with them was never like what you and I had. You never would have abandoned me like they did. Even when you and I fought, I knew we'd eventually get past it. And besides, I did absolutely nothing wrong—"

"Please, Kai." I stare into his face, catching his gaze and holding it. "You don't have to agree with me. Just hear me out. I remember that first argument, when we didn't talk for a day or so, and I felt like the rug was pulled out from under my feet. I realized that you could leave at any time—disappear, whenever you wanted, and there would be nothing I could do about it. I didn't like the feeling, so I vowed to distance myself. I would never be dependent on you, which I thought meant that I would never get hurt."

Kai nods. He looks down at our intertwined hands. I can tell he's listening.

"But I was wrong, of course. So wrong! Distancing myself from you was hurt that I inflicted on myself. I was too scared of the waves, so I played in the shallow waters, which meant that I never got to feel the exhilaration of letting myself fall. Of honoring my true feelings. Of loving you in this deep and beautiful and terrifying way."

"But you did." Kai rubs his thumbs against mine. "This week, you did."

"Yes. Thank god for this week. But I'll always regret not choosing this sooner. When I think of all the time I wasted being scared and proud and hiding behind my excuses … " I shake my head, blinking away tears of frustration. "What I'm trying to say, Kai, is that it doesn't matter who's right. Sometimes you need to apologize even if you think you've done nothing wrong. Your friends are hurting. They miss you. And I can tell you miss them too." I lean over and kiss his cheek, scratchy with stubble. "Now I'm going to head over there, make myself a plate of cheese and crackers, and say hello. You get to decide if you want to come or not. You get to decide what you want to say to them, if anything."

I let go of his hands, square my shoulders, and begin the long walk across the room. Chin up, head held high. I can't tell if Kai's friends notice me or not. Instead of looking toward them, I look around at the artwork on the walls.

Eons pass. I'm halfway across the wide wooden floor. I am the *Titanic* gliding through the lonely ocean. *No, that's not a good metaphor—I am* not *going to sink.* Chin up, squared shoulders, head held high. Finally, when I've almost given up hope, I feel Kai's hand slip into mine. Sweet relief courses through my veins. I glance up at him and smile. He smiles back, but I can still see a tightness there, around the edges.

When we reach the table, I grab a plate and hand it to Kai, who immediately lasers all of his attention onto the cheese display. Nadia is standing right there, on the other side of the table. Arms crossed over her chest, as if to shield herself.

"Hi," I say to her. "Nadia, right?"

She nods.

"I thought it was you, when I bumped into you the other day. I've seen so many photos of you over the years." I reach out my hand. "I'm Tegan. It's nice to finally meet you!"

Nadia accepts my handshake. She seems taken aback by my friendliness. *Good.* I've decided the best way to handle things is to channel my dad and pretend like I have no idea there is any sort of tension happening here. It's how Dad always handles interactions between my mom and his series of girlfriends, and while it used to annoy me, I'm beginning to think he might be onto something. My feigned obliviousness just might be the bridge that enables them to talk to each other with their pride intact. No one has to make the first move, because I've already bumbled my way into it.

"I loved your piece," I tell Nadia. "The painting of the starfish? Kai told me it was yours. The colors are gorgeous. How long did it take you to paint it?"

"About four months, overall," Nadia says. Her arms drop down to her sides. "You know, working on it here and there, after school and on weekends."

"You're super talented. It's one of my favorite pieces in the show. I was drawn to it from across the room."

She waves off my words, but her face opens up a little. Maybe she can tell I'm being sincere with my praise.

"This is a neat gallery. So you work here?" I ask.

"Yeah, I interned here last summer and stayed on through the year. Last season, I helped curate a show consisting purely of ephemera. It got a lot of interest."

Ephemera? I have no clue what that means, but no way am I asking. Is she purposely using art lingo to make me feel out of my element?

"Kai was a huge help with that show," she continues. "I never would have been able to pull it off without him." She glances at Kai, but he doesn't look up. He's standing a few feet away from us, chomping on cubes of cheese like it's his job.

Even though I want Kai to reconnect with his friends, I bristle at the warmth in her voice. I imagine the two of them here in the gallery, spending hour after hour together, immersed in their shared world of art. I want to bare my teeth and snap at her to stay away from my boyfriend.

But he won't be mine for much longer. I need to prepare to let him go.

"So what's coming up in the fall?" I ask, attempting to shift the conversation back to neutral ground. "What show is up next?"

"The next big show opens in September and features local

printmakers. Chine collé, drypoint, and all that. I won't be here in the fall, though. I'm going to California College of the Arts to study painting." I can tell she is trying to act nonchalant, but she can't fully hide the pride in her voice. "What about you?" she says. "Are you going to college?"

"Yep. Georgetown."

"Wow. Where is that, again? The East Coast?" The words she's not saying echo in my ears: *Somewhere far, far away from here?*

"It's in Washington, DC."

For the first time in our conversation, she smiles fully. "Awesome. Congratulations."

"Thanks." My gut sinks in despair. *You have no idea how far away I'll be.*

Like I suspected, Nadia is the gateway to the rest of Kai's friends, and before long I've introduced myself to the whole gang: Skeeter and Kaylee and Noah. Even R.J. shakes my hand, pretending like we didn't already meet the other night at The Blue Oasis. I guess if his sister seems cool with me, then he is too. I don't think R.J. hates Kai either. Kai just happened to be the guy Nadia fell for, and no brother wants to see his sister get hurt.

Eventually, Kai abandons his cheese plate and wanders over to our little group. He wraps his arm around my waist, and I lean into him slightly, trying to say with my body, *It's okay. They won't bite.* I watch his friends registering this new information. Nadia chews her lip and looks down at her feet.

What was it Kai had said, that day we got shave ice? *My friends liked to give me crap for being in love with this mainland girl who barely even knew I existed.* I wonder if us being a couple changes their minds about anything.

"Hey, Nadia?" Kai asks. "Can I talk to you for a minute?"

"Sure," she says, tucking a strand of hair behind her ear. They walk over together to the corner of the gallery, next to a watercolor painting of a volcano spewing lava.

I half-listen to Skeeter and Noah debate the merits of the food table's bread selection, crispy cracker versus baguette-style. I sense they are only talking to fill the space. All of us are watching Kai and Nadia, while trying to seem like we're not actually paying them any mind. I force myself to laugh along with the others as Noah bites off a chunk of Skeeter's baguette, spewing crumbs all over his black shirt. In the distance, Kai leans in and gives Nadia a hug. She wraps her arms around him, and my throat tightens.

Yep, it's still there—that spark of jealousy, even though this is what I wanted to happen. Now my jealousy of Nadia stretches so much deeper. I'm jealous she gets to keep living beyond this week. I'm jealous of all the time she has left—time to make mistakes and learn from them, to take wrong turns and right them. I'm jealous of all the Sunday afternoons and silly adventures and monotonous Wednesdays she has in store, time to be bored and lazy, time to daydream and argue, time to fritter away without counting every grain of sand slipping through the hourglass. I'm jealous of Nadia, but really I'm jealous of my past self. I wish I still had that arrogant innocence—assuming that my life would keep going and going and going.

My Best Week is almost over. How long will it take for Kai to move on? How long before his memories with me begin to blur around the edges? How long before he forgets me?

Nadia will be here, waiting in the wings. She'll be eager to help him forget.

Watching her and Kai amble back toward us—the tension is gone from his shoulders, and his manner is easy, relaxed—I wonder if his feelings for her will change into something more. When I'm no longer here, will there be anything to stop him from falling in love with her? I mean, really, how could he not? She is beautiful, and creative, and she loves him. Yes, she still does—it is obvious from the way she is looking up at him, right now, her smile wide and hopeful. If his feelings for her changed, hers would leap up to match his in a heartbeat.

What will Kai's Best Week be? One day, hopefully a very long time into the future, will I get to relive this week again, with him? Is my Best Week his Best Week too?

Selfishly, there is a part of me that wants it to be so. But the bigger, more generous part of me—the part of me that loves him more than I love myself—hopes that the Best Week of Kai's Life is far into the future. I don't want his life to peak at eighteen. He has so much more living to do. So many more magnificent adventures and fantastic surprises in store. I pray his Best Week is yet to come. Which means I am praying for it to be wholly apart from me.

Maybe it will be the week of his wedding and honeymoon. Or maybe he'll spend the week playing with his kids. Or grandkids. Or even great-grandkids.

As I watch Kai and Nadia walk toward us, I have the sense that I am watching Kai's future. And I want this future for him. I want him to remember me, but I don't want him to pine for me forever. I want him to fall in love again—to have a rich, full, passionate life. Yes. I want him to end up with someone like Nadia, after I'm gone.

A bittersweet feeling wells up inside me, happy-sad tears filling my eyes. I try to blink them away, but Kai notices as he comes up and slips his arm around me again. "You okay?" he asks softly.

He is a steady anchor. I belong here, in this space between his chest and his arm. I fit here so perfectly. A Tegan-shaped space.

I nod, smile a watery smile. "I'm going to miss you, is all."

His eyes darken with sadness—with realizing, with remembering—and I wish I hadn't said anything. He tightens his arm around me, leans down and kisses my hair.

"You guys are cute," Nadia says. With her words of approval, it's like the entire group exhales and relaxes.

Skeeter leans closer to me. "We all thought you were way out of his league," he stage-whispers, and everyone laughs.

"Yeah, Kai," R.J. says. "How did you finally convince her to go out with you?"

Kai glances down at me. I wonder what he is going to say.

"I got her to come visit me," he says. "I knew if Tegan came back to Hawaii, there was a good chance she would fall in love with the island. Then I just tried to be in the background of the picture so she would fall for me too. By default."

Everyone laughs again. Their eyes shine with happiness to have Kai back within their fold. They ask where he's taken me around the island and offer suggestions of places we should go, their voices rising with excitement.

"How long are you here?" Noah asks me.

"Just till Sunday, unfortunately."

I focus on the solidity of the floor beneath my feet, the warmth of Kai's skin brushing mine. Here. Now.

"A bunch of us are going on a picnic tomorrow, if you guys want to join," Nadia says.

Kai wraps both arms around me in a bear hug. "Thanks for the invite, but I'm going to decline before Tegan can answer. I want to hog her all to myself these last few days of her trip."

I squeeze his arm gratefully. I am greedy to soak up every last precious minute with him. Just the two of us.

"Well, next time, then," Nadia says. She smiles at me, a real smile. If we weren't both in love with the same guy, she seems like someone I could actually be friends with. "Maybe you and I can grab coffee, Tegan. I'd like to get to know you better."

"I'd like that too," I tell her. "Let's definitely do that, next time."

When she hugs me goodbye, I send her a silent wish: *Please, be good to him. Take care of him for me.*

dear t,

you were in my dream again last night. i was really glad you were there. the dream was mostly about theo—he was in trouble, and we went to rescue him. he was all beaten up by those guys he hangs with, the high school dropouts who deal drugs and think they're tough shit. i've been warning theo about them for ages, but he never listens. in the dream, he was shattered. i felt so helpless. he's my little brother, and i didn't protect him. i didn't keep him safe.

maybe it's a subconscious message about you, about how i've been feeling so helpless just sitting here refreshing social media, waiting for a new update from your mom about how you're doing. maybe theo in the dream was a symbol for you. i should be there with you. i feel sick that i'm not there. but what would i do? saunter into your hospital room and hold your hand? your mom barely even knows me. they'd probably kick me out.

i wish you weren't so far away. i wish you'd just come to hawaii like we'd planned. the truth is that i'm angry, t. i'm angry at you for getting into this accident. i'm angry that you might die. i'm angry at myself for loving you all this time and not doing enough about it. i'm angry at you and me and trains and airplanes and cell phones and the whole world. i guess being angry feels better than being constantly terrified.

you can't leave me, t. please, don't leave me. please, keep fighting.

in the dream i made up with my friends too. because of you. even though in real life, you don't even know about all the drama that went down with me and my friends. anyway, nadia called me today. which is a big deal—i haven't talked to her for months. she heard about your accident and asked how i was doing. at first i was going to give some gruff, terse response and hang up, but i couldn't keep the tears out of my voice. so we ended up talking for a while, and it was actually pretty nice. normal. like the old days. she invited me to this picnic with a bunch of my old friends tomorrow, and i think i'm gonna go.

i told my parents about theo today. about the guys he's involved with and how he's started selling weed. they're grounding him for, like, ever. he's gonna be so pissed at me. but it was the right thing to do. you were the one, in the dream, who convinced me to do it. so, thanks.

have i said this already? i love you.

—kai

PART THREE

FRIDAY

*D*eep, pillowy darkness. Like being underwater, so far down below the surface that no light reaches you. A steady beeping. Voices. No words, just an urgent tone. I want to help. Can't move my body. Are my eyes closed? Can't open them. My head splits in pain, and I—

I open my eyes. Headache. My vision is blurry, and my chest is tight. Weak morning light streams into the room, and it takes me a second to place where I am. Then I remember: *Kai's bedroom. Hawaii.*

Kai.

He is breathing softly beside me, his eyelashes long and dark against his cheeks. I wish I could be around to see him grow older. I try to picture him with gray hair and wrinkles, but it's impossible.

The worst thing about being on borrowed time is the forgetting, and then the remembering. Every morning, I wake up thinking that I still have a wide-open future waiting for me to live it. And then I remember, and the stone sinks back down into my gut, and I have to come to terms with The End all over again. So much regret. So much I would do differently, if I had the chance.

But I don't. So there's no point in thinking about it.

Instead, I study Kai's face as he sleeps. He looks peaceful. What is he dreaming about? I memorize the slant of his nose and the muss of his hair, the thickness of his eyebrows and the curve of his lips. I want to be able to close my eyes and see his face for eternity.

His eyes blink open, and he catches me staring at him. We both blush.

"Good morning," he murmurs, pulling me toward him. "You know what I could never get tired of?"

"What?" I run my fingers up the knob of his spine.

"Waking up and seeing you. I used to always roll over and reach for my phone first thing, to check for an email from you."

"Me too. I felt unmoored for those last few weeks, when we weren't talking."

"Unmoored. That's the perfect way to describe it. How are you so good with both numbers and words?"

No, I'm not. Numbers, maybe. Not words. I haven't been able to write my letter for you. And I'm running out of time.

Kai nuzzles his face into my shoulder. "It feels so cozy, here with you."

I kiss his hair. "Wanna go back to sleep?" *Maybe I can slip out and try to work on his letter.*

But Kai flings off the covers dramatically. "No, the Hulk has risen! We have so much to do today!" He leaps out of bed and flexes one arm, then the other. I laugh, reaching out and touching his bicep.

"I still don't know when you got these muscles," I say. "Where was I?"

"You were too busy trying to keep me in the friend zone."

I bring his hand to my lips and kiss his palm. "I wish my friends from home could see what a hot boyfriend I snagged."

Kai raises one eyebrow. "Boyfriend, huh?"

I drop his hand. My cheeks grow warm. "Well, um, I thought— is that okay?"

"Are you kidding me?" He smiles. "Of course it's okay. I'm thrilled to be your boyfriend, T. I've been wanting this for *years*. I guess it just surprised me, to hear you say it."

I pull the covers around me. "Are you sure? It doesn't freak you out?" *Though I guess if it does, he only has to stand it for a few more days. Stop it, brain. Stop it.*

Kai suddenly crouches down to the carpet. *Did he drop something?* But then he rises up on one knee and takes my hands in his.

"Tegan Rossi," he says in an exaggeratedly deep voice—his Hulk voice. "Will you ... be my ... girlfriend?"

He's grinning, and so am I, and it's all a silly game, a joke, just pretend. Like when we were kids playing make believe, running across the seaweed-strewn beach, turning what we saw into something else. All it took to transform an object was to name it out loud, whatever you wanted it to be, and the other person would believe you wholeheartedly. *Pretend that rock is a hidden temple. Pretend this stick is a magic key. Pretend this shell is a diamond ring.*

Only it's different now. If we were kids—or even if this was another reality, and I was here in a life that wasn't ending in two days—then this moment could be light and airy and giddy. A sparkling placeholder for some future possibility. But now, it's like staring down a dark tunnel at a future that is never going to happen. Kai on bended knee. Asking me a real question, for real life. Asking me about forever.

The moment stretches out, heavier now. Kai looks up at me, a smile still wide across his face, but a deeper question in his eyes. He's thinking it too. Imagining.

I want this moment, right now, to be more than itself. I want it to hold both the present and also the future that might have been. In Kai's face, I try to imagine an older Kai, with a few wrinkles around his eyes. I imagine him down on bended knee, asking me a very similar question. I can almost see it. The impossible-future, the never-future, glimmering, superimposed over this moment unfurling right now.

"Will you?" Kai asks softly, in his normal voice.

"Yes." My voice comes out croaky. "Yes."

There's true happiness in his eyes, and my heart swells. He pumps his fist in the air and rises up to kiss me. "I love you, girlfriend."

"You're cheesy, boyfriend." I smile at him. "I love you too."

This is it, I remind myself. *This moment. This is what you've been given. You need to let this be enough.*

As usual, Kai drives with the windows down. The morning air is cool and damp. Mist obscures the mountaintops. We successfully managed to sneak out of the house before the rest of Kai's family got up, and now, driving through the quiet morning, it seems like we are the only two people on Earth. As if this world—the sky and the trees and the lava rock and the road stretching out like a black snake before us—as if everything exists just for us. And maybe it does. Not in the real world, but in *this* world, whatever it is. *What if all of this is here to guide me to some crucial wisdom? What if all of this is a puzzle*

designed for me?

If so, where are the pieces? How do I fit them together into something cohesive and whole, something that makes sense?

Even though I told Kai that we need to accept my fate and not waste time trying to change it; even though the majority of my brain believes that this week is nothing more than a dream; even though my scars are gone, and I have an hourglass tattoo over my heart that is changing by the second; even though I know that in real life, I died, boom, end of story; even though most of me believes all of this, there is still a tiny defiant place deep within that refuses to give up hope. *What if Kai was right? What if there is some sort of clue at Akaka Falls? What if Okalani and Keone weren't only using the* o'opu alamo'o *as a metaphor—what if the fish hold an answer?*

With every mile that takes us closer to Akaka Falls, my nerves clench tighter. And my expectations heighten, despite my efforts to tamp them down. As hard as I try, I can't give up my desire to live. I can't hush that niggling question in the back of my brain: *What if?*

One reason I've always loved math is that, in a math problem, you always know what you are solving for. And the answers don't change. Three plus three equals six, every single time. Three plus three will always equal six. No two ways about it. But now, I can't shake the feeling that there is something I should be looking for— only I don't know what it is. *How can you solve for* x *if you can't even figure out what the equation should be?*

"You hungry?" Kai asks, breaking me out of my reverie. "Ready to stop for breakfast?"

I'm not hungry, but Kai must be. Besides, I don't want to pass up an opportunity to see whatever he wants to show me. "Sure," I tell him. "That sounds perfect."

A few minutes later, we pull off the highway into a small shopping center. Kai parks in front of a restaurant called TEX Drive In.

I'm confused. "Tex?" I ask. "Like, Texas?"

Kai shrugs. "Nobody really knows. My best guess is that it refers to the size of their portions, which are huge. In any case, this place is the best. Puts all other malasadas to shame."

"Mala what?"

"Malasadas. C'mon, I'll show you."

He leads me inside the restaurant, which is an order-at-the-counter-style place. This early in the morning, only a handful of guests are seated in the wide sea of tables and chairs. Giant menu boards hang above the counter. I stand back, studying the menu, still confused what exactly it is that we're going to eat, when Kai grabs my hand and tugs me across the room.

"Where are we going?" I ask. He's leading me *away* from the counter where you order. "I thought we were eating breakfast here."

"We are. But first, I want to show you something."

We approach a big glass window—not facing the parking lot but looking deeper into the building. I peer inside and see an industrial-sized kitchen, with pristine countertops and gleaming steel appliances. A woman in an apron and hairnet stands under a sign: MALASADAS. Next to her rests a giant slab of dough; she fries a large basket of round golden shapes.

Kai flings one arm out dramatically. "I give you … malasadas!"

"Those things she's frying?"

"Yep. Deliciously fried golden dough. You might know them as *doughnuts*."

I laugh. "All this fuss for doughnuts? You've been acting like this is the holy grail of breakfast foods."

"Malasadas are not *just doughnuts*, T. They are the best doughnuts you'll ever taste."

I'm skeptical. I've eaten some pretty amazing doughnuts in my life. There's a place called Unc's in my hometown that makes the best apple fritters. Supposedly, the secret is potato flour. Unc was Irish.

I needle Kai with my elbow. "What are you willing to bet?"

He strokes his chin thoughtfully, then points at me. "Loser carries the pack on the hike." We have a small backpack filled with water bottles and sunscreen.

"Deal."

We shake on it. Then Kai pulls me in, and we kiss on it, too, for good measure.

Up at the counter, Kai orders us a variety of malasadas, filled with plain custard and chocolate custard and apples and mangoes. I grab napkins, and we go sit at a picnic table outside. In the distance, the mist has burned off the mountains, and around us the air has turned warm and humid.

"Careful, they're hot," Kai says, handing me a malasada wrapped in wax paper. The golden dough is covered in sugar granules. When I take a bite, chocolate custard oozes out one side.

"Ooh!" I say, trying to cool off my bite before I swallow. "You were right! These are hot malasadas!"

Kai watches me in amusement. "Tegan," he says, "you want to know something?"

"What?" I ask. I blow ferociously on the fried dough, waiting to take another bite.

"You're my hot malasada."

He winks. I burst out laughing.

How am I ever going to say goodbye to him?

"Okay," I admit. We're back on the road again, the taste of chocolate still on my lips and a sugar high buzzing in my blood. "You were right."

"What?" Kai shouts, though I'm pretty sure he heard me. The breeze isn't *that* loud.

"You were right!" I shout back.

"What?" He grins, and I *know* he heard me.

"You were right! Those were the best doughnuts ever!"

His hand finds my knee. "I'm glad you liked them," he says in his normal voice. "We can get more tomorrow, if you want."

Tomorrow. Just like that, it's back—The End, lurking.

"Okay," I say. "Maybe."

We're mostly quiet for the rest of the ride to Akaka Falls, each of us wrapped up in our own thoughts. Even though I'm willing to bet we're both thinking about the same thing.

One thing I love about being with Kai is that we don't always need to be talking. Even when we were long-distance, sometimes we would sit on the phone in comfortable silence, just being present with each other. He doesn't feel the need to rush in and fill a silence, and neither do I. At least, not with him. Sometimes with other people I get awkward and anxious when the conversation lapses, and I stumble over my words to say something, anything. But with Kai, that's never been the case. He has an easy openness that makes you feel comfortable letting your guard down and relaxing into yourself. Maybe I can say something about that in my letter to him.

When we pull into the entrance for Akaka Falls, it is after 10:00 a.m. The parking lot is already half-filled with SUVs and minivans. Mothers smear sunscreen onto kids' faces, and vendors stand beside ice chests, selling bottles of coconut water. I reach for our backpack on the floor of the Jeep, but Kai grabs it first.

"I lost the bet," I remind him. "I'll carry it, fair and square."

"No, it's fine. I'll carry it."

"Kai, don't be ridiculous. It's not even that heavy. I can carry it myself."

"Please, T," he says, and his eyes are serious. Pleading. "Let me."

This isn't really about the backpack. I imagine what it would be like if our roles were reversed, if I had to stand by and watch Kai's time tick away, knowing there was nothing I could do to stop it. That would be torture.

"Okay," I say, relinquishing the backpack. "Thanks."

He slings it over his shoulders, locks the Jeep, and takes my hand. Together, we walk through the parking lot to the start of the trail. The posted map shows a loop that will take us down to Akaka Falls, and then over to the smaller Kahuna Falls, and then back up to the parking lot. According to the map, the entire loop is only a mile or so.

"Ready?" Kai says.

"Ready!"

A neon-green lizard scuttles across the asphalt. I point as it disappears into the undergrowth.

"Did you see that?" I ask.

"What?"

"The lizard!"

"They're everywhere, if you know where to look," says a voice behind us. I turn, and a middle-aged woman with flowing silver hair is smiling at us. At her feet is an open ice chest, full of bottled coconut water. I smile back uncertainly.

"The geckos," she says. "They're everywhere, but did you know they are not native to the islands?"

I shake my head and catch Kai's eye. He shoots me a look like, *Don't let this lady suck you in ...*

"The geckos were introduced here," the woman continues. "They have flourished on the islands over thousands of years. Sometimes life, like love, springs forth where you least expect it. Isn't that right?"

She winks at me, as if we are in on some joke together. Kai tugs at my hand, and while part of me wants to turn away from this strange woman and follow him down the path to the waterfall, another part of me is intrigued. *What if she knows something important? What if she has information that can help me? What if, what if, what if?*

I step toward her. "You seem to, um, know a lot about the geckos," I say lamely.

"Oh, I have lived here all my life. The geckos are our guardians, and I'm not just talking about bugs." She laughs, throwing her head back. Her laughter is unrestrained, like a child's, and I relax into trust. *Maybe she's just an overly friendly woman, or maybe she has a message specifically for me. Whatever the case, I want to listen.*

"Have you ever heard of the *mo'o*?" she asks, brushing aside a lock of her silvery hair. Her earrings jangle.

"No," I admit. I turn to Kai, who still seems impatient. I wonder if, despite his promises, he really does have a plan to spend the day searching for the *o'opu alamo'o*, hoping to find some magic ingredient that will keep me here beyond this week.

"Have you heard of the *mo'o*?" I ask him.

"Old legends," he says dismissively. "They're supposed to be evil spirits."

The woman shakes her head sadly. "Good and evil, life and death—they are intertwined, no? Impossible to separate one from the other. The contrast provides truth. We would not know what light is, without the darkness."

She looks down at the ice chest at her feet, filled to the brim with bottles of coconut water. For a moment, I think that our conversation is over. I expect her to reach out her hand for money, trying to sell us some of her wares.

Instead, she leans toward me, her bright eyes sparkling.

"Legends are stories," she says. "Stories that carry wisdom. But sometimes, years pass, and the wisdom gets distorted. Do you want to know the truth?"

I nod, spellbound.

"In truth, the *mo'o* is not evil. The *mo'o* is a great magical dragon, powerful and benevolent, protecting us from harm. The gecko is its representative on this earth. Some believe that the great *mo'o* manifests itself inside the body of a gecko."

My heartbeat quickens. *Maybe the gecko, not the* o'opu alamo'o, *is the answer I have been searching for. Maybe the gecko can protect me. But how?*

The woman reaches into the pocket of her jean shorts and pulls out a bright-green string. "May I?" she asks.

I nod.

"Hold out your left wrist."

I do as instructed, and she ties the string onto my wrist. A bracelet. In the center is a small silver charm: a gecko with a tiny tail curled up like a spiral. "This will keep you safe," she says, tying a triple knot. "Do not worry. The *mo'o* will protect you."

"How much is it?" I ask.

"No charge," the woman says, smiling so wide I glimpse a crown on one of her back teeth. "You just seemed like someone who would understand the *mo'o*. Take care, Teacup."

Teacup. I do a double take, staring into the woman's face.

"My mom used to call me Teacup," I say.

The woman smiles but doesn't say anything more.

"Thank you," I say. And then, surprising even myself, I throw my arms around her. It's instinctual—a reflex, a muscle memory. The woman hugs me like she expected this all along. Her palm rubs circles on my back. My mom used to rub my back like this when I was a little girl and had trouble falling asleep. I feel warm and comforted, and very close to tears. *Goodbye, Mom*, I think—the first time I have let myself think these words. *I love you infinity.*

And then I feel a sob building ferociously in my chest, and no matter what world this is—a dream or alternate reality or third dimension or Heaven or nowhere but my own mind—I do not want to be sobbing in a stranger's arms on the edge of a parking lot surrounded by gawking sunburned tourists. I sense that once I start crying, it will be a long time before I'm able to stop.

Time is already seeping away so quickly, minutes and hours dripping out of my pockets like loose change. *I don't have any time to spare. I don't have time for a breakdown.*

Pulling away from the woman, I wipe my eyes and do my best to swallow the gigantic lump in my throat. I push away the memory of my mom rubbing my back. I push away the image of her round cheeks, her warm smile, her voice saying, *I love you infinity, Teacup.* I push it all away, and I take off down the path, away from the woman, past Kai, not looking back.

I'm not aware of Kai's voice or presence until I feel his hand on my shoulder. It is as if I am underwater, swimming alone among the undulating currents. All I hear is the buzzing in my own head. All I feel is the frantic beating of my heart. My entire being is focused on not falling to pieces. *Let it go, it's okay, let it all go …*

It's not like my life was perfect. I had problems and worries and stress. My mom wasn't perfect either. We argued sometimes. She annoyed me and drove me crazy. *So why does it seem like saying goodbye to her is the same as saying goodbye to myself? Why is letting go of my imperfect life so utterly, painfully impossible?*

Kai touches my shoulder, and I jerk around, yanked out of my reveries, back to this time and this place. I must look stormy-eyed, because he holds his hands up like he's trying to calm a wild animal.

"What happened back there?" he says. "You okay?"

Let it all go …

You don't have any time to spare. You don't have time for a breakdown.

"Yeah, I'm okay." I release a big breath. "I just—I miss my mom, you know?" On the last word, my voice quavers. I bite my lip, trying to steady myself.

"I know," Kai says, and then his arms are around me, and I'm breathing in his Kai scent. I think about how my mom seemed disappointed when I canceled my trip to visit Kai. She would be happy to know that I am here, soaking up this week with him. Doing all of these things I kept putting off until later.

I lean back, looking up into his face. "My mom really liked you."

Kai laughs. "She hasn't seen me since I was eight years old! I was easy to love then."

"You were a pretty adorable kid," I agree, smiling. "But I'm serious. She always told me how lucky I was to have a friend like you. She saw that I was truly myself around you. No judgments, no pretentions. She was disappointed in me when I bailed on our summer plans."

Kai pulls me in and kisses my forehead. "Your mom was crazy proud of you, T."

I close my eyes, letting my forehead rest against his chest.

"And not just for all your awards and accolades," Kai adds, as if reading my mind. "She was crazy proud of the person you are. You know that, right?"

I do know. *I love you infinity.* Mom and I still had a million words left to say to each other. But at the same time, when you get down to it, there were no words left unsaid.

"Thanks," I say. I give him one more squeeze and pull away, ready to put this behind us. To keep moving down the path, toward what's left of today.

Kai reaches for my hand. The sunlight catches the gecko charm on my new bracelet, and it shines like it could light up this whole rain forest.

"I love you," I say, feeling a rush of joy that I'm still around to say it.

"I love you too," Kai replies. Another rush of joy: I'm still around to hear it.

The path is paved and narrow, bordered with lush ferns and flowering bushes. There are lots of people here already, mostly families and members of a tour group wearing identical red baseball caps. I keep my eyes peeled for geckos, but I don't spot any.

After a few minutes, the path widens into an outlook over a breathtaking cliff, green with foliage. There it is, across the ravine. Akaka Falls.

The falls are narrower than I anticipated, like a single spigot of water streaming down, down, down. Taller than I expected too. Turbulent white at the peak, the waterfall gradually dissolves into blue mist by the time it reaches the murky pool at the bottom. It is mind-boggling to imagine a fish climbing up this waterfall. It seems a thoroughly impossible feat.

My mind flashes to something my mom said once, when I was frustrated over a big homework assignment in middle school. "It's impossible!" I had exclaimed, dropping my pencil onto the table in resignation. "I'm never going to finish this in time. I might as well give up now."

I had expected my mom to frown, to lecture me about the importance of following through, to try to coax me forward with stories about how important a good education is, how school is a privilege, how she wished she had finished four years of college. How the future was wide open for me, and I only had to work for it.

Instead, she had smiled. There was a mischievous glint in her eyes. "Isn't it fun?" she said. "Achieving the impossible?" Then she squeezed my shoulder and walked away.

Is that what this week is meant to teach me? Is that the wisdom of the o'opu alamo'o? *That it should be fun?* Maybe that's the crucial piece of the puzzle. This week is impossible, after all. I died. Yet I'm still here, with Kai, hiking through a Hawaiian rain forest on a humid summer morning. I'm still here, breathing, thinking, feeling. Maybe all I'm meant to do is to have fun. Soak it all in. Make it count.

"Excuse me." Someone taps my arm. I turn and see a young woman, maybe five years older than I am. "Could you take a picture of us?" Behind her is a guy around her age, with a new-looking haircut and pale skin. Both of them are pretty pale, actually—and not sunburned. Either they've been super vigilant with sunscreen, or they arrived in Hawaii, like, this morning.

"Sure," I say. As she hands me her phone, I notice a sparkling diamond ring on her left hand. *I bet these two just got married. I bet they're honeymooning.*

She joins her guy, fitting into the crook of his shoulder like it's a space made exactly for her. They beam at me. He says something, and she laughs. I snap a few photos in a row so they'll have options to choose from. Watching them is watching a future I'll never have.

I'm jealous, because I want this so badly for myself. But I'm happy for them too. Because I can tell they're enjoying it.

"Thanks!" the woman says as I hand back her phone. "Want me to take one of you?"

"Sure!" Kai steps in, pulling his phone out of his pocket. "That would be great." He and I walk to the walled edge of the overlook, and we pose together like the honeymooners had—his arm around my shoulders, my arm around his waist, our bodies pressed together like two halves of a zipped-up sweatshirt. We haven't taken many photos together this week, which is unusual for me. Andrea might be the photographer of my friendship group back home, but I'm the documentarian—the one who pulls out her phone to capture a random Tuesday lunch, or the striking shadows against a brick wall, or the sunset on my way home from school. This week, I haven't really thought about taking photos. It's been a nice change. I've relaxed into each moment, no longer worrying about trying to preserve everything in pixels. Where I'm going, there's no need for photos. But I do want Kai to have a keepsake from this week. A new picture he can frame for his nightstand. One of us together.

I smile so wide my cheeks ache.

Suddenly, Kai leans down and kisses me, dipping me backward like we're in a movie. Honeymoon Guy whoops.

"Got it! A perfect shot!" Honeymoon Lady exclaims.

Kai pulls me back up to standing. I try to catch my breath.

"You two are adorable together," she says, handing back Kai's phone.

"She's a keeper," the guy puts in, winking at Kai. "I can tell."

"I know," Kai replies, his hand finding mine.

"Good man. Don't let her go." Honeymoon Guy wags his finger.

"Don't worry," Kai says. "I won't."

Later, after we've sipped water and people-watched in the shade for a while, Kai turns to me and says, "What next?"

I've been thinking the same thing. Here we are, at Akaka Falls, the place Okalani and Keone told us about, with the whole day stretching before us. And while the falls are striking, and while I'm glad we came to see them, there's a small part of me that is ... disappointed. Restless. I bounce my knee up and down, the way Kai does when he's nervous. I don't want to admit that I was hoping for *more*. Even though I keep insisting we can't change my fate, I've been secretly wishing and searching for puzzle pieces. I thought there would be an important piece here. But Akaka Falls seems like any other Hawaiian tourist destination: beautiful, vibrant, humming with people. No secrets in sight.

I shrug. "I don't know."

Maybe Kai can read my emotions on my face. Or maybe he's feeling the same way. He stands and pulls me up with him.

"C'mon," he says. "Let's go."

"Are we leaving? Already?"

Kai grins like a puppy that's stolen a sock out of the laundry. "We're leaving the beaten path, if that's what you mean."

"What are you planning, Kapule?"

"I want to get closer to the falls. Let's hike down farther. I want to see the *o'opu alamo'o*."

"Is there a path?"

"Maybe. If not, we'll forge our own path."

This sounds dangerous. This sounds like a not-entirely-smart idea. I look down at my silver gecko charm.

"Okay." I lift the backpack onto my shoulders before Kai can grab it. "I'm in."

It's actually not that hard to slip undetected off the official trail and into the rain forest. Kai and I stroll casually to the far end of the viewing platform, past all the people taking photos of the falls and drinking coconut water, past the little kids chasing each other in spur-of-the-moment games of tag, just like Kai and I used to do. At the far end, making sure that no one is watching us, we quickly climb over the low wall, dropping down about three feet to the sloped mountainside. Akaka Falls shoots out over a cliff, but this side of the canyon descends more gradually. Kai plans to wind our way down in switchbacks, steadily snaking back and forth. We follow a narrow strip of rocks and dirt between the ferns and vines; it might be a path, or not; it's hard to tell.

We've only been hiking for ten minutes when my doubts about this plan rear up. I'm all for adventure and spontaneity. I pride myself on not being afraid of anything. And I'm not afraid now. But there's a difference between being brave and being reckless. We haven't made any discernible progress down the mountain. If anything, Akaka Falls seems farther away than it was from the viewing platform. We can't possibly make it all the way down to the falls, close enough to see the *o'opu alamo'o*. All we'll do is get lost, or get bitten by a snake or a spider, or fall and break a bone trying to navigate down steep, slippery rock.

"Kai?" A bead of sweat slowly courses down my back under my thin T-shirt. "Are you sure about this?"

"Yeah," he says, half-turning to look at me. I recognize the focused set of his eyes. Stubbornness. *Once Kai Kapule sets his mind on something, it is very hard to change it.*

"Isn't this great?" he continues. "We're in the rain forest—actually *in it*, for real. This is true hiking. We're trailblazers, T!"

The light is different down here. Up on the real trail, even the parts shaded by leaves and branches, it was very sunny. Down here, everything is dim. I look up, and the sky has turned a steely blue-gray color.

Only a minute or two later, I feel the first drop.

"Um, Kai?" I point up at the sky.

But I don't need to tell him. Suddenly, a waterfall opens up right above our heads. Buckets of water pour down, drenching us.

Kai shouts something I can't make out. Then he starts laughing. We both do. I close my eyes. Water streams down my face. I let the backpack fall off my shoulders, onto the ground. Kai sloshes over to me and wraps his arms around my waist. He kisses me, and he tastes like rain, and I can feel his muscles through his soaking-wet T-shirt. I think of that scene in *The Notebook* that Andrea and Mel and I always swooned over, how we thought life couldn't get much more romantic than Ryan Gosling declaring his undying love for you in the hammering rain. And here I am, in a Hawaiian rain forest in a summer rainstorm, kissing this boy I love who loves me back, kissing him as if it's my last day on Earth, because it is, almost. And it's even better than *The Notebook*.

Move over, Ryan Gosling. Real life is infinitely better than any image on a screen.

How did I not realize that before? How did I not know that being with Kai in person would be a million times better than FaceTime and texting, that kissing him would be worth the risk a million times over?

Maybe that's the answer. Maybe this moment is the puzzle piece I'm meant to collect.

Kai tightens his arms around me. Our kisses deepen, and I forget about everything else except for him, and me, right here, right now.

Then, as quickly as it swept in, the rain lets up. The gray clouds disperse, and the sun comes out again. Kai and I collapse onto a big slab of rock. Our clothes are soaked, but it feels nice in the humid heat. I wring out my hair. Kai shakes his head like a dog after a bath.

"It's all the *'Ohi'a* tree's fault," Kai says.

"What?"

"The rainstorm. My favorite picture book as a kid was a legend about Akaka Falls. There's a stone around here somewhere, called *Pōhaku a Pele*. When a branch of the *'Ohi'a* tree strikes this stone, the sky will darken, and a rainstorm will come."

"I love all the legends and stories here." I hug my knees to my chest. "Do you believe it? About the *'Ohi'a* tree?"

Kai tilts his head thoughtfully. "You know, if you had asked me that question last week, I would have scoffed and said definitely not. But with all that's happened—with you appearing here like this—it's changed how I see the world. There's a lot more mystery and magic than I believed was possible."

"I know what you mean. I used to try to find answers to every question. Research, rationality, and logic—those were my touchstones. But now, I think it's actually okay, not being able to explain everything."

Kai rests his hand on my knee, and we lapse into a comfortable silence, gazing across the ravine at Akaka Falls. The clouds part, and the sun shines upon the waterfall like a spotlight, and—

"Look!" I point at the falls. "A rainbow!"

The colors glimmer, luminous and clear, alive in the misty waterfall.

"*Waianuenue*," Kai breathes. "You really are my lucky charm, T."

"*Waia* what?"

"*Waianuenue*. *Wai* means 'fresh water' and *nue* means 'colorful' or 'dancing.' *Waianuenue* means the rainbow you can sometimes see—if you catch it just right—in waterfalls."

"What a perfect name. It does look like the colors are dancing." The rainbow seems like a message meant for us, about magic and mystery, things explained and not explainable.

I take a deep breath. I don't exactly want to have this conversation, but I need to ask. I only have two more days left here. I can't leave any words left unsaid.

"Kai?" I ask gently. "What are your plans, you know ... after this?"

"Well, tomorrow I have a surprise planned, and Sunday we're going snorkeling with the mantas, right?"

"No. I mean, yes. We are. But what I meant was—what are your plans for, you know—the future?" *Because I'm not going to be around to see for myself.* "Are you still planning to stay in Kona instead of going to college in the fall?"

His face shuts down a little, his expression immediately more guarded. *He doesn't want to have this conversation either. He's tired of this conversation.*

"Yep," he says. "I'll be working at the Tiki Room during the week, helping out on the boat on weekends."

The boat means his parents' business—Mrs. Kapule filled me in about how it's expanded since the manta snorkel I went on with my parents all those years ago. These days, Mr. and Mrs. Kapule mostly work in an office, managing the business stuff and marketing, and they hire employees to handle the boat tours. I imagine Kai likes being out in the water, guiding the tourists. And I bet he is great at the job—he's so cheerful and calm and friendly. But it's not like Kai's parents *need* him to help out. Their business is thriving. They can afford to hire people. Working on his parents' boat should not keep him from following his own dreams.

"Are you sure that's what you want?" I ask quietly.

"Yes." Kai's tone is firm, unyielding. "I love it here. Why should I leave?"

"You don't have to leave. You could go to the University of Hawaii."

Kai waves his hand. "I want to be an artist. I don't need college."

"My mom always told me that college isn't only about what you learn in books. It's about expanding your horizons. Trying new things, meeting new people, venturing out into the world on your own. All of that would be amazing for your art. Not to mention, you could study business too, and you'd be able to help out your parents even more than you do already."

Kai's eyes bore into mine. "Why are you pushing me on this, T?"

"Because I'm not going to be around to push you later." I bite my lip, swallow the lump that's appeared in my throat. "I just—I'm sorry, I don't mean to fight about this."

"No," Kai says. "Go on. I want to hear what you think."

I look out at the falls. The rainbow is still there, but fainter than it was a few minutes ago. "I don't want you to regret it later," I begin. "Both my parents got their community college degrees but never went on to a four-year university. My mom always wished she had been able to. It's a gift, you know? To go to college. To keep learning and studying and growing." I take his hand, trace the lines on his palm with my fingers. "I know how much you love it here. And I can see why—it's paradise. But it's not the only paradise in this world. There are so many other incredible places to explore. The lake by my grandparents' house in Pennsylvania is its own paradise. I've never been to Paris, but I imagine the narrow cobblestone streets and the grand avenues and the Eiffel Tower are paradise too."

Kai nods. I sense that he really is listening to what I'm saying. That's all I can ask. He doesn't have to agree with me—I only want him to hear me out.

"I'd hate for you to stay here because you're playing it safe," I continue. "Because you're afraid to venture beyond what you already know and love. Do you want to know the truth?"

"What?"

"You're not just great here on the islands, Kai Kapule. You're great anywhere. You would be amazing in college."

A smile tugs one corner of his mouth. "You're just saying that because I'm your boyfriend."

I playfully squeeze his knee. "Only a little. Mostly I'm saying it because it's true."

A gecko darts out from the bushes, flashing neon green in the sunlight before disappearing again into the ferns.

"When it comes down to it, this is your life," I say. "This is one hundred percent your decision. No one else's."

I look into his eyes, to make sure he is listening. He is. His normally laughing eyes are serious.

"But if there's one thing I've learned this week, it's that life is too short to be dictated by fear. I read once that we regret most of all what we don't dare to try. I think that's true."

Kai looks down at our knees, side by side in a row. He wraps his arm around me. "I'm glad you finally dared to give me a try," he murmurs.

"Me too." I lean my head against his. "Best decision of my life."

After a few minutes, I stand up and stretch. The rainbow has disappeared. No sign of the gecko either. I'm tired, and hungry, and my feet ache.

"Can we go home now?" I ask.

"We're already home."

"What?" I laugh. "No we're not."

"Yes, we are," Kai says. His eyes are serious, like they were this morning, when he got down on one knee and asked me to be his girlfriend. "My home is wherever you are, T."

I hug him close because I don't know what to say. I feel the same way about him—and it's such a sweet sentiment—but his words make me unsettled. Because, in two days, I won't be here anymore.

I don't want to take his home away. I guess he'll have to find his own home apart from me. Because where I'm going, he can't come. And if he tries to follow me, I won't let him.

He won't try to follow me, will he?

Kai hoists the backpack onto his shoulders, and we start climbing the makeshift path through the ferns, back up the ravine to the lookout point, back to where we began.

"Can Tegan come?" Paulo asks. "To my championship game?"

We're sitting around the kitchen table, having dinner with Kai's family. By the time we made it back from Akaka Falls, it was early afternoon, and I was so exhausted that I fell asleep while Kai was taking a shower. He let me rest, only waking me up when dinnertime rolled around. I asked him to wake me up sooner next time. *If there is a next time.* I don't want to waste any more precious hours napping when this week is nearly over. Thinking about it makes anxiety spiderweb across my chest.

I swallow a lump of poi and meet Paulo's hopeful eyes. My heart squeezes. "I'm sorry, buddy. But I won't be here then. I have to go home on Sunday."

"Sunday? That's in, like, two days!" He looks at Kai, then at his mom and dad, with distraught eyes.

Mrs. Kapule reaches over and touches his shoulder. "It's okay, Paulo. Tegan will come back to visit again soon."

Paulo turns his pleading eyes on me. "Please, Tegan! Can't you stay a few more days? Please! I really want you to see my game!"

"Plane tickets are expensive," Mr. Kapule puts in. "You can't just change them willy-nilly. You'll understand when you're older."

"You can call Tegan and tell her all about your game. How about that?" Mrs. Kapule suggests.

Paulo crosses his arms, his lip thrust out in a pout. But he mumbles, "Okay."

"I wish I could stay longer, buddy," I say, swallowing another lump in my throat that has nothing to do with poi. "Believe me—if I could be there, I would."

"So tell us, Tegan," Mrs. Kapule says, obviously trying to change the subject. "What are your plans for the fall? Kai told us that you're going to Georgetown?"

I nod, feeling hollow inside. *Not anymore …*

"What a great school. Congratulations," Mr. Kapule puts in. "Maybe you'll rub off on Kai. We can only hope!" He laughs, but there's tension there—an old argument, unfinished. Kai shoots him daggers.

"Do you know what you're planning to major in?" Mrs. Kapule asks.

"Not exactly. I'm going in undecided." *I'm only eighteen! I thought I had all the time I needed to discover what I wanted to dedicate my life to. I thought I had nothing but time.*

I can tell Kai's parents are waiting for more. So, even though

215

I really don't want to talk about this, I elaborate. "I love math and science ... but it's so hard to choose a specific area. There are lots of things I'm interested in, you know?"

Kai's parents nod eagerly. "It's wonderful to have so much curiosity about the world," Mr. Kapule says. "That will serve you well, your whole life."

Under the table, Kai squeezes my hand. *Can he tell that I'm beginning to hyperventilate?* All of this discussion about my future—a future that is never going to happen—is twisting the knife in my chest, sharp and painful.

"This was delicious, Mom," Kai says. "Is it okay if Tegan and I are excused? I want to take her outside before the sunset disappears."

"Sure," she says. "Just drop your plates in the sink—that's fine."

"Nothing quite like a Hawaiian sunset, huh?" Mr. Kapule says to me.

"Nope," I agree, following Kai out the back door onto the patio. "Nothing beats this."

Kai leads me to the far end of the yard, where we sit in the grass under the mango tree, watching the colors soak into the sky.

"Sorry about that," he says.

"About what?"

"My parents, like, bombarding you with questions."

"It's okay. They were trying to show interest."

"They're always trying to bring everything around to college. Just to make sure I know, one more time, how disappointed they are in me."

"What was that between you and your dad? That part about me 'rubbing off' on you. You looked pissed."

Kai pokes in the grass with a stick. "He's still upset about me turning down CalArts."

"CalArts? Wait—you got into CalArts? Kai, that's huge!" It's an incredible art school outside of Los Angeles. He's been talking about their programs for as long as I can remember.

Kai shrugs with a half-smile. "I was wait-listed, but I found out a couple weeks ago that I got in. They sent a big packet in the mail and everything."

"That's amazing! Haven't you always wanted to go there? I thought CalArts was your dream!"

"It was. It *used* to be. But dreams can change."

"Yeah, I guess … but why did yours change?"

Kai rubs the stick between his palms. "I *barely* got in, T. It's proof that I don't belong there. I'd be at the bottom of the barrel. What if I can't handle it there? What if my artwork's not, you know, up to par? Plus, Los Angeles is far away, and most people already have their housing and roommate situations all figured out, so I'm behind the curve. It's easier to stay here and stick with what I've been planning to do."

Two birds fly above us, silhouetted against the cotton-candy clouds. I drop back on my elbows, watching them grow smaller and smaller in the distance. I don't say anything.

After a couple minutes of silence, Kai groans and hugs his knees. "Okay, Tegan. Just come out and say it."

"What? It sounds like you've already made up your mind. Does it matter what I say?"

"Yes, it does."

"I think you already know what I'm going to say."

"Please, get it out in the open. I want to hear it."

"Bullshit," I say. "That's my response to everything you said. It's all complete and utter bullshit. You're building up these walls of excuses because you're scared. And I understand being scared, Kai. Believe me. Change can be terrifying. But you know what? Change can also be exhilarating and eye-opening and wonderful. This is the perfect opportunity for you! Passing it up because of housing assignments or wait-lists or whatever other bullshit excuse you decide to use is—it's the worst thing I've ever heard. Letting go of your dream like this is a total slap in the face to your enormous talent. It's not who you are, Kai. You're braver than this. You don't give up so easily."

Kai's eyes are wide. I buzz with red-hot energy. I take the stick from him and begin digging in the grass, simply because it's something to do with my hands.

A few moments pass. I'm not sure what Kai is feeling. Angry? Attacked? Defensive? I study the grass, unwilling to look at him. I've said my piece. Now it's his turn to talk.

He puts his palm on my back, a gentle warmth through my thin T-shirt. "I hear you," he says softly. "I'll think about it. Okay? I'll think about it."

He wraps his arm around me. I sit back, letting myself lean into him. I'm still upset about what he said. But it's not my decision. *It's his choice. It's his life. Not mine.*

"Not all of us get to go to college," I murmur. "My parents never did. And now I won't. I was really excited about Georgetown, you know."

"I know. That's why you got on the train instead of coming here."

"That was an excuse. That was my own bullshit."

Kai laughs. Then he squeezes my shoulder. "Let's not think about the past anymore. Let's focus on tomorrow. Remember what I said back at Akaka Falls?"

I rack my brain, trying to remember the details of our conversation. "No ... "

"Tomorrow, I have a surprise for you," he says with a wink. "And I think you're really gonna like it."

dear t,

it only took 3 years of real life and 5 days of dream life, but i did it. i finally did it. in my dream last night, i asked you to be my girlfriend. and you said yes. now if only that could happen in real life. when you make it through this, t, i promise i'm going to stop beating around the bush in phone conversations that we can both pretend later never happened. i'm going to get down on one knee, take your hand in mine, and ask you to be my girlfriend. and hopefully you'll say yes. but either way, i need to ask the important questions instead of putting them off for later. i need to stop making excuses for myself.

that was a theme of my dream last night too. you always know how to call me out on my bs, and your dream self is no different. she is fierce. in the dream, you asked me about my plans for the future and why i'm not going to college. and i didn't have a good answer. you could see right through my lines about wanting to keep working at the tiki room, wanting to stay and help out my parents. you knew they were just excuses. when you found out about CalArts, you guessed the real reason i'm turning it down: i'm afraid. here, i'm a big fish in a small pond. it's familiar, and comfortable, and i don't need to really push myself. CalArts is a wide-open terrifying huge-ass pond, and i'm worried that if i go there, i'll drown. what if i don't make it? what if i'm not good enough? what if i don't have what it takes?

the truth is, it's not that i want to stay here in kona forever. but leaving and coming home with my tail between my legs would be so much worse than never leaving at all.

at least, that's what i used to think. now, i'm not so sure. what's that famous line from that famous poem? "'tis better to have loved and lost than never to have loved at all." i agree. it's infinitely better to have loved you (even if you don't love me back) than to have never loved you. and as far as losing you, that's not an option. okay, t?

when i woke up this morning, there was this loud voice in my head, insisting: go to her. go. go. go. so guess what? i went online and bought a plane ticket, and i messaged your mom so she knows i'm coming. i was surprised when she wrote back right away. she thanked me and said you would want me there, and she asked for my flight number so your dad can come pick me up from the airport.

so i'll be there soon. i'll see you tomorrow. don't let go. keep fighting.

love, kai

SATURDAY

*D*eep, pillowy darkness. A steady beeping. Voices. *"Tegan." Is that my mom? "Teacup." Mom! Mom, I'm right here! I try to reach out to her, but I can't move a muscle. I try to open my eyes, but I can't escape the darkness.*

I wake up reaching for my mom. My hand grazes Kai's bare stomach, smooth and warm. With his eyes still closed, he grabs my hand and brings it to his smiling lips. A good-morning kiss. I'm going to miss waking up with him to a brand-new day. *Or will I? Do dead people actually miss being alive? Do they miss the people from their lives?*

I shake my morbid thoughts away. "What's the surprise?" I ask.

He laughs. "Good morning to you too."

"C'mon, what is it? I can hardly take this suspense! You know how much I love surprises."

"Yep. That's why I'm not telling you."

He pulls me on top of him, and his lips meet mine, and I forget about surprises for a little while.

Since Kai won't tell me where we're going, I decide to bring my floral suitcase along rather than trying to pack a smaller bag. Even though I don't know the rules of this dream world / alternate reality / wherever this is, my suitcase seems to be magical. Filled with things I need that I don't remember purchasing. I keep hoping that some new clue will appear when I open the lid. A secret key? A message from my mom? It's doubtful—I don't think that's the way the suitcase works—but it doesn't hurt to hope.

"Should we bring snacks for the road?" I ask Kai. My mom is a big car-snack person, so I always associate road trips with snacks. The only reason I didn't bring any snacks on our trip to Akaka Falls yesterday was that I knew we'd be stopping for breakfast.

"Sure," Kai says with a bemused expression. "Good thinking."

He hands me an insulated lunch bag, and I fill it with a couple of apples, sliced cheese and crackers, and a bag of trail mix. Kai slips in a package of something sugarcoated and rainbow hued.

"Are you stealing Paulo's candy?" I tease. For as long as I've known him, Kai has been obsessed with gummy candy.

"You better be nice, or I won't share any with you," Kai teases back.

"You're right," I admit, weaseling a neon-blue gummy shark out of the bag and popping it into my mouth. "These things are pretty addicting."

"Wait till you try the sour rainbow belts," Kai says. "They'll blow your mind."

We pile into his Jeep and make our way down the street. I inhale the salty sea breeze, savoring the warm sun brushing my skin through the window. One word resounds in my head in a loop, no matter how much I try to push it away: *Tomorrow, Tomorrow, Tomorrow …*

We've only driven a few minutes when Kai pulls off the main highway. I know exactly where we are: the parking lot for the resort. The same place we parked that first night, after our date at The Blue Oasis.

"What are we doing here?" I ask.

"Follow me," Kai says, opening his door and stepping outside.

Maybe he has to pick something up. Or maybe he wants to go to the beach again. I take his hand, and we walk together toward the fancy tiled entrance to the hotel.

Kai leads us straight into the main lobby. Open-aired and high-ceilinged, it feels like stepping inside a palace, with a panoramic view of the sparkling blue ocean below. Kai strides over to the check-in desk. I trail behind, slightly dazzled by my surroundings. This hotel is even larger and more impressive than I remember from when I stayed here three years ago.

When I reach Kai's side, he's already in conversation with the receptionist behind the desk. It doesn't take long for me to realize that he's not asking for directions or booking some excursion package for us. He's paying for a room.

A hotel room. For us. For tonight.

I grab his hand and pull him aside.

"Sorry, can you hang on a moment?" he says to the woman behind the desk.

"Kai," I whisper urgently. "This place is super expensive."

"I know," he says.

"You don't need to do this."

He smiles. "I know. I *want* to do this."

"I don't need some grand gesture from you."

"It's not a grand gesture. I've been working a lot. I have some money saved up. This is how I want to spend a little of my money."

I tug at his hand. "I don't need a fancy hotel room. I would be just as happy crashing in your bedroom tonight."

"Please, T. Please stay here with me. Please let me pretend."

I look at him quizzically. *Pretend? Pretend what? That I'm not going to die?*

"I booked a room here," Kai explains, "because, just for one day, I want to be a kid with you again. I want to run around the hotel grounds and splash in the pool and eat Popsicles until our tongues turn into rainbows. And I also want to be an adult with you, staying in a fancy hotel room and wearing those fluffy hotel robes and eating breakfast together on the terrace tomorrow morning. I want to get a taste of that future with you."

I bite my lip. "I want all of that too," I whisper.

"Okay then, it's settled." Kai strides back over to the check-in desk.

I hurry after him. "Let me pay for half. We can split it."

"I have a better idea." Kai hands me one of the room keys. "Let's stay here again sometime in the future. How about … a year from now. You can pay for our room that time. Okay?"

I can't decide whether it's more or less painful to make believe like this—to imagine that my life will continue on beyond this week. *But if Kai wants to pretend, I can pretend. For him.*

"Okay," I promise. "It's a date. Oh, and Kai? One more thing."
He looks at me.

I put my hands on my hips. "We definitely did *not* need road trip snacks for this surprise."

He winks. "You know I can't resist any excuse for gummy candy."

Kai pushes open the door to our hotel room, and my breath catches. It is like stepping into a dream. Completely different from the rooms I remember sharing with my parents. Those rooms were nice, but in a regular-hotel-room way: a little cramped, with narrow aisles between the beds and not much space to store your luggage. This room is huge, actually composed of multiple rooms—there's a separate living space with two couches and a giant TV, and a kitchenette with a full fridge and stovetop. On the granite counter, I spot a plate of chocolate-covered strawberries.

"What are these doing here?" I walk over to inspect them.

Kai shrugs, smiling. "I guess they're a gift from the management."

"Why would they give us a gift?" There's a card with a picture of the resort on the front. I flip it open.

Happy honeymoon!
Best wishes for many blissful years ahead.

"Honeymoon!" I exclaim. "Kai, what did you do?"

"I *may* have stretched the truth a *little* bit so we could get a room upgrade." His smile is the same smile from when we were kids and he would sneak extra towels from the resort down to the beach.

"I can't believe you would do that! It's totally lying!"

Kai wraps his arms around my waist. "Please let me pretend," he says softly. "All right?"

My indignation falls away as I remember Kai on bended knee the other morning. I guess this is the closest we'll ever get to a honeymoon.

"All right," I say, and then, to prove that I really am okay with this, I pick up a strawberry and take a bite. The chocolate melts on my tongue, and the sweet juice slides down my chin.

We roll our suitcases into the bedroom. Soft yellow walls, crisp white sheets, a vase of fresh plumeria on the end table. Kai opens the sliding glass door, revealing a private patio. I kick off my sandals and fall backward onto the enormous bed—yes, it is just as soft and comfortable as it appears. Before long, Kai joins me. We both scoot up so our heads rest on the pillows, turning toward each other like two halves of a cutout heart.

"So, what should we do first?" I ask.

His hand finds my hip. "Well, we could go snorkeling. Or search for the Popsicle cart. Or walk on the beach and look for shells. Or splash in the pool and put all the little kids to shame."

"That all sounds fun. I should go change into my swimsuit."

"Okay. Me too."

Neither of us moves.

I am aware of the loud beating of my heart, echoing in my ears. Kai's eyes drink me in. I see so much love in his eyes when he looks at me. He's always looked at me this way.

Butterflies dance in my belly. I feel excited and ready. Not just my body; my mind and my heart are ready too. I lean in and brush my lips against his, knowing exactly what I want.

Kai must taste the urgency in my kisses. When I reach down and touch the zipper on his shorts, he pulls away.

"Are you sure, T?" he asks. His voice is husky. "I never want to pressure you. This isn't what this is about—the hotel room, I mean—we don't have to—"

"I know." I pull him down toward me. "And I'm sure. I'm ready. All this time, I've been waiting for you, Kai. Waiting for us to happen. Even though I didn't admit it to myself. Does that make any sense?"

Kai nods. "Perfect sense. I've been waiting for you too."

"I love you."

"I love you." Then his eyes slowly widen, and he smacks his forehead. "Crap. This is embarrassing. I totally, um, forgot to bring ... "

Condoms. I remember the white paper bag from the clinic. *Where did I put that?* I picture it tucked somewhere in between my dresses and sweaters. I'm grateful that I brought my entire suitcase with me today.

I sit up and scramble off the bed. "Hang on. I think I have one."

"You do?" Kai sounds shocked. "You brought condoms from home? You really were secretly in love with me, weren't you? Or else you just couldn't resist my sexy charms."

I laugh, rummaging through my suitcase. "Both. Er, neither. I didn't bring this from home." *Ah-ha!* I pull out the folded white paper bag and open it up to reveal a small chocolate bar, a pamphlet on safe sex, a travel pack of aspirin, and three wrapped condoms.

I rip off one of the condoms and toss it at Kai. "They gave me this 'women's health packet' back at the clinic, the first day I was here. So don't thank me. You can thank Aunt Sarah for this."

Kai squeezes his eyes shut. "I'm going to pretend you didn't bring my aunt into this moment right now."

"Sorry. Where were we?" I climb back onto the bed, stretching out beside him. My bare feet brush his shins.

"My sexy charms," Kai says with a grin.

"Oh, yes, right. Of course. Irresistible."

We smile goofily at each other. Before this week, I never realized that real-life romance isn't like the movies. Things don't have to be so serious and intense all the time. You can have intensely serious feelings for someone and be silly with them. You can go from making out to laughing, and back to making out, and that's okay.

Actually, it's better than okay. It's perfect.

Perfect. I've always wanted my first time to be perfect. But I don't exactly know what I'm doing, and I get the sense that Kai is in the same boat. He slips down the straps of my tank top, and we kiss for a solid minute while he tries, and fails, to unhook my bra. Eventually, I smile and reach around to help him out.

"Thank you!" he says with evident relief. "That thing is like a bank vault!"

"I thought the Hulk could bust through bank vaults," I tease.

Kai swallows. "I guess Hulk's a little nervous."

There's vulnerability in his eyes—no masks, no mirrors, no pretense. He's all in. I'm all in too. I feel safe and known and whole. There is so much love here between us. We'll fumble through this together, and it will be imperfectly perfect.

Andrea says that she doesn't get why people make such a huge deal over sex. She says we're just a collection of body parts, and it's really not all that complicated. It is true that I've never been as aware of my body as I am right now. Kai makes a slow trail of kisses from my neck down to my belly button, and goose bumps flutter across my skin. I'm hyperaware of my breathing, my flushed cheeks, his hands on my breasts, the ache between my legs. It's like my body has taken over control, and my brain has quieted down, my thoughts disappearing—for once—into the background.

Only not quite. I'm not just a collection of body parts, and neither is Kai. What's happening *is* complicated, and it *is* a big deal. It matters that Kai's smile lights me up inside and that his eyes make me feel completely seen. It matters that he knows my favorite shave ice flavor and what the scar on my knee came from and that I secretly love Hallmark movies and all of my other details. It matters that I feel a little nervous and a little scared, but, mostly, what I feel right now is trust. I trust him with my whole being. That matters a lot.

"Are you sure?" Kai asks one last time, right before, and I know that I could turn back now—I could change my mind, tell him that I don't want this—and it would be okay. He would understand.

But I am sure. I do want this.

"Yes," I whisper.

Kai's eyes find mine. I don't think I've ever felt so connected to another person. I'm naked in more ways than one. My walls have all been stripped away, and what's left is me, just me, at my essence.

"Are you okay?" Kai asks. "Is this okay?"

"Yes." I kiss him, and he kisses me back. We move together, forward and back, forward and back, and all those clichés are right, it is sort of like waves gently rocking a boat. It is both simpler and bigger than I thought it would be, both ordinary and extraordinary, both completely normal and completely amazing.

And I don't feel scared. Not at all.

Afterward, Kai collapses on top of me, and I wrap my arms and legs around him, wanting to keep him this close a little bit longer. Eventually, he rolls over, and we curl up side by side.

"Whoa," he says.

"Whoa," I say back.

Kai's hand cups my knee, his fingers gently tracing my scar. Wait. *My scar?*

I sit up and hug my knee to my chest, bending down to examine it. My scar is definitely back, the familiar dimple winking at me as if it never left. I turn my wrist, my fingers brushing the delicate skin under my arm. Yep—that scar is back too. *What is going on?*

Part of me is relieved to see my scars again. It was eerie to have them gone, like bits of my life had been erased. But another part of me is dismayed that my scars have returned. Maybe this is happening because I'm so close to The End.

"What's wrong?" Kai asks, his brow furrowed.

"Nothing. It's fine." I shove my arm toward him. "My scars are back. They completely vanished all week, and now suddenly they reappear. What do you think it means?"

Kai's voice is hopeful. "Maybe it means we're not in the dream world anymore. Maybe somehow we made it back to reality … " His voice trails off, but we both know the words he's not saying: *Which would mean tomorrow isn't the Last Day.*

I look down at my chest; the tattoo is still there. Only a little bit of sand remains in the top half of the hourglass. Still, it's worth a shot …

I slip my T-shirt and shorts back on. I don't care what universe this is, it seems wrong to call my mother when I'm naked in bed with a boy. As I dial the familiar ten digits, my heart hammers in my chest. *Pick up, pick up, pick up, pick up …*

I have never wanted anything more in my life than I want my mom to answer the phone in this moment. I want it so badly, and I can imagine her voice so clearly, it feels as if I can will it into existence.

But the phone rings. And rings. And rings. That same hollow ringing.

I count eight rings, and am just about to hang up, when—

"Hello."

I'm so startled to hear her voice, I nearly drop the phone.

"Mom! Mom, it's me—"

"This is Marie Rossi. I'm sorry I missed your call."

Not Mom. Voice mail.

"If you leave your name and number, I'll be happy to return your message as soon as possible. Thank you!"

There's a mechanical *beeeeeep.*

I fumble for words. "Hi, Mom, it's me. I'm in Hawaii right now, with Kai. We're having a great time. It's so beautiful here. I really miss you, though. I can't wait to come home and see you." There's the lump again, filling up my throat. "I guess I mostly wanted to say thank you, Mom. Thank you for everything you've done for me. You're the best mom I could imagine." The tears are burning my eyes now. I wipe them away with the back of my hand. "Oh, and Mom? I love you. I love you infinity. Okay. Goodbye-for-now." I hang up the phone and let it drop onto the bed.

"Voice mail." I sigh. "This whole week, I've never gotten her voice mail. What do you think it means?"

Kai shrugs. "I don't know, T. Maybe it's a good thing. Maybe she'll call back! Or you can try calling her again later."

"Yeah, okay." But in my heart, I know she isn't going to call back. And I'm willing to bet that I won't get her voice mail if I try calling again. I think it was a one-time gift from the universe. A chance to say my last words. To leave nothing left unsaid. I'm pretty sure that

the voice mail, and my scars, are simply more proof of what I don't
want to believe:

Tomorrow is Sunday.

Sunday is my Last Day.

It's almost time to say Goodbye.

Not Goodbye-for-Now. Goodbye-for-Ever.

"Watermelon, pineapple, or mango?" Kai asks.

"What about cherry? I always get cherry."

Kai looks pained. "The man said they don't have cherry anymore."

"Oh, okay. That's fine. I'll, um, try … mango."

"Mango. Great. Be right back!"

Kai heads toward the other side of the pool, where the Popsicle
cart has set up camp for the afternoon. I stretch my legs, savoring the
sunlight filtering in through the trees above our lounge chairs. We
found the perfect mix of shade and sun. Behind us, the ocean waves
thump the shoreline. In front of us, the bright-blue pool sparkles.
Right now the pool is crowded; Kai and I are hoping it might clear
out in an hour, during the lunch rush. I watch a group of laughing
kids spray water guns at each other. A few grown-up couples float
around on inflatable rafts, hands linked to keep them from drifting
apart.

I'm embarrassed by my disappointment that they no longer have
cherry Popsicles. What was I expecting? It's been, like, a decade since
Kai and I got Popsicles as kids. We're lucky they still sell Popsicles
here at all.

What was it my grandma used to say? *Things change. Change is the only constant of life.*

"One mango Popsicle, my lady." Kai bows with a flourish, holding out my wrapped Popsicle like an offering.

"Thank you, kind sir."

Kai settles on the lounge chair beside me. We unwrap our Popsicles and watch the kids splash in the pool and the adults float around together. It is like we are watching a tableau of our past selves and our future selves. The mango is sweet on my tongue, less tart than the cherry flavor was. But it tastes good.

Despite what I said to Kai yesterday—about how he should embrace new experiences and leave the island and give CalArts a try—the truth is, I've never really liked change. I guess it's one more thing I've been secretly afraid of, and a big reason why I never let my feelings for Kai emerge. Maybe because of my grandma's death or my parents' divorce, I associated change with negativity. Things are humming along great, and then a big change happens and shatters everything to pieces.

But something I've realized this week is that change can actually be wonderful. I mean, I knew that on some level—I was excited for the change of going off to college. When it came to my dreams and goals, I embraced change because it meant that I was moving forward. But in my personal life? No, thank you. Change was moving backward. Change meant loss. I didn't like moving into a new place with Mom, while Dad got a separate apartment. I didn't like any of Andrea's boyfriends, because she suddenly had zero time to spend with anyone else.

Then this week happened, and I guess I'm changing my mind about change. Even when your life is already humming along great, big change can come along and make things not worse, but better. Kai and I were awesome as friends. But being in love with him is a million times sweeter than what we had before. I used to spend so much energy frantically protecting our friendship boundary because I was terrified that things would fall apart if we went any further. *Oh, past self. Loving him is way worth the risk of things falling apart.* I know that now.

Even if change doesn't make things better, it can at least give you some variety. Like this mango Popsicle. I still like cherry best, but this one is a close second.

"What's your joke say?" Kai asks after we both swallow our last bites.

I turn my Popsicle stick sideways. "Huh. I don't think they're printing jokes anymore. It looks more like … advice."

"Interesting. So what advice does the universe have for you, T?"

I read the stick aloud: "Make each day a masterpiece."

Kai smiles. "We've been doing that this week. A masterpiece week."

"Yeah. It sure has been." On the pool deck, a little boy chases a little girl. They cannonball into the water, one right after the next. "What does yours say?" I ask.

"Fortune favors the bold," Kai reads. "I think I've read that quote somewhere."

"It's Virgil. One of my favorites." I nudge him with my elbow. "Maybe it's telling you to go to CalArts."

"Maybe." Kai doesn't take the bait. Instead, he sighs. "I wish I'd been bolder before this week. With you."

"I wish I'd been bolder too. But we can't go back and change the past. All we have is this moment." Now I'm talking in Popsicle-stick quotes.

I reach over and grab his hand. He squeezes my palm. We sit in our lounge chairs, holding hands like the couples on the rafts in the pool. Not wanting to drift apart.

"Hey, T?" Kai says after a little while. "Can I ask you something?"

I shift my body toward him. "Of course. Shoot."

"What if this whole week is some crazy dream? What if, come Monday morning, you wake up in your own bed, and you're back in your old life—we're both back in our old lives—and it's like this week never happened? We're still in the middle of that stupid fight, not talking, and we just ... go our separate ways?"

"That would never happen, Kai. We wouldn't stay in that fight forever. You're my best friend. I couldn't stand to lose you." I bite my lip, regretting my choice of words. After all, Kai is going to lose me. Tomorrow.

"You're my best friend too. But at the time of our fight—" He shakes his head, looking down at the plastic weave of his lounge chair. "It was getting so painful to be, you know, *just* friends with you. I don't know how much longer I'd be strong enough. To keep pushing down my feelings like that."

I remind myself that none of these hypotheticals matter. Because I'm not going to wake up in my own bed on Monday morning. I died in a train accident. Tomorrow is my Last Day. But still, panic hits my gut to think that, in another world, Kai and I might have lost our friendship. That would have been the capstone experience for my change-is-always-bad philosophy.

"Kai, look at me."

He meets my eyes. I can tell that what I say next will matter a lot to him. I wonder how long he was thinking about this hypothetical before he brought it up.

"Kai, I love you. I couldn't stand to be just friends with you either. Not after everything that's happened this week."

"But that's exactly it, Tegan. What if you don't remember any of this? What if this week is a dream that fades away to nothingness as soon as you wake up?"

"That wouldn't happen. Of course I would remember." *I would remember. I would remember.* I think about waking up in the lava tubes on Monday, with no recollection of how I got there or what had happened. When trying to remember was like trying to read words on a blank piece of paper. What if Kai is right? What if I don't remember any of this? What if, in real life, I'm too scared to leap off that cliff into the unknown, and I never admit to myself that I love Kai, and our lives become two divergent paths wandering away from each other?

Is any of this even real at all? Does anything that's happened this week count?

Reality is a matter of perception, Okalani had said. *You perceive this to be real, so yes, it is real.*

A little girl wades into the pool wearing a snorkel mask. As I watch her duck her head below the water's surface, a new thought hits me. "Maybe it's like snorkeling," I offer. "Or riding a bike."

Kai's eyes are confused.

"What was it you said to me the other day, before we went snorkeling?" I ask. "When I was afraid that I had forgotten how to do it?"

Kai smiles. "I said, 'The body always remembers.'"

I lean over and kiss him softly. "The body always remembers. And my body would never forget this. Not in a million years. I'm sure of it."

Eventually, the pool does clear out a little, and Kai and I jump in and swim around, chasing each other like we used to do as kids. I wrap my legs around his waist, and he carries me like a monkey. We float on the rafts side by side. The water on my skin dries just in time for me to jump back in and get wet again. We eat hot dogs and curly fries. We people-watch from our spot in the shade. We apply and reapply sunscreen. We go snorkeling and see a lot of beautiful fish, but we don't find our sea turtle friend.

I hold tight to Kai's hand and to his smile, to our laughter, to the sunshine and the fresh breeze and the salty-air smell. I run my fingers through the soft grains of sand and think about how even if we lived for a billion moments, we would never have enough time to count it all.

The sun wheels through the sky. The light changes. The kids climb out of the pool, and the parents gather up towels and sand buckets and water wings. Daytime slips to afternoon slips to dusk.

Kai prods my foot. "Ready to go back to the room?"

"Not really. But I know we should."

"I made dinner reservations for tonight."

"You did?"

"But we don't have to go if you don't want to."

"No, I want to. Reservations! That's so sweet of you." I remember what his mom said on that first day. *He's never made reservations for anyone before.*

I stand up and wrap my towel around my waist. A truth about

life: sometimes it's time to head inside before you feel ready to leave the water.

Our hotel bathroom is bigger than my bedroom at home. There's a walk-in waterfall shower and a Jacuzzi tub. Fancy bath products are arranged on the counter between the sinks. I want to try them all.

Nothing compares to a long, hot shower after a day in the sun and the sand and the ocean. Under the stream of water, I close my eyes and try to imagine all of my worries running off my body and disappearing down the drain. It works a little bit.

Kai and I don the fluffy hotel robes and sit out on our private patio, polishing off the rest of the chocolate-covered strawberries. Then, already, it's time for dinner. I've decided to wear my red sundress, the same one I wore on our first date. There's a kind of poetry in it. Things are coming full circle. Reservations, a dinner date, butterflies in my stomach. So much has changed since that first night, and yet some things remain the same. Like this incredibly handsome guy, with his hair still wet from the shower, looking oh-so-grown-up in a button-down shirt and khaki slacks, a slow molasses smile spreading across his face when I step out of the bathroom and announce, "I'm ready!"

His eyes dance. He puts his hand on his chest like I'm lightning and he's been struck. "Man, T, that dress. You look stunning."

"You don't look half-bad yourself. I still can't get used to seeing you in pants."

Kai laughs and waggles his eyebrows.

"I mean, instead of shorts! I'm used to seeing you in *shorts!*" I throw a pillow at him.

He catches me around the waist and nuzzles my neck. We grab the room key and head off to dinner, two sort-of grown-up little kids out on their first last date.

Kai leads me down the path from our hotel room to the resort restaurant, nestled snugly against the cliff. The hostess escorts us to a table on the patio with a spectacular view of the ocean stretching as far and wide as the eye can see. The sun is sinking down, washing the sky in bright orange. *My next-to-last sunset. It's a beauty.*

"Have you been here before?" Kai asks.

I look around. "I can't remember. Maybe I came here with my parents, when I was little. Have you?"

"Only a few times—for big occasions. The last time wasn't that long ago, actually. My high school graduation. My parents made reservations here after the ceremony, to celebrate. Paulo tried to steal the saltshaker off the table." Kai tilts it toward me. The ceramic saltshaker is shaped like a seahorse. The pepper grinder, disappointingly, is a normal pepper grinder shape.

"We got all the way to the parking lot," Kai continues. "And suddenly, Paulo started crying. He pulled that saltshaker out of his pocket and explained that he'd wanted to take it home as a toy. But the poor kid was so racked with guilt, he didn't even make it off the property before he confessed! We took him back here, and he apologized to the manager, who was really nice. He said Paulo could take the saltshaker home as a souvenir, but Paulo didn't want to."

I rub my thumb over the ridges in the seahorse. "He's such a sweetheart. I wish I could see him grow up. He's gonna be a great guy, just like his brother."

Kai smiles. "You mean Theo?"

"Theo's a good kid too. I'm serious. You're a role model for both of them, Kai. They look up to you so much. Anyone can see that."

"Thanks, T. I'm far from perfect. But I try."

"They're lucky to have you." I set the saltshaker back down on the white tablecloth and rest my hand on top of Kai's. "Hey, will you apologize for me? To Paulo? Tell him I'm sorry to miss his soccer game."

"Of course I will. He'll understand."

For the rest of dinner, we don't talk much. Our silence is like a friendly dog—like Olina—curled up in a ball at our feet. I am so filled with emotion that I could overflow. I don't need to talk about anything. It's enough to simply sit here, drinking in the fading sunset, holding Kai's hand across the table. He orders the seafood pasta, and I choose the salmon. Every bite is perfection. I scrape my plate clean.

When the waitress comes with the dessert menu, I'm about to offer apologetic eyes and wave it away—*too much; too full; no, thanks!*—when something out of the corner of my eye catches my attention, and I change my mind.

Across the patio, a couple is sitting down to dinner. They are a little less pale than they were yesterday, and they're dressed up in nice clothes rather than hiking gear, but it is definitely them: the honeymooners who took our photo at Akaka Falls.

A memory sweeps in. *Wait a minute—I have been to this restaurant before.* It was the first time I came to Hawaii, ten years ago. My parents and I ate dinner here the day we arrived. We sat on the other side of the patio, facing the resort instead of the ocean. But I'm sure it was this place.

We'd had a long day of travel and sun, and I was tired. After we finished our meal and the waiter cleared away our plates, it took forever to get the bill. It was so hard to keep my eyes open. I was a little girl with a full belly who was up way past her East Coast bedtime.

Eventually, my dad flagged down the waiter and handed over his credit card without even seeing the bill. "I'm sure it's fine," he said. "I don't need to check it first."

"I'm sorry, sir, but I can't do that," the waiter said with a grin. "Your meal has already been taken care of."

I didn't understand the details at the time. But, later, my parents explained that a man dining at the restaurant had secretly paid for our meal as a random act of kindness. He told the waiter it was because we looked like a really nice family, enjoying a meal together. He requested that they wait to bring our bill until he left, so we did not get a chance to thank him or even meet him. But that added to the sense of magic. He could have been anyone, and so he was everyone. The whole world seemed a more generous place.

Years later, when my parents told me they were separating, I was angry. I clung to those half-remembered words from a stranger, brandishing them as evidence that a divorce wasn't possible. *A really nice family, enjoying a meal together. How could we have fallen so far? How did we get so lost? We had been a happy family. Hadn't we?* Somehow my parents had reached an impassable broken place, full of tense silences and bitter words, and by the time my dad moved out, everything had this air of inevitability.

But thinking about it now, the memory of that stranger's kindness doesn't make me sad. And my parents' divorce no longer makes me angry. It doesn't mean that the love we felt as a family was any less real or true. We *were* a really nice family, enjoying a meal together. And we still can be. If I got to do things over again, I would tell my parents, "No, I am not having two separate graduation parties. This is my big day, and all I want is to have dinner with the two of you, together. You are still my family."

In truth, the divorce was probably for the best. They both seem much happier now than they were in those final months, when they were fighting constantly. Maybe one day I'll understand everything better. And maybe one day they'll reach a truce—even a friendship.

I hope that I can watch them from Heaven, or wherever it is that I'm going after I leave this world. I want to see what happens next. Do they find their way through the mess together? Do they find a way not to hate each other anymore? I want to see how their story ends.

"What sounds good to you?" Kai asks, interrupting my thoughts. He holds up the dessert menu. "I'm pretty stuffed, so you should order what you want. I'll only have a bite or two."

"Maybe the chocolate lava cake?" I tell Kai what I'm planning to do.

He grins and says, "That sounds perfect." Then he gets a funny look on his face. "Tegan, no one else comes even close to you."

I think of Nadia, with her burgundy-streaked hair and dark-rimmed eyes, her artistic talents and kind bravery, and the way she gazed up at Kai like he was her favorite star in the night sky. I think of the millions of other girls out there, any one of whom Kai might meet in the future—here in Hawaii, out in Los Angeles, somewhere else in the wide-open world. I think of how much I'll miss him, and how much I want him to fall in love again. I don't want him to become a sad-eyed soul, clinging to my ghost.

I point my finger at him and make my tone very serious. "Kai Kapule, I expect more from you. Don't you go putting me up on a pedestal. I'm not perfect. I want you to remember me for all that I am. Yes, there are good things about me. But I'm a regular person, with flaws and insecurities and plenty of regrets. Remember me as, well, *me*. All of me. Okay?"

He nods. "Okay. But it's still true, what I said. No one else is like you."

Before I can reply, the waitress returns. I order the chocolate lava cake. "Not for us, though." I point to our honeymooner friends across the patio. "We'll pay for it now, and when the time comes for their dessert, will you please bring the cake to them? Just say … " I remember the card in our hotel room. "Best wishes for many blissful years ahead."

Instead of going back to our room, Kai announces that he has one more surprise. We walk across the beach to the more densely packed sand near the water's edge. At this hour, we are the only ones here. It is as if we are stepping back in time—or trying to step back in time—returning to Monday night, when Kai brought me here after The Blue Oasis. Farther down the beach, I spot the chaise lounges we slept on that night. They are covered with towels, waiting for morning.

Kai fiddles with his phone, and I can guess what he is searching for. The glow from his phone screen lights up his features: his straight nose, long eyelashes, strong cheekbones. The face of the boy I loved a long time ago, and the man who—I hope—will eventually learn to love someone else.

Kai tucks his phone into his shirt pocket, and soon the delicate ukulele melody winds its way into the night. "Magic by the Water." He lifts one hand in the air. "Miss Tegan Rossi," he says in a formal voice, "may I ask you for this dance?"

Please, T, his eyes say. *Please let me pretend.*

So I smile, playing along. "I would be honored, Mr. Kapule." I place my hand in his.

Kai pulls me close, wrapping an arm around my waist. I put my other hand on his shoulder. He smells like spicy cologne and hotel shampoo. Closing my eyes, I rest my temple against his cheek, and together we sway to the music. A breeze gently lifts the hem of my dress and plays with tendrils of my hair. Our feet shuffle a circle in the sand. I can hear the waves rolling in and receding, rolling in and receding. Goose bumps spring up on my arms. Kai's hand shifts on my back, drawing me closer.

Kai is trying to be romantic. Returning to slow dance on the beach is a super sweet gesture. The murmuring of the waves, the soft breeze, the gentle moonlight—in another world, all of this would be perfect.

But here, now, in this world … everything is wrong. I don't know how much longer I can make believe. I want to scream at him that we can't go back in time. This isn't Monday night, when the whole future seemed to stretch before us like a fresh swath of beach brushed clean by the tide. This is Saturday night. My Last Night. Our future is a beach littered with kelp and driftwood, half-smashed sandcastles and broken seashells. Relics of memories and regrets and might-have-beens. The tide is closing in, and no matter what I do, I can't escape it. Tomorrow, I'll be crushed against the rocks. And Kai wants to pretend the inevitable isn't happening.

My face is hot, and my heart is beating rapidly—I wonder if Kai can feel it through the thin fabric of my dress. The tears are building behind my eyes, and I can hear my blood pounding in my ears. I try to swallow, but it's no use.

Kai tucks a strand of hair behind my ear. "I love you," he whispers.

When I open my mouth to reply, the dam breaks. I mean to say, "I love you too." Instead, I let out a sob.

Kai pulls back. "Hey, hey. What's wrong? Are you okay?"

The music notes unfurl delicately into the night, but we are no longer dancing. The breeze picks up, flinging sand against my bare legs. It stings. The sobs rear up inside of me like an unstoppable, unknowable force. I pull away from Kai and cover my face with my hands. My whole body shakes. I can't remember the last time I cried like this. Not at the lava tubes. That was gentle and delicate compared to this. A desperate, animal sadness keens out of my lungs. I've never sobbed like this in front of Kai. I didn't even cry on the phone when I told him about my parents getting divorced. I always told myself that crying was for Other Girls; I was too strong to cry. When the world knocked me down, I would brush myself off and Get Over It, as quickly as possible, with no drama. Now a lifetime of stored-up tears are erupting out of me.

"It's okay," Kai says, rubbing my back. "Let it out. It's okay, T."

I had thought he might be scared of my unrestrained crying. But he's not. He doesn't seem fazed at all. *I don't need to hide from him. Why did I used to think I needed to hide?* I'm flooded with such strong love, it makes me cry even harder.

Kai's hand on my back is a warm, gentle presence, letting me know I'm not alone.

Gradually, the flow of tears slows, and I'm able to catch my breath. I wipe my face with my fingers. My eyes are hot and puffy. The music from Kai's phone has completely stopped. All I can hear is the heartbeat of the ocean waves against the shore, and my own heartbeat in my ears gradually calming down to a normal rate.

Kai kisses my forehead. "You want to go back to the room?"

"Not yet. Can we stay here a bit longer?"

"Of course."

My legs are still a little shaky, so I plop down right there on the beach, folding my legs beneath me. The sand is cold against my bare skin. Kai sits down next to me, wrapping his arm around my shoulders.

"I'm sorry for bringing you back here," he says. "It was a bad idea."

"No, no—it was a lovely idea. It was so sweet of you."

"I should have realized it would be painful. I know—" He clears his throat and digs his bare toes into the sand. "I know that we can't go back, T. As much as I want to."

"We both want to. Believe me, that is my biggest wish."

He leans his head against mine. We stare out at the dark waves.

"Thanks for pretending with me today," Kai says softly.

I thought I had already squeezed out every single teardrop, but new tears brim in my eyes. My words come out in a whisper. "I can't believe it all went by so quickly."

Back at the room, I try calling my mom once more. No answer. Not even voice mail. The phone rings and rings and rings, echoing through my mind, taunting me.

Tomorrow. Tomorrow. Tomorrow ...

I don't want to go to sleep. But I don't especially want to stay awake either. My body is wrung out, and my spirit is exhausted. Mostly, I crave normality. My biggest wish is to have my normal life back. I curl up under the covers with Kai because it's the normal thing to do.

"Good night," Kai says.

Your last "good night," my brain thinks.

"Good night," I whisper.

It doesn't seem possible that I'll ever be able to fall asleep.

It doesn't seem possible that I'll ever be able to let go of this life.

Maybe that's what sleeping prepares us for. That liminal moment between wakefulness and dreaming, when you have to relinquish control and let yourself drift over to the other side. Maybe that's what it's like to cross over from life into death.

Soon, I will know.

dear t,

i'm not gonna lie. it is scary as hell to see you in that hospital bed, hooked up to all those tubes and beeping monitors. it breaks my heart to see you like this. so still.

but i'm glad i came. as soon as i walked

into your hospital room, i immediately knew that this is where i'm supposed to be.

i brought along a snowflake i carved for you out of wood. it's a new thing i've been working on for the tiki room: wooden snowflake ornaments. i was planning to give this one to you for your birthday, but i finished it early. so i asked your mom if i could hang it in your window. she said yes, i should. i like to imagine you opening your eyes and seeing that snowflake. would you know it's from me?

my dream last night was the most real-seeming one yet. we were staying in a hotel room together at the fancy resort. just us two. it was the best dream i've ever had. this morning, i swore i could smell you on my pillowcase. crazy, huh?

but i woke up from the dream with this enormous sadness welling up inside me. uncontrollable. just, like, this huge wave of despair. i can't shake the feeling that it was my last dream of you. that you saved the best for last. that it was your way of saying goodbye.

you always said you were horrible at goodbyes. so, i'm begging you, tegan—don't say it. say hello instead. open your eyes and say hello. i'll be here, waiting for you with my sexy and charming smile. that's an inside joke, from my dream last night. i really want to tell you about it. i want it to become a real inside joke between us.

i can't bear saying goodbye to you. not in my dreams. certainly not in real life.

please, don't say goodbye, t.

i love you.
—kai

SUNDAY

I'm underwater, so far down below the surface that no light reaches me. A steady beeping. I'm so cold. My whole body aches. I look around for the mantas, but I don't see them. I don't see anyone. I'm alone. Forever. My chest constricts in panic. Wait. I don't want this. I—

I wake up in a panic, shivering, tangled in the sheets. The room is dark, the curtains pulled closed, and it takes me a few seconds to remember where I am. *The hotel room. Kai.* My relief to see him there, sleeping beside me in the dim morning light, is pummeled away by the crushing realization that today is Sunday. My Last Day. *There will be no more waking up like this.*

The bedside clock reads 5:18. I nestle my body against Kai's warm back, hugging my arms around him, breathing him in. I wish I could fall back asleep and hold him forever. I wish I could freeze this minute on the clock so we could stay like this. I wish that time wasn't so merciless, so fiercely intent on marching forward, forward, forward.

But I don't have the luxury of falling back asleep. There is so little time left. I kiss Kai's back and gently extricate myself from the bedcovers. Then I slip on my fleece pullover, tiptoe into the bathroom, and ease the door shut. I think back to that night so many nights ago, when I was staying in a hotel room like this one, and I snuck into the bathroom to get ready before I crept out to meet Kai at the lava tubes. I remember being so nervous. I didn't know what to expect. In some ways, it was a reckless decision. A giant leap of faith.

I'm so glad I took that leap.

Lines from a poem we read in a long-ago English class flit through my mind: *'Tis better to have loved and lost than never to have loved at all.* I wish I could remember who wrote those words. I never realized, before this moment, how agonizingly true they are. Saying goodbye to Kai is one of the hardest things I've ever had to do. But the joy of loving him is worth the mountain of pain to leave him. Given the choice to make again, I would venture out to those lava tubes every time. I would keep choosing him and choosing him and choosing him. Even knowing how it all has to end, I would still take the risk of loving him. I only wish I had been brave enough to jump off that cliff sooner.

I flick on the light and pull the notepaper from my pocket. I have a letter to write.

You know that final-day-of-vacation feeling? Your trip is quickly coming to a close, and you are uncomfortably straddling two worlds:

the magical, relaxing vacation one and the everyday-life one waiting for you on the other side of the calendar page. Soon, you'll be heading to the airport. Soon, it will be back to reality. You try to soak up every last minute of vacation time, but it's already tainted with the knowledge that it will be gone before you know it. Like the last dregs of Kona coffee—still there, in the bottom of your cup, but it won't be long before you swallow those final sips and the taste disappears from your tongue.

Today is like the last day of vacation. Only a million times worse.

Kai and I make a valiant effort to pretend like this vacation isn't ending. After I finish writing his letter, I climb back into bed and snuggle up with him. Somehow I fall back asleep, a shallow dreamless sleep, and then Kai is waking me up with kisses, and then we're making love again, and my mind goes there—*the Last Time, this is the Last Time*—and when the tears flood my eyes, I tell Kai it's because I love him so much. Which is the truth, and yet also a lie. Because he doesn't know what I'm planning to do later.

Afterward we shower and get dressed and head out, walking hand in hand down the hall to the open-air veranda, where the hotel serves breakfast. We sit at our table looking out at the glimmering blue ocean, and Kai orders scrambled eggs, and I order the macadamia nut pancakes with homemade coconut syrup, just like I remember from my childhood, and when they come, I swallow bite after bite of sticky sweetness, even though I'm not hungry, not at all. I smile at Kai and whisper, "Your pancakes are better."

After breakfast we still have some time—checkout isn't until noon—so we change into our swimsuits and splash around in the pool. We're surrounded by children and families, but I feel entirely alone. Time is somehow moving in slow motion and fast-forward at once. My smile is brittle, cracking across my face. I feel like I've been hollowed out. I feel too much to feel anything at all.

In the pool, Kai lifts me in his arms like I'm a damsel in distress, swinging me around. "I am the HULK!" he shouts, so enthusiastically that some kids glance over with curious eyes, wondering if this is a new game they can join. I reach up and kiss him, which makes the kids look away in boredom.

"Hulk love you," Kai grunts.

"I love Hulk," I say, feeling a sudden rush of desire to tell him everything. But I don't. I can't. If he knew, he would try to stop me.

Kai thinks we're both going back to his house tonight after the manta snorkel. We'll curl up in his bed together and talk. Or we'll just lie there quietly, listening to each other's breathing. Maybe he thinks we'll stay up all night like that, until eventually morning comes, and the last grain of sand trickles through my hourglass tattoo, and ... what? A blinding white light? Oblivion? Or maybe he thinks we'll drift off to sleep together, and I simply won't wake up. The End.

What that sounds like to me is a long, drawn-out, heartbreaking goodbye. And Kai knows I'm terrible at goodbyes. I can't bear the thought of him waking up on Monday morning to find me gone. Or, even worse—what if he wakes up to my still, silent body beside him? No. I refuse to put him through that. I remember what he said, back when we first reconnected in the lava tubes, about putting his dog Makana to sleep. About how he couldn't escape that final image of his beloved dog as a lifeless shell. That is not how I will leave Kai. No way. I want to choose how our last goodbye unfolds.

So I haven't told him my real plan. My secret plan.

The truth is, I'm not coming back from the manta snorkel.

I'll be the last one out in the water, the last one clinging to the raft.

And then I'll disappear. I'll let myself sink down, down, down into the water. Into the land of the manta rays that I so desperately yearned to visit as a little girl. I guess dying means I'll finally get my wish.

It will be best, for both of us. It will be easier to simply slip away.

After checking out of the hotel, we walk around downtown Kona and hit up Kai's favorite local Mexican restaurant for a lunch of fresh fish tacos. We laugh about old inside jokes and memories from when we were kids. Both of us carefully avoid mentioning anything about the future, about what is coming—the train barreling toward us, unavoidable. On the drive back to Kai's parents' house, we lapse into silence. I'm grateful to stare out the window and let the fragile smile fall from my face. *Only a handful of hours left now.*

In Kai's room, I rummage through my floral suitcase for what I'll need for the manta ray snorkel: bathing suit, shorts, T-shirt. The tour guides will provide wet suits and snorkel masks. I duck into the bathroom to change. My reflection stares back at me with numb acceptance. The sand in my hourglass tattoo has nearly run out. I look completely different from the giddy-eyed girl who twirled in front of this mirror in a new red dress before her first date with Kai at The Blue Oasis. I've aged centuries since then. I feel ... tired. I'm so tired of dreading this Last Day.

I step out of the bathroom as Kai is returning from the laundry room with two beach towels, Olina at his heels. She comes up to me and whines, licking my hand. *Does she know what is coming?* Kai hands me a beach towel, and something brushes against my bare leg.

I look down, and my heart splinters.

My neon-green gecko bracelet is on the floor. It fell off my wrist. Maybe I snagged it on something, or maybe it's a cheap bracelet that wasn't made to last.

Kai bends down and picks it up. "Do you know what these are called?" he asks. "These bracelets made from a single thin thread?"

I shake my head.

"They're called 'wish bracelets.' When the thread breaks, and the bracelet falls off, your wish comes true."

"I like that idea," I say. I like that idea much better than what I was thinking a moment ago. Which is that the bracelet broke, which means I'm no longer protected by the magical *mo'o*, which means I'm not safe. I'm not special. This is really, truly, my Last Day.

Kai pours the bracelet into my palm, and I look down at it, a tangle of neon-green thread and one tiny silver gecko charm.

"What's your wish?" he asks softly.

I lean against the wall, attempting levity. "You know I can't tell you that, or my wish won't come true."

"Oh yeah. Good call, T. I really want your wish to come true."

"Me too."

We stare at each other. We both know what my wish is. We both share the same wish. *Just one more day, one more week, one more month, one more year ...*

Just one more, one more, one more ...

There is such sadness in Kai's eyes, it breaks my heart.

I hate goodbyes, and this one is the worst ever.

"Here." I hand the bracelet to Kai. "I want you to keep this for me."

"What? No. It's yours."

"Please, I want you to have it. Let me tie it on you." I reach for his wrist and loop the thread around it. But my heart sinks. The bracelet is too small—it won't reach around his wrist.

This is my real wish: if I can't have more time, I want Kai to live all of my unlived days. I want the *mo'o* to protect him.

I remember the carved wooden box that I noticed on his bookcase that first day in his room. I walk over and slide it off the shelf. It's my Last Day. I don't care anymore about being a snoop. I just want to know.

"What's this box?" I ask Kai.

He doesn't seem upset that I'm holding it. "It's my box for special things."

Perfect. "Did you make it?" I ask, already knowing his answer.

He nods.

"It's beautiful."

The box's lid is carved with a crisscross pattern, bordered by intricate flowers. Vines creep along the sides. If I can't tie my bracelet around Kai's wrist, at least I can leave it with him. This box will be the perfect place for safekeeping.

"Can I open it?" I ask.

"Sure. Nothing in there you haven't seen before."

His words reach my brain as I open the lid, and for a split second I'm confused. *How could I have seen the contents before? Does he think I secretly opened this box while he was out of the room?*

And then I see what's inside, and my insides leap with recognition. Memories pour out of the box, overflowing like gushing water.

The tiny pink seashell he gave me after the wave ruined my sandcastle. Dried-out Popsicle sticks imprinted with knock-knock jokes—we would read them to each other by the resort pool, dissolving into giggles before the other person even finished the punch line. Postcards I sent him from the lake and notebook-paper doodles from when I was bored in class. My wallet-sized school pictures. A pressed flower from my garden. The sea glass I found in the school parking lot and mailed to him ensconced in Bubble Wrap. There's even that photo I sent him last year, of us as kids—a little blurry and off-center, but perfect—taken by my mom with a disposable camera.

This box is brimming full of *us*.

"This is amazing, Kai. I can't believe you kept all of this."

He shrugs. I can't tell if he's embarrassed, or proud, or something else. "Memories are all we really have, right?" he says. "Memories with you are my treasure."

I carefully place everything back inside the box, setting my thread bracelet on top. The silver gecko charm gazes up at me, like it knows a secret, but it's not telling.

Please keep him safe. Please, mo'o *or God or whoever might be out there listening—please protect him for me, okay?*

Gently, I close the lid and set the box back on the shelf.

"Ready to head out?" Kai asks. "We need enough time to sign in and get our wet suits and everything."

"Yeah, I'll be right there. I'm gonna run to the bathroom—meet you out at the Jeep?"

"Sure." Kai kisses my forehead. Then he leaves, whistling for Olina to follow. She leaps off the bed and trots after Kai.

Feeling like a thief, I step around to Kai's side of the bed. Only, I'm not stealing anything. I'm leaving something.

I pull the folded sheet of paper out of my pocket. Bring it to my lips and kiss its smooth, flimsy surface. Press it gently onto Kai's pillow.

It seems so light, so insubstantial. *What if it blows off his bed? What if he doesn't find it? I need something to weigh it down. An anchor.*

My hand retreats into my pocket, touching the rock I picked up from the lava tubes when I first woke up here in Hawaii, when I didn't even know where I was. Slipping this rock into my pocket was an instinctual act—but, then again, maybe not. Maybe it was more than that. Could it have been the first piece of a puzzle? Perhaps a deep place within me knew that I would need this lava rock for exactly this purpose.

I close my fingers around it, squeezing hard, as if this rock can contain all of my wishes and hopes—for me, for Kai, for this life and the next one. I press the lava rock onto the paper, securing my note to Kai's pillow. Where he will find it tonight. When he returns home. Without me.

Blinking away tears, I gaze around Kai's room one final time. His posters. His photographs. A wooden snowflake ornament he carved hangs in the window, casting diamonds of shadow onto the floor. I say goodbye to my floral suitcase, grabbing my mom's gray sweater and slipping it over my shoulders. Then I open the door and step out into the hallway without looking back.

Dear Kai,

I want to say thank you. Thank you for being my best friend, and for loving me, and for teaching me what it means to trust someone enough to fall in love. You are my anchor and my limitless blue sky. You are my hot malasada and the perfect halo-halo. Loving you is as steady and easy as the waves crashing endlessly onto the shoreline. I hope you know this already, but in case not, I'll say it here: I loved you in my heart long before I admitted it to you, or to myself. I've always loved you.

I know you won't understand what I'm choosing to do, but remember that this is my choice. This is how I want everything to end. The mantas will take good care of me.

Please don't miss me for too long. Please don't ever stop making your beautiful artwork. Know that it is okay to smile, and laugh, and be happy. I want you to be happy, Kai. I want you to live freely and fearlessly and joyfully and without regrets. And I want you to fall in love again. Whoever she is, she will be very lucky.

Thank you for the Best Week of My Life.

Love,

Tegan

Kai parks at the docks as the sun is setting, rivers of pink and orange streaming across the sky. Such a gorgeous sunset makes a fierce ache bloom in the middle of my chest. I guess God or the universe or whatever you want to call it is giving me a proper send-off.

I follow Kai down the ramp to where the boat waits. Its name is painted in blue letters along the side: LUCIE IN THE SKY WITH DIAMONDS. The same boat from when I snorkeled with the mantas as a girl. I remember my mom humming the Beatles' song and my dad pointing out that *Lucie* was spelled wrong, until my mom suggested that maybe *Lucie* was how the boat owner spelled her name, and then my dad thought it was clever. A constellation of blue stars decorates its hull.

"Who's the boat named after?" I ask Kai.

He bites his lip hesitantly. Then he says, "My mom's sister."

"Sarah?"

"No, her younger sister."

"I didn't know your mom had another sister."

"I never met Aunt Lucie. She died when my mom was in college. Car accident."

"Oh my god. That's terrible." The next words come rushing out of me before I can stop them: "I wonder what her Best Week was."

"Maybe she spent it with my mom," Kai says. He looks like he might start to cry. He pulls me in for a tight hug, kissing my hair. We stay like that for a little while, the dock swaying softly beneath our feet. Eventually, a man calls us over. Time to go.

The boat deck is already half-filled with sunburned tourists struggling into their wet suits. Kai greets the captain and crew—guys he's worked with many times before—and signs us in, handing me a wet suit and a snorkel mask.

I climb into the cramped below-deck bathroom to change into my swimsuit. Stripping off my clothes, my fingers brush against the chain of my puka shell necklace. I can wear it underneath the wet suit, but then it will be lost with me. I want Kai to have it when I'm gone. I unclasp it and slip it into the pocket of my jean shorts. Then I fold the shorts and place them carefully back in my bag, along with my T-shirt and sandals, my underwear and bra, and Mom's gray sweater, all pressed into a neat stack and waiting patiently for my return after the manta snorkel. They don't know I'm not coming back either.

Up on the deck, I take my seat next to Kai. The boat slowly pulls away from the dock, winding through the narrow harbor and out to the open sea. A crew member comes around and sprays a clear liquid into our snorkel masks. "Antifog," Kai explains. "It keeps your mask from fogging up underwater."

Another crew member explains what will happen when we reach the raft, in the middle of the ocean, where the manta rays flock at night to feed. Under the raft, bright lights shine down into the water, illuminating the plankton. Dozens of handles jut out from all four sides of the raft. When we reach the spot, we will swim the twenty meters from the boat to the raft and each grab on to a handle. Then our only job is to duck our heads into the water and peer down through our snorkel masks at the giant gliding mantas swooping up to eat the plankton right beneath us.

The boat rocks in the current as we motor through the shadowed water. I breathe in the cold salt spray and look out at the horizon. Nearly all color has leached from the sky; the pinprick stars blink awake. Kai squeezes my hand. I squeeze his back.

Soon. Very soon now.

Eventually, we spot the small raft floating in the ocean like a miniature wooden island. The boat stops and drops anchor. One by one, we waddle in our swim fins to the edge of the boat. One by one, we fit our snorkel masks over our eyes, and then one by one we dive off the edge into the cold water.

I swim for a handle on the far corner of the raft, as far away from the boat as possible. This way, it will be easy for me to be the last one out here. No one will notice if I am the last one back to the boat. Or rather, if I never make it back to the boat.

That's not true, of course. Kai will notice. But I push the thought away. *This is my life. This is my choice, no one else's. He'll read my letter, and he'll understand.*

Kai swims over and grabs the handle beside mine. He grins and gives me a thumbs-up before fitting his snorkel tube into his mouth.

Will he understand? I picture him up on the deck of the boat, alone, waiting for me. I imagine his face when he realizes that I'm not coming back. *No, no. Don't think of that.* I push the thoughts away, all of them, and duck my face into the water.

It takes my eyes a few moments to adjust. Columns of bright-blue light beam down into the dark ocean. Silvery fish dart everywhere, going after the dots of plankton, thousands of plankton, illuminated by the lights.

There are no mantas, and there are no mantas, and there are no mantas, and I'm worried they might not come after all. *What if the mantas don't show up? How will I ever find the strength to let go of this handle and drift down into the deep, alone? I need the mantas to be here. I need them to catch me, to cradle me. To rock me to sleep for the last time.*

Suddenly, they arrive. Gliding through the water, dark giants with graceful wings. They spin toward us, upside down, swooping and swallowing the plankton. Their white bellies shine in the light. They are beautiful. Elegant dancers spinning a magical ballet. I could watch them for hours. I could stay here, just like this, forever. Oh, how I wish I could.

The mantas come so close, we could reach out and pet them. Once, twice, their rubbery skin brushes against my arm in a gentle gesture of hello.

Hello, hello! I think. The beams shine down into the water. My entire being fills with light. I think of Kai's wood carving. The girl and the manta rays. The mantas and the girl. Homecoming. After all these years. *It's nice to see you again too.*

I'm not sure how long it's been. A few minutes. An hour. An eternity. I'm not sure how long it's been, but it's almost time.

Around us, the other snorkelers begin to break away from the raft and swim back to the boat. Kai touches my arm, asking without words if I'm ready. I turn toward him under the water. I can't see his eyes, only the outline of his snorkel mask.

I hold out my hand. Five more minutes.

Soon it will be time.

Last year ...

"Tegan," Kai said that night on the phone. "You know how I feel about you. And I think you might feel the same way about me. What if we gave this a shot?"

"I have no clue what you're talking about." Even though I did.

"Listen, I know the situation's not ideal. I know we live far apart.

But I'm crazy about you, T. I lo—"

My heart pounded, out of control. "Kai, you're my best friend. You know me better than anyone else in the world. I can't—I can't afford to lose you."

"That could never happen, T. I promise."

"You're saying that to be nice, but you don't know what will happen. No one stays friends after they break up."

"Who's to say we'd break up?"

"Oh, Kai. What's so wrong with keeping things the way they are?"

"Because we could be so great together. Because I can't stand it when you talk about other guys. Because I go to sleep every night thinking about you. Because I've fall—"

"Stop. I'm sorry, Kai. I just—I can't. It's risking too much."

He was silent.

"You want to know the truth? I'm scared."

No response.

"Kai, are you still there? Please say something."

"Tegan Rossi, you surprise me. I thought you weren't afraid of anything. And suddenly, you're letting fear rule your life."

We rise above the water's surface. We are the last two out here on the raft. Everyone else has returned to the boat.

I spit out my snorkel tube. "Go on," I tell Kai. "I'll follow right behind you."

Kai takes out his snorkel tube. He leans in and gives me a kiss. He tastes of salt water. If I were crying right now, he would taste like my tears.

I pull away. He hesitates. *Does he know what I'm about to do? Will he try to stop me?*

But then he jams his snorkel tube into his mouth and dives into the water.

Goodbye, Kai, I say in my head. *I love you. Thank you for the Best Week of My Life.*

I force myself to take a deep breath. Then another. Then I close my eyes and dive down into the frigid water.

And with a flash of insight, I remember the actual first time we met.

Ten years ago ...

I sat wedged between my parents, the boat rocking gently beneath us. We were still tied to the dock as more people boarded the boat, their shoes clomping on the deck.

"Are you scared?" my dad asked, bending down. "You seem quiet."

I shook my head no. I was never scared.

But actually, deep in my belly, fear unfolded its snaking tendrils.

"Your mom and I will be right beside you," Dad said. "No reason to worry." Then he and Mom began to talk over my head about some grown-up thing.

Across the deck, a boy around my age passed out snorkel masks. My eyes trailed him as he moved around the boat. When he approached us, I looked away and pretended like I hadn't been watching him.

"Hi," he said, handing me a mask. "I'm Kai." His dark hair flopped down into his eyes, and he brushed it away.

"I'm Tegan." I took the mask from him. "Thank you."

"You're welcome." A warm smile spread slowly across his face.

I smiled back. The sparks of anxiety inside me died down. I wasn't afraid anymore.

Darkness. Cold. The mantas dance around me. They are so beautiful, so graceful. Their smooth flippers brush against my skin. Up above, plankton glitter in the light beaming down from the raft. It's mesmerizing.

I thought I would be filled with a sense of peace, but I find myself wishing for Kai. Wishing he could see this.

I push the thought away and let myself sink lower, deeper. Into the cold. Into the darkness.

What if everything had unfolded differently? What if I had made a different choice, that long-ago night in the lava tubes?

"We could still do it," Kai said. "Run away." His eyes met mine in the lamplight. I could see a question in his expression—I knew what he was asking. And I knew what I wanted to answer. But it was beyond terrifying, letting yourself go. Relinquishing control.

Kai's eyes were so kind, so strikingly familiar and new at once. He leaned toward me.

And this time, I didn't give in to my fear.

This time, I didn't turn away.

Two sides of the same coin. Two hermit crabs sharing one shell.
I leaned toward him, and gently, softly, our lips met.

I'm underwater, so far down below the surface that no light reaches me here. I'm freezing. My whole body aches. I look around for the mantas, but I don't see them. I don't see anyone or anything. I'm alone. Forever. My chest constricts in panic. *Wait. I don't want this. I—*

Suddenly, a hand grabs my ankle. I'm yanked backward. Arms close in around my torso. Upward, upward. The mantas surround me, waving their flippers. *Goodbye-for-now. It's not time yet.*

Kai's mouth on mine. Breathing into me. A heavy pressure on my chest. Then I'm coughing, sputtering. Shivering. I'm cold. So cold. The boat rocks beneath us. I'm aware of people crowding around, someone on a walkie-talkie. I close my eyes. I'm so tired. I don't know if I've ever been this tired.

Kai pulls me to him, wraps his arms around me. He is an anchor. Strong, steady. He hugs me so tightly, like he can change destiny with sheer physical will. Like he can split infinity, like he can arm wrestle time and win. Like this, right here, right now—me and him, him and me—like we can go on and on and on.

"I love you," he whispers fiercely in my ear. Water drips from his hair onto my cheek. "I love you, Tegan. Listen to me. This *wasn't* the

Best Week of Your Life. It wasn't. Not even close. Okay? This week never happened. The Best Week of Your Life is yet to come. Listen to me."

I try to listen, but I can't keep my eyes open any longer. *I'm sorry,* I want to tell him. *I love you too. But I'm so tired.*

I feel myself drifting off, and then everything fades away.

TODAY

It takes an enormous effort to lift open my eyelids. The room is bright. So bright. I have a pounding headache, and my mouth is dry.

"Hi there, Teacup," a voice says.

Slowly, my eyes adjust, and the blurry figure sitting on my bed becomes clear. Curly brown hair, round cheeks, warm eyes filled with tears.

"Mom!" My voice sounds raspy and soft. "Mama!" My heart leaps. It seems like I haven't seen her in years, like I thought I'd never see her again. I reach toward her, and she gently wraps her arms around me, and even though I pride myself on not being a Girl Who Cries, the tears flow down my cheeks. She smells like lavender shampoo and home. *Mom.*

"Hey, sweetie," a deep voice says.

Mom pulls back, and I look behind her. *Dad.* I can't believe he and my mom are here in the same room. Dad's brow is creased in concern, and his smile is tentative, unsure. "How you feeling, my girl?"

"Good. I'm good. I'm so happy to see you guys."

Dad sits down in the chair next to my bed. He reaches over and holds my hand.

"What's going on?" I ask. My throat is raw. "What am I doing here?"

My parents exchange a look, but not of anger or frustration or annoyance. It's something different. Like they're together on the same team.

"You were in an accident, sweetheart," my mom says softly. "But everything is okay. You're going to be okay."

Dad explains that we've had this conversation a few times already. I woke up for the first time in the early hours of the morning, but I keep falling back asleep and waking up again, and I don't remember the previous conversations. The doctors say this is completely normal, similar to patients coming out of anesthesia.

"Like my wisdom teeth?" I ask.

"Yes, like that." Dad smiles. After I got my wisdom teeth removed, Dad was with me in the recovery room, and I kept waking up and asking him if my jaw was supposed to hurt.

"Can I get some water? My throat is on fire," I say.

Mom brings me ice chips and explains that I had a breathing tube. The nurses just recently took it out. My voice is raspy, and my throat aches.

Later, after the doctors come in and run a bunch of tests, and after my parents make some phone calls to relatives, and after the doctors explain a little bit about what happened and ask me questions about what I remember, and I do my best to answer although my memory of the past few weeks is pretty hazy—after all of these things, everyone leaves the room except for Mom and Dad.

"Are you hungry?" Mom asks. "Thirsty?"

"Thirsty," I say. Dad refills my paper cup with ice chips. Mom pulls some granola bars out of her purse and hands one to Dad.

"Thanks, Marie," he says. "You're always so prepared."

Did my dad just give my mom a genuine compliment? What world is this?

We sit there together, the three of us, a family. My parents stare at me, wonder shining in their eyes, like I'm a newborn baby and they can't believe I'm theirs. I suck on my ice chips. The coolness soothes my throat. My parents chew their granola bars. I remember that restaurant in Hawaii where the stranger paid for our dinner. *A really nice family, enjoying a meal together.* That's what we are.

A small slip of ice falls from my fingers and melts against my neck. I reach up—I can feel something smooth against my skin, underneath my hospital gown. It's ...

"My puka shell necklace! But I lost it! Where did you—how—"

Dad smiles. "Your mom found it."

"I was packing a suitcase to bring for you here," Mom explains. "Your necklace was in the pocket of your jeans."

"My jeans? Which ones?"

"Your jean shorts. The new ones. They were already inside your suitcase, actually—with that cute red sundress. When did you buy that?"

"A while ago." *Back before my fight with Kai. Back when I was planning to go to Hawaii this summer.*

Kai. I'm hit with a sharp pang of missing him. *Does he know about the accident? Does he know where I am?*

I touch the smooth shell. "Thank you. I'm so glad you found it."

Dad squeezes my hand. Mom kisses my forehead. "We're so glad you found your way back to us," Mom says.

"Now, why don't you get some rest, sweetheart," Dad suggests. "We'll be right here if you need us."

We're. We'll. I forgot how much I missed my parents as a "we."

They both stand up, like one solid unit, and move to the chairs by the window. I drift off to the sound of them murmuring gently to each other. They sound like … friends.

Everything is dark. The air is cold. I'm sitting on a boat in the middle of the limitless ocean. The sky is full of stars. My skin is damp, my hair wet. I'm enfolded snuggly in a soft towel. A warm body sits beside me. Kai. He wraps an arm around me. I snuggle closer and lean my head against his shoulder. I feel effortlessly, completely safe.

I open my eyes. A hospital room. I blink for a few moments, and then I remember: *I was in an accident. But I'm going to be okay.*

The monitors beep steadily. The edges of my pain are sharp, but mostly my body aches in a diluted, blurry way. My room is empty. Mom's book sits on the chair beside my bed, facedown to save her place. *Maybe Mom and Dad slipped out to grab food. How long was I asleep?*

My attention is snagged by something hanging in the window. The blinds are open, and the light catches its smooth surface, casting diamond-shaped shadows onto the bedcovers.

It's a snowflake ornament, paper-thin and intricately carved. It tilts slightly, this way and that, as if waving hello. My throat tightens, and a surge of joy floods my chest. I'm not even sure why, but I'm thinking of Kai.

And then, like I've magically summoned him, I sense a presence in the doorway. I glance over.

His smile spreads slowly across his whole face, lighting him up.

My heart quickens. The heart monitor *beep, beep, beeps.*

Am I dreaming? Is this real?

Reality is a matter of perception. You perceive this to be real, so yes, it is real. The words flit across my mind. I don't know where they come from.

"Hey," he says softly. He approaches my bed tentatively. "You're awake."

"Hi," I say, reaching out for him. My best friend. My person. He sits down gingerly on the edge of the bed, taking my hand in his. His fingers are warm, and it is so natural, so right, to be holding his hand like this.

"I missed you," I say. "You're really here?"

"I had to come. I needed to see you."

My head is fuzzy. I know we had a fight, but I can't remember the details. Which doesn't even matter. I'm just relieved he isn't mad at me anymore.

It seems like I've been away for a long time, on a long journey. How long has it been since Kai and I last spoke?

"How are you feeling?" he asks.

"Okay. Sore. A little fuzzy-headed." I look at our hands, holding each other. I notice something on my wrist—a thin red line, a scratch. I turn my hand over. The scratch encircles my wrist like a bracelet.

Must be from the accident. I imagine this red scratch healing into a threadlike scar. A sense of calm washes over me. *I'm going to be okay.*

I lean back against the pillows. My mind is still reeling that Kai is actually in my hospital room. "I can't believe you came all the way here."

"You better believe it. And I'm not going anywhere." His smile is contagious.

He tells me about a really tall waterfall in Hawaii, about how there are these little fish that literally climb up the waterfall using these suction fins on their bellies, or maybe their mouths, he isn't really sure—but the point is that they climb all the way to the top of the waterfall, back to where they were born. Back to where they began.

"I think that's why I kept asking you to visit me in Hawaii," Kai says. "I wanted to return to where we began. I thought if I could bring you back to the place we first met, then maybe you would feel the magic too. The magic I've always felt with you."

I squeeze his hand. "I feel it. I've always felt it. I was just … I was scared."

Kai looks down at the bedcovers. Around us, the monitors beep. Footsteps patter down the hall. Here, now, Kai and I are wading into uncharted territory. Uncharted, raw honesty. This is the topic we never broach: him and me. Us.

And yet, somehow, it seems like we've already had this whole conversation before.

"Why did you come here?" I ask. "I mean, I'm happy you're here. *So* happy. But what made you decide to come all this way?"

"You're gonna think I'm weird."

"Kai, I'm your best friend. I already know how weird you are."

He grins. "Touché."

I nudge him with my foot. "Tell me."

"Well," he begins, "the past week or so, I've been having these super vivid dreams about you, T. About us, in Hawaii, doing things together. A couple nights ago, I had a dream about hiking to Akaka Falls with you."

Akaka Falls. I can picture it—like a photograph flashing through my mind. A tall, thin stream of water flows down vibrant green cliffs. In the foreground, a couple is kissing. The guy is dipping the girl like something out of a movie, her hair a dark curtain, his arms wrapped solidly around her waist.

I don't know where the image comes from. I don't know how I know this. But the guy is Kai. And the girl is me. I *feel* it, as if the scene were real. I *feel* it, even though that's impossible.

"And you were so honest with me," Kai continues. "In the dream, just like you are in real life. You didn't buy any of my crap. You didn't take any of my excuses. You kept telling me that I needed to trust in myself. That you believed in me and would never give up on me. When I woke up, I was filled with this overwhelming desire to take action. I needed to see you. I listened to that voice in my head that was insisting, *Go to her, go to her.* I trusted that voice. So here I am."

He gives a sheepish half shrug, looking so much like his little-boy self that, for a moment, I'm eight years old again. I'm ready to grab his hand and yank him along behind me—out of this bed, out of this hospital room, two kids trolling the hallways for lollipops. Time is a needle skipping between the grooves of a record.

"My dream self sounds like a badass," I say.

Kai laughs. "She is. Just like your real self." He leans in and smooths a strand of hair away from my forehead. His eyes lock onto mine. "Tegan Rossi," he murmurs. "You dazzle me, you know that?"

I laugh, looking past Kai's shoulder at the wooden snowflake spinning gently in the afternoon sunlight. I don't think I have ever dazzled anyone. Right now, in this scratchy hospital gown, in this bruised and swollen body, I feel the furthest thing from dazzling.

"I'm a mess." I sigh.

The machines beep and whirr. Everything seems fragile. I think of my heart, expanding and constricting in my chest, and my tender bones, healing. I think of the faraway ocean waves in Hawaii, sweeping their graceful rhythm onto the sand, right at this very moment, and the next moment, and the next.

"I'm serious," Kai says. The room narrows around us. Everything fades away but his face. "You are a blaze of light. I'm so glad you held on. You didn't leave."

There is a question in his eyes. I ache to answer it. Because I finally, wholeheartedly, know my response. *Yes, yes. Bring on the cliff. I'm ready to leap.*

I reach up and pull him down toward me, meeting his lips with my own. His mouth is warm and tender, and he tastes like sweet mint gum, and I have the strongest sense of déjà vu. Like, somehow, this isn't our *first* first kiss. Maybe because Kai is my best friend. Kissing him is both new and familiar. Both a dream and reality. The past and the present and the future, all wrapped up in this one moment.

When we pull apart, we simply sit there for a few seconds, grinning goofily at each other.

"Whoa," Kai says.

"Whoa," I say.

Later—after my mom comes in with smoothies and a fresh change of clothes, then hugs Kai hello and retreats with a knowing smile; after we FaceTime with Kai's family so I can say hi to his mom and dad and brothers (who look so much like him, it's adorable); after I promise them, and Kai, that I'll come visit Hawaii soon; after Kai tells me that he's going to CalArts in the fall, and we calculate the time difference between California and DC (only three hours!); after he carefully climbs into the hospital bed next to me, and we both doze off, and I wake up to his hand in mine, the clouds glowing pink through the window—later, after an afternoon that feels so full, it's like an entire week has passed, a nurse comes in and says that visiting hours are almost over. Five minutes.

"I'll see you in the morning," Kai says. "Rest up. Get a good sleep."

"I will. Let's hang out more tonight, okay? In our dreams."

He smiles. "I'd like that. I'll meet you at our hideout."

"The lava tubes. Good plan."

Gingerly, he sits up and scoots off the bed. "You're really coming to Hawaii?" he asks. "Promise?"

"Promise. You're really going to CalArts?"

"Yep. As long as you come visit."

"It's a deal." We shake on it. And then we kiss on it, too, for good measure.

"I can't wait to show you around Kona," Kai says. "There's so much I want to do with you." He rattles off a list of activities— snorkeling, shave ice, hiking Akaka Falls, dinner at The Blue Oasis. I have the strangest sense that I've done these things with him recently.

"It's gonna be awesome," Kai says. His smile is his grown-up self and his little-kid self, melded together.

"Yeah," I agree. My heart swells with excitement for the big wide-open future, for all the mysteries and magic waiting in store. "It's gonna be The Best."

Acknowledgements

Ever since I was a little girl, it has been my Big Dream to publish a novel. I am eternally grateful to my wonderful literary agent, Mark Gottlieb, for reading my query in the slush pile and being my champion every day since. Thank you to editor and publisher extraordinaire, Georgia McBride, for bringing Tegan and Kai's story into the world and making my Big Dream come true. It has been a delight to work with the entire Month9Books team, especially Dr. Emily Midkiff, Jackie Dever, Danielle Doolittle, Jennifer Million, and Nicole Olea. Many thanks to my fellow Month9Books authors who have been so supportive of my journey as a debut novelist.

As a writer, I have been fortunate to be nurtured by many encouraging mentors and teachers over the years. Thank you to Aimee Bender, Susan Segal, Richard Fliegel, James Ragan, and Viet Thahn Nguyen at the University of Southern California; Trezza Azzopardi at the University of East Anglia; Porter Shreve, Bich Minh Nguyen, Sharon Solwitz and Patricia Henley at Purdue University; and Paul Douglass and Nick Taylor at the Martha Heasley Cox Center for Steinbeck Studies at San Jose State University.

Thank you to all of my teachers, classmates and friends from elementary school onward who have encouraged my writing over the years. Too many to name, but you know who you are!

Thank you to my students and clients, who continually remind me of the joy and magic that comes from unleashing words onto the blank page. Special thanks to Lenore Pearson and Shana Lynn Schmidt, who have become my good friends—your brave vulnerability on the page is humbling and inspiring.

Thank you to Jeffrey Dransfeldt for taking such lovely author headshots for me.

A giant hug of gratitude to Connie Halpern and Mrs. Figs' Bookworm. Connie, you are such a ray of sunshine for me, and for countless others!

Thank you to the talented and generous authors Jennifer Niven, Anna-Marie McLemore, Vanessa Hua, Ken McAlpine, Natalie Lund, Tommy Mouton, Amberly Lago, Hilma Wolitzer and Carand Burnet. I feel so fortunate to call you my friends.

Thank you to my family and to friends who have become family: Allyn McAuley, Laurel Shearer, Colin McAuley, Mary Blasquez, Ann Silvestri, Arianna Silvestri, Amanda Rackley, Julie Hein, Melissa Kaganovsky, Erica Roundy, Dana Boardman, Lauren Baran, Chidelia Edochie, Michael and Luana Swaidan, Ben Raynor, Tera Ragan, Shavonne Clarke, Tiffany Chiang, Wayne and Kathy Bryan, Tavis Smiley, Barry Kibrick, Julie Merrick, Rima Muna, Patti Post, Jess Ahoni, Justin and Fawn Nishioka, Alicia Stratton, Tania Sussman, Henry Fung, Joan Redding, Annette and Ron Schmidt, and all of my aunts, uncles, and cousins.

Special thanks to my aunt Kym Woodburn King for her constant love and kindness. Thanks also to Grandma and Grandpap, Mary Lou and Gene Paschal, for making me feel like a best-selling author ever since I was a kid; and to Gramps, Dr. James Dallas Woodburn II, for all the phone calls, lunch dates, and stories.

Boundless gratitude to my amazing mother-in-law, Barbara McAuley, for your fierce belief in me and my writing—and the countless hours of babysitting Maya so I can have time to write! And a big hug to my sister-in-law and favorite librarian, Allyson McAuley, whose opinion matters so much to me, and who has always treated my writing with such respect. Thank you for reading an early draft of this book and giving me invaluable feedback.

Thank you to Holly Mueller, my wise friend and first reader, for all of the exclamation-point-filled emails cheering me on as I drafted this book, and for being a listening ear during the long road to publication.

I wrote this novel in memory of my dear friend Céline Lucie Aziz and my grandma Audrey Woodburn (Auden). My grandparents traveled to Hawaii often, up until Auden died when I was five. We scattered her ashes in the ocean. As a little girl, when I thought of Heaven, I always imagined my grandma relaxing on a beach in Hawaii. The Big Island is still the place I feel closest to her. The idea of a "Best Week" sprang into my mind after my treasured friend Céline passed away in a car accident at the age of 26. We had daydreamed about one day traveling to Hawaii together, but we never made it. Céline did spend time in Hawaii with her family shortly before she died. Hawaii is a place that has touched me deeply, in the same way it is a touchstone for Tegan in the book.

To my brother Greg: thank you for being my best friend since the day you were born. Your wisdom keeps me grounded during the highs and lows of the journey, and your enthusiasm for life is contagious. Thank you for teaching me about patience and faith, and thank you for your open-hearted feedback on early drafts of this book.

Thank you to my mom, Lisa, for your deep listening, for taking care of Maya so I could write, and for devouring the first draft of this book even though you don't typically read YA. As Tegan says to her mom: "I love you infinity."

Thank you to my dad, Woody, for being my role model, my

biggest fan and my favorite writing buddy. You inspired me to become a writer, and you have taught me to find joy in the creative process. One of my most treasured memories is when you called me after reading my first draft of this novel—you read it straight through in one sitting!—and told me how proud you were. Making you proud lights me up inside. Don't ever forget!

To my husband, Allyn: you are my anchor and my limitless blue sky. You are my hot malasada and the perfect halo-halo. Loving you is as steady and easy as the waves crashing endlessly onto the shoreline. Thank you for being the inspiration for Kai and Tegan's love story. I am the luckiest.

To my daughter, Maya: thank you for sparking a renewed sense of purpose and love for my work as a writer—and as a human being. Thank you for all of the Best Weeks you have already given me. I hope your Best Week is always yet to come.

Dallas Woodburn

Dallas Woodburn published her first book, *There's a Huge Pimple On My Nose,* when she was in fifth grade... and she hasn't stopped since! Her published books include the YA novel *The Best Week That Never Happened*; the YA short-story collection *3 a.m.*; and the adult short-story collection *Woman, Running Late, in a Dress.* She has won numerous awards for her writing including the international Glass Woman Prize and the John Steinbeck Creative Writing Fellowship. A passionate champion of young writers, Dallas is the founder of Write

On! Books, an organization that empowers youth through reading and writing endeavors, and is also editor of the book series *Dancing With The Pen: a collection of today's best youth writing*. She lives in the San Francisco Bay Area with her amazing husband, adorable daughter, and overflowing bookshelves.

Connect with her at www.dallaswoodburnauthor.com.

CONNECT WITH US

Month9Books

GMMG
GEORGIA MCBRIDE MEDIA GROUP
GEORGIAMCBRIDE.COM

Find more books like this at http://www.Month9Books.com

Facebook: www.Facebook.com/Month9Books
Instagram: https://instagram.com/month9books
Twitter: https://twitter.com/Month9Books
Tumblr: http://month9books.tumblr.com/
YouTube: www.youtube.com/user/Month9Books
Georgia McBride Media Group: www.georgiamcbride.com

OTHER MONTH9BOOKS TITLES YOU MIGHT LIKE

THE LADY ALCHEMIST

GARDEN OF THORNS AND LIGHT